-THE-
- PIRATES OF -
-MARYLAND POINT-

Dot Gumbi

THE PIRATES OF MARYLAND POINT

A comedy by Dot Gumbi

Email: dotgumbi@gmail.com

Twitter: @DotGumbi

First published 2012 by Lulu.com

in association with P'Nut & Carn Publishing

ISBN 978-1-4717-6813-2

Second edition published 2014

Cover by Marcel Baker

www.marcelbaker.com

LEGAL

ACKNOWLEDGEMENTS:

This novel could not have been written without the help of a great number of people.
Thanks to everyone who gave support and spread the word.

Special thanks to the following for going above and beyond in their help:
Marcel Baker (for his cracking illustration work).
My Dad (for drawing the map).
Steffi (for proof-reading).
Dr. Monika (for her awesome promotional work).
Rich and Jarvis (for helping make the book trailer).

Extra special thanks to Joe Dearman, who, much like a boxing trainer, yelled encouragingly from the ringside,
offering valuable comment and suggestion as I flailed between rounds/

This novel is dedicated to Maryland Point.
And the best landlord in the world

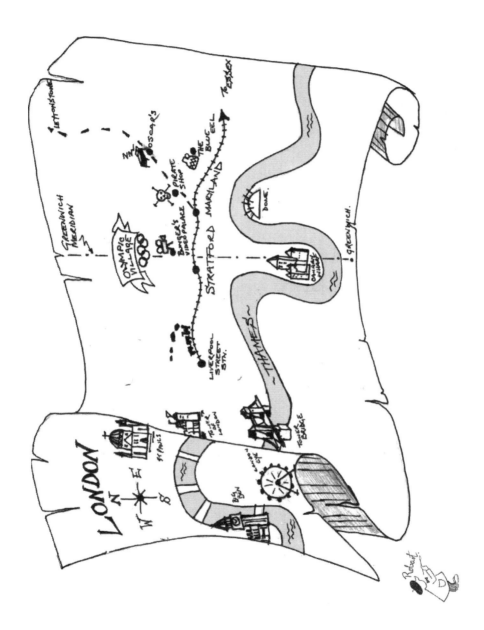

- 1 -

INTERROGATION

I adjusted my glasses and grinned at the two police officers opposite me. They didn't grin back. In fact they sat there, looking bored. Or maybe unimpressed. I couldn't be sure anymore. We'd been in the same grey interview room for well over twelve hours now. Surely it was time to let me go? Or at least let me sleep?

It was DI Ken Bludwyn who eventually broke the silence. He was a weather-beaten specimen with a grey moustache and heavy bags under his eyes like hammocks.

'Oscar, let's go through it one more time.'

I stopped grinning. 'Oh, c'mon! How many more times have I got to tell it to you?'

Bludwyn shrugged. 'Until it makes sense.'

'I've got rights y'know!' I cried, pointing a finger at an imaginary charter on the table. 'You can't keep me here any longer.'

To Bludwyn's right a pale-faced beanpole began bouncing up and down excitedly in his chair. 'Can I tell him, sir? Can I?'

This was DC Lloyd "Slick" Peasworth. A rookie. And an annoyingly keen one at that. For the last twelve hours he'd had his tongue up Bludwyn's arse looking for a promotion, or a biscuit. Either way it had made for uncomfortable viewing.

Bludwyn's tash smirked. 'Go ahead, Slick. Let's see how the suspect takes the news.'

I didn't like the sound of that. I sensed danger.

Words burst out of Slick's mouth. Horrible words. But he said them with such joy it sounded like he was accepting an Academy award. 'You are now on a terror charge! We can hold you for an entire month! Isn't that great?'

I didn't think it was that great, to be honest. And what did it mean anyway? A terror charge? Were they really stupid enough to try and pin everything on me? I could tell them what happened a million times, nothing would stick. How could it? They were barking up the wrong spruce.

'You know, you're wasting valuable police time,' I said. 'You should be out there looking for them, not questioning me.'

'Them?' Slick's tone was sceptical, like he didn't know what I was talking about. 'You mean, the pirates?'

'Of course the bloody pirates!' I snapped. 'I've told you three times now! Haven't you been listening?'

'You seem a little stressed. Maybe you need something to calm your nerves.' Slick reached into his blazer and carefully placed a box of cigarettes on the table. He gave them a gentle tap. 'Help yourself.'

'You bastard.'

'Now now,' said Bludwyn. 'You can't swear at an officer.'

'Of all the low stunts you could pull. You know I've given up.'

'Oh?' said Slick. 'Since when?'

'When do you think?' I spat. 'How can I smoke again after what happened? Just thinking about it makes me sick.' I flicked the box back to him.

Bludwyn gave his partner a nod. Slick returned the cigarettes to his pocket.

'Well, Oscar,' said Bludwyn, 'There's no other option. Unless you are going to confess, I suggest you start at the very beginning, again.'

Slick nodded. 'And when you get to the end, stop.'

'Okay,' I said, rubbing my forehead. 'We'll go from the very beginning, again...' I cleared my throat and looked up at the ceiling, ready to relive the nightmare once more. 'It all started out quite innocently I suppose, but it ended up being about the fate of the planet. And you know what? I didn't even see it coming.'

- 2 -

AN UNEXPECTED VISITOR

London ain't like the films say.

If you believe the films everyone goes about in a bowler hat singing *'God Save The Queen'* and drinking tea all day. They'll tell you that Tower Bridge is always up. That every flat has a stellar view of the Thames and that jolly policemen are always skipping about in front of Big Ben saying "allo, allo, allo."

None of that's true. And if it is, then I was short-changed.

When I moved to the city I got something never seen on film. I got Maryland Point, a dirty run-down spot on the arse of Stratford, seven miles east of Downing Street. And evolutionally, about seven millennia behind it.

The Friday night it all began was much like any other. Sirens screamed by my window, drunks hollered up from the street and cockroaches marched across my wood-chip walls, whilst I lay in bed with a pillow round my ears trying to block it all out.

I don't know why I bothered. In the five months I'd lived there, it'd never worked.

The area was a war zone, though my landlord saw it differently. He'd advertised my flat as a: *"Original Edwardian Penthouse situated in an up-and-coming area less than a mile from the venue for the 2012 Olympic Games."*

Trade Descriptions could have him on that as I'd have described it as a pokey attic room above a launderette in an East London slum.

My landlord also described the *penthouse* as having *"spectacular views"* which I suppose was true. Since moving in I had seen some *spectacular* things such as a mugging at dawn, some kids using a shopping trolley to ram-raid an off-licence at dusk, and even once seeing a tramp trying to pick a fight with a full moon.

After five months it had reached the stage where I didn't even bother looking at the spectacles anymore. I'd just lay in bed at night and listen to them. The sound of someone puking beneath my window, the sudden screech of wheel-spin. Was it a car backfiring or a gunshot? Who cared? It was all noise.

And that's exactly how it was that Friday night.

I don't know the exact time, sometime after midnight I reckon, I was laying in the darkness waiting for sleep when a blitz of car horns went off followed by a bang...a very loud and very familiar bang...a bang that a person who lives alone shouldn't hear. It was the sound of my front door slamming shut.

Panic shot through me and I sat bolt upright and listened. From downstairs I heard floorboards creak. I quickly groped about under my bed for a weapon. As I searched I could hear slow and heavy footsteps coming up the stairs. I was done for. I'm not much of a fighter, never have been, and despite being armed and knowing the terrain, I felt the odds were still massively stacked against me, especially considering the best weapon I could find under my bed was a large red onion.

My bedroom door flew open with a bang and instinctively, in what I can only describe as blind panic, I bit into the onion and lobbed it through the darkness like a grenade, hoping its fumes might temporarily blind the intruder so I could bundle him.

There was silence.

For a second I thought the onion had worked, but then a large shadowy figure staggered through the door. It stood in the middle of my room and began howling, laughing and attempting to sing, crowing a couple of ear-splitting lines in the style of *The Copacabana*.

   'They call it Mary...Maryland PoynTAA!'

- 3 -

JIMMY STRONGBOW

I recognised the voice instantly. There was only one man I knew that had a voice that sounded like a clapped-out gearbox, and that man was my landlord, Jimmy Strongbow.

I threw on my bedside lamp. Cockroaches scuttled for the shadows, dashing past the feet of the figure stood in the middle of my room wearing a bright glittery blue blazer and a Barry Manilow wig that was squashed down on his smiling head.

'Jimmy! What the bloody hell are you playing at?'

'They call it Mary... Maryland PoynTAA!'

'You prat!' I shouted. 'I was armed! I could've killed you!'

I had no idea what was going on, so I reached for my glasses to get a better look at the situation. Two things became immediately clear. Firstly, my landlord was farcically drunk. Secondly, the onion I'd thrown at him had no affect whatsoever aside from leaving a rank taste in my mouth.

'I'm the ghost of Christmas yet to come,' he laughed, waving his arms about. *'OooooOoooo.'*

'It's July!' I spat, 'and the middle of the night. Do one!'

'No, Oscar...calm down, me ol' son...I'm celebrating,' he said, doing a little dance, at least it looked like a little dance, a shuffling of feet, but I suppose in hindsight he was just trying to keep his balance.

'What we celebrating, Jimmy?' I said. 'You finally decided to do something about the cockroach problem?'

He started chuckling. 'Gordon Bennet! You don't half tickle me.'

I crossed my arms. 'It might be some big joke to you. But I pay to live in this dump. I should have a rent reduction or something.'

'Rent reduction!?' I can't explain it, but talk of losing money seemed to sober him up. 'Oscar, me ol' china, do I need to remind you how lucky you are? You are living in a *penthouse*. Only playboys have pads like this.'

'No playboy would have wooden flooring like mine.'

'No,' agreed Jimmy. 'You're right. Yours is superior. Bespoke, you might say.'

I frowned. 'It's made out of fruit boxes! I'm *Granny Smith* by the door and *Banana Republic* by the window.'

Jimmy nodded. 'Designer labels. I should raise your rent for that. You're mugging me over this penthouse.'

'Stop calling it a penthouse! It's a bloody loft! I'm up here with the water tank. It's behind your head, look.'

'An internal water feature.' He turned and patted it affectionately. It gave a worrying crack. 'Very bespoke.'

'I've got enough water features already.' I sat forward in bed and pointed at the buckets dotted about the room. 'When you going to get the roof fixed?'

Jimmy unzipped his trousers.

'Wait!' I protested, but it was too late. I could already hear the sound of a bucket filling up.

He let out a satisfied sigh. 'Loft, penthouse, call it what you will, Oscar, it's worth a pretty penny. When the Olympic Games turn up here, we are going to be millionaires, me ol' son.'

I overlooked the fact that he said "we", by the time the Olympics came I would be long gone. I'd either be priced out of the place and on the street, or bounced out into the nowhere of Zone 6.

I shook my head. 'Jimmy, just because two weeks of hop-scotch and pin-the-tail-on-the-donkey are being held about half a mile away doesn't mean that this whole area is paved with gold.'

'Aha!' he exclaimed, zipping up his flies. 'That's where you are wrong, my pedigree chum. You know the model shop?'

'What? Your model shop?' It was so called because it was the width of a size-zero model, a strip of space that had been in Jimmy's family for generations. And it had stood empty for just as long, waiting for someone who had more money than sense to snap it up. Problem was, it was just too narrow. You really couldn't do anything with it, even sell it.

'Sold it!' beamed Jimmy.

'You're joking!' I cried. Apparently the stupid thing had been on the market since Queen Victoria had fallen off her perch. 'How much you get for it?'

'One million quid.'

'One million?!?'

Jimmy beamed. 'One million smackeroonys, me ol' china.' He started singing again. *'They call it Mary! Maryland PoynTAA!'*

I wrapped a pillow round my ears. 'Shut up!'

He stopped suddenly and started sniffing. His smiley drunkenness turned to a look of anger. 'You been smoking in 'ere?'

'No,' I lied.

'This is a non-smoking penthouse.'

'I know that.'

He patted the wooden beams, or maybe he was leaning on them to steady himself. 'Listen, this place is a tinder box. You can't smoke in 'ere, it will go up!'

'Don't worry,' I said. 'I'll use my "water-features" to put it out.'

'Watch your lip.'

'Whatever,' I said. 'I don't smoke.'

Jimmy looked about the room. 'Then why you got ashtrays up 'ere?'

Snookered. 'They ain't ashtrays,' I blagged. 'They are camouflaged cockroach traps.'

'You what?'

'Honest,' I lied. 'Cockroaches are smart. Some scientists reckon smarter than dolphins. They reckon they can do a sudoku and everything.'

'Sudoku?' Jimmy's eyes crossed. 'But...but...how'd they hold the pen?'

Confused, he staggered into my wardrobe. It gave an almighty crack and collapsed on top of him. From beneath a pile of clothes he gave a muffled sigh.

'I remember when all this was fields.'

- 4 -

NEXT MORNING

You don't need to set an alarm clock in Maryland Point. The dawn chorus will wake you up. At 8am sharp the sound of a billion pneumatic drills will fill the sky. After that getting back to sleep is impossible.

I rolled over and reached for my glasses. The room pulled into focus to reveal my landlord still sparko in the wardrobe. His feet poked out from beneath a pile of clothes that rose and fell as he snored. His bucket of piss stood nearby, already starting to ferment in the early morning heat.

Somewhat depressed by the way in which the day had started I reached for my cigarettes. I fished one out and sparked up. I wasn't worried about Jimmy catching me. The place needed fumigating.

I sat there for a while, puffing large clouds of blue smoke, trying to ignore the dirty onion taste that was still burning my lips. Thoughts drifted through my mind, the way they always do when you smoke. Thoughts like, where had my life gone so wrong? How had I ended up living here? Would I ever have enough money to move somewhere else? And how was it I had a millionaire pensioner passed out in my wardrobe dressed up like Barry Manilow?

Had Jimmy really sold his little shop for a million? It was hard to believe that something that small was worth so much, but, ever since the government had announced that some nearby land was going to be turned into an Olympic stadium, property prices had gone berserk.

Suddenly everyone felt they were sitting on a goldmine. All they had to do was put their feet up and wait for a compulsory purchase order to roll in.

I didn't believe that would ever happen. Maryland Point was too much of a dump. Rather than pay out, I expected the government to turn up one night with a bulldozer and push everything into the Lea River and pretend Maryland Point never existed. I mean if the world's TV cameras caught one glimpse of the area during the Games, viewers would think the feed had been hijacked by an Oxfam appeal.

I climbed out of bed. My cigarette hissed as I dropped it in Jimmy's bucket. I slipped on some jeans and looked out of my window. The Olympic site lay half a mile away. A row of cranes stood above the rooftops. All working like crazy to get things finished in time. That's all anyone seemed to care about round here: the Olympics and what it could do for them. It could do nothing for me, unless cockroach extermination became an Olympic sport. That's the only thing I really cared about.

I picked a t-shirt from the pile of clothes and gave it a sniff. It seemed clean. I put it on and gave Jimmy a kick.

'Now you're minted, get my cockroach problem sorted. I mean it.'

He didn't reply. He just carried on snoring.

- 5 -

BATHROOM TROUBLE

I'll be the first to admit my flat was unusual. The weirdest thing about it was my bathroom being outside the front door. I mean, it was still in the building, on the first floor landing to be exact, but was in a strange no-man's mezzanine between my flat and the launderette below.

I'd pulled Jimmy up on it when he first showed me round, but he assured me it was all to do with "feng-shui", and that, even though the bog was outside the flat, it was for my use and my use only, and that nobody working in the launderette would use it, ever. Which if that were true meant that, as well as cockroaches, I had to deal with a sodding poltergeist, as I left the flat that morning to find my bathroom door shut and the toilet flushing.

The door opened and Berol stepped out, smoking a roll-up. She's a fierce looking East End sort with cheap gold earrings and electric white hair in a vicious short back and sides. She flapped a newspaper behind her. 'Cor! I'd give that a few minutes if I were you, Oscar.'

'Berol!'

'Oh, don't you start.' She turned and headed back downstairs to the launderette. 'Ere, come with me. I want a word with you.'

I didn't like the sound of that. Berol ran the launderette with an iron fist and was known for flooring troublemakers with a well aimed kick to the plums. As such I made sure that when I gave her any washing my pants were always pre-rinsed.

I followed her down the creaky stairs into the cloudy steam of the ground floor. The back of the shop was always like this when the launderette was open. Wood-chip walls dripped with condensation and there were black bags everywhere stuffed with dirty clothes.

'You want to be careful,' I said, nearly tripping over a bag. 'All this is a health hazard.'

'And this building ain't?' She propped herself by a door that led to the back office and took a long drag on her roll-up.

'Jimmy's upstairs,' I said.

She shot me a confused look. 'He's where?'

'He passed out in my room last night.'

'Typical,' she croaked. 'Down The Eel, I bet. On the sauce again. That's where all my wages go, on that pissed up sponge.'

I waved my hands for her to calm down. 'I'm just letting you know.'

She blew smoke into the steam. 'I can smoke where I bloody want. And if Jimmy wants to stop me, he'll have a fight on his hands. I'll get Jaggers on it.'

I smiled and lit a cigarette of my own. 'You reckon you could afford Jaggers?'

'He's a good man. A real Robin Hood. After what he did for The Eel, he could do anything. I'll tell you now, Jimmy ain't gonna stop me smoking – he's got more chance handcuffing a ghost.' Her eyes suddenly lit up as if remembering something. 'Listen, you and me got to have words.'

I braced myself, fearing an imminent kick in the plums.

'How many times have I told you about deliveries?'

'Deliveries?' I said.

'I've told you before, I don't mind accepting stuff, so long as I don't have to sign nothing.'

This was true. I regularly ordered films online, but as I didn't officially have a front door, I had to have them sent to the launderette.

Berol would accept them and leave them in the hallway. She didn't mind so long as she didn't have to give her name to anyone. She was very particular about that.

'Something come for you this morning,' she said. 'And the postie tried to make me sign for it...*three bloody times!* I told him, I ain't signing nothing, but he was a proper jobsworth. He must have been here five minutes giving it chat. In the end I took his pen and wrote "up the hammers."'

'*Three times?*' I said. 'Sorry.'

'You will be.' She disappeared into the back-office and returned with a parcel. It was the size of a shoebox and covered in skulls and crossbones and yellow biohazard symbols.

'Oscar, if it becomes regular, them wanting me to sign stuff, I ain't doing it.'

I examined the parcel closely. It looked like someone had had a poke at the plastic wrapping with a pen but thought better of it. All the seals were intact.

'Cheers, Berol,' I smiled, tucking the package under my arm. 'Don't worry. You won't need to sign for anything like this again.'

- 6 -

THE WALK TO WORK

If there was one feature about my "penthouse" I actually liked, it was the location. I know I've not painted a rosy picture about what I thought of the area. I didn't really care about the Olympics or any of the other urban redevelopments the newspapers were always banging on about. The sole reason I lived in Maryland Point was because it was round the corner from work. Ten minutes walk, if you want to be exact. Although in the five months I'd lived there, I'd never been exact. I mean, what's the point in being early for anything? All it means is you've got to wait, and who likes waiting? It was a small ambition of mine to arrive exactly on time, or with one second to go, just like I was James Bond turning up to diffuse a bomb, or something.

That morning a glorious summer sun was rising over Maryland Point. A gentle breeze played at my t-shirt. High up above planes criss-crossed the flawless blue roof of the capital. On street level, things weren't quite so peaceful. In fact, as ever, Maryland Point was gridlocked with red double-decker buses and illegal mini cabs. Death-wish cyclists in Lycra weaved past, screaming at the traffic and flipping the world the finger.

I cut across the road and examined Jimmy's model shop. The FOR SALE sign had already been taken down, though when it had been up it had almost been as wide as the shop itself. I tried to look in through the whitewashed glass and see if I could spot the new owners. I was intrigued to know what sort of nutter thought it was worth a million notes. But it was too dark. I couldn't see anything.

'Ere, watch your back, mate.'

I turned round to find two deliverymen, struggling with a mattress.

'Much obliged,' said one of them as I stepped out of their way. I wondered if they might be the shop's new owners, so I watched them. They carried the mattress past the model shop to a darkened doorway a few doors down. Above it a dirty neon sign flickered: **Stratford Tanning Depot. Open 24 hours.**

I glanced up the road. Six or more mattresses were sitting on the lip of a lorry, all wrapped in plastic and waiting to be unloaded.

I grinned and continued my walk to work. On the way I stepped over a fresh piece of graffiti on the pavement that said: VIVA CASPER!

* * *

Bludwyn's tash studied me. 'And that's all you saw?'

'Yup.'

'Are you sure?'

'I've told you three times already! I don't know how much more you need me to flesh it out. I walked to work. I've told you about the weather, the traffic, the sign on the shop being taken down, the mattress delivery to the Stratford Tanning Depot and the VIVA CASPER! graffiti. I mean, what more do you need?'

'You must have seen something else? Heard something?'

'C'mon, London's knackering on the senses. It's like staring into the snow-screen on a TV that needs tuning. There is just so much moving, so much going on, you can't say that you're seeing the full picture. For all I know the pirates were probably doing doughnuts and cart-wheeling down the street. But if they were, I didn't see them that morning.'

Bludwyn scribbled something in his notebook, probably about doughnuts.

- 7 -

BUNGER'S VIDEO PALACE

I arrived at Bunger's Video Palace at precisely 9:09am. Not quite what I'd call a personal best, but not far off. The shutters were already up, so I went in through the front. The shop bell gave its usual bored ring.

Inside, I couldn't see anyone about, but then, I couldn't really see a lot. The shop is dark. It's always dark. It's down this dirty little back alley, you know the type London seems to specialise in: uneven grey flagstones, a superfluous black bollard, and the dull tired brick of nearby buildings built too close, long ago, by people who probably still took a horse and cart to work and drank to Queen Victoria.

Some would say it sounds quaint. They are the same people who think the new *Star Wars* films are better than the old ones. They don't know what they are talking about. I have to work down this dark little alley and I say it's shit. I spend five, sometimes six, days a week working in shade like a lizard under a rock or something. If it weren't for going out for fag breaks, I'd never see the sun. Who said smoking was bad for your health?

We couldn't even turn the shop lights on, they flickered so bad it was like being in a disco, and Bunger was too tight to replace them. Which was probably a wise business decision as the shop wasn't much to look at. It was made out of whitewashed walls, with a low slung grey ceiling and green lino, the likes of which I'd only even seen used in schools and hospitals.

Sometimes I didn't know what was worse. Where I worked or where I lived. Both were in Maryland Point. Both should've been condemned. Oh, another day in paradise…

I clutched my parcel and walked toward the rear of the shop. As I passed the counter a voice floated up from beneath it. 'You're late.'

I didn't bother replying. Instead I stopped and peered into the bargain bin. *The Three Amigos* was still in there. I picked it up and read the blurb. I swear those blurb writers can polish any turd. 'Your onion trick didn't work.'

'Onion?' A head poked up from beneath the counter. It belonged to my colleague Duncan. His eyes were confused. 'What onion?'

'Jimmy broke into my gaff last night,' I replied, tossing the DVD back into the bin. 'Drunk as a Lord he was. I tried that special GM onion trick you told me about, but it didn't work. I told you it was bullshit.'

Duncan's eyes darted left, like he was trying to look into his ear for an answer. 'Maybe Jimmy had been drinking Guinness…sometimes that cancels it out.'

'You're full of it.'

'No, I'm serious,' he protested. 'Was he drinking Guinness?'

I waved him down. 'I'm not in the mood, Duncan. I didn't sleep well. You want a brew?'

'Erm…yeah, cheers,' he drawled, turning his attention to his clipboard. 'I'll have a Julie.'

I picked up my parcel and headed to the "staff area". I use that term extremely loosely. If the shop was so ugly we had to keep it in darkness you can guess how bad things were behind the scenes. The "staff area" was nothing more than a glorified toilet at the back of the stock room. It had a dirty sink and stinky fridge that nobody had ever found the time or energy to clean. The white seals had gone grey and were working their way towards black.

I tucked my parcel safely under the sink and switched the kettle on. I glanced back through the shop. Duncan had his back to me. He was stood at the counter processing the returns, carefully sniffing each DVD case before ticking it off on his clipboard.

I liked Duncan. I didn't understand him, but I liked him. He had a cheeky boyish smile and laughed nervously a lot of the time. It was kind of endearing. He was easy company, if you could put up with his occasional crackpot theory about talking animals, crystals, ley-lines or whatever other nonsensical voodoo he was into that week.

His hair was like his mind, a complete mess, pulling in multiple directions. And his dress sense wasn't any better. Everything was too tight. His trousers too short. And he always wore this faded old leather jacket that looked like it had been made from the hide of a hippo. Apparently he'd been working at Bunger's Video Palace for about nine years now. Nine years in this dark and dingy East London armpit. If that doesn't prove he's not the full ticket I don't know what does.

Bunger had hired him at the height of *The Lord of the Rings* frenzy. He thought it would be good business to have a Kiwi behind the counter. And it sounds like it was. From what Duncan told me every punter who came and rented part of the trilogy was regaled by his tales of New Zealand, and how he'd been on standby to be an extra in the movie, and that his cousin knew Peter Jackson, *personally*. It didn't matter if any of it was true or not, it gave the punters a warm and fuzzy feeling, a closer connection with the movie and, more importantly, put money in Bunger's till.

Money always went in Bunger's till. Hardly any came back out.

'So…what happened with Jimmy?' drawled Duncan, as I came back with the teas. 'Why'd you need the onion?'

'Did you stitch me up with that?' I said, setting the drinks down. 'Was that a prank?'

A nervous laugh escaped from the corner of his mouth. 'No, it's serious. I always have an onion. For defence. Under my bed. It's cheaper…and Jaggers says it's legal. The law can't touch you.'

'Forget the law – it didn't work.'

'Maybe you had the wrong type of onion,' said Duncan. 'Was it red or white?'

'It doesn't matter now.'

'Large or small?'

'It doesn't matter.'

'Did you bite into the middle or just the edge?'

'I said, it doesn't matter! The point is it didn't work. I was lucky it was just Jimmy and not a real burglar.'

'What was Jimmy doing in your flat anyway?'

'Celebrating, I think.' I swigged my tea. 'He'd been at The Eel all night. Someone's bought the model shop off him.'

'I knew he'd sell it,' said Duncan. 'I read that it's a developers dream.'

'Pfff…where'd you read that?'

'Erm…on the back of a toilet door somewhere.'

'In Jimmy's handwriting, I bet. That shop ain't worth a penny, let alone a million notes. You can't do anything with it. I mean it extends back a fair way but it's no wider than a phone box.'

'I wonder who bought it?' drawled Duncan.

'Who knows?' I said. 'Everyone wants a piece of this area now. Since the Olympics got the green light everything has been snapped up, bought up and done up. If Jimmy can sell his model shop it wouldn't surprise me if Bunger cashes in on this place. A DVD shop can't have long left.'

Duncan didn't register my ominous prediction that a store renting home movies was doomed in the current technologically advancing climate. In fact Duncan didn't register a lot of things anyone said, they'd just bounce off him, he'd just carry on as if you'd said nothing, often too tangled up with his own bizarre thoughts. 'Maybe they'll make it into a dog showroom.'

'A what?'

'Y'know...a place where they sell dogs.'

'You mean a kennel?' I gave him a puzzled look. 'What are you on about?'

'Round here lots of people talk about seeing a dog man. I reckon he's going to have to open a shop sooner or later to keep up with demand.'

'Prat!' I said. 'They ain't seeing a dog man! They're seeing a man about a dog!'

'That's what I said,' said Duncan. 'Lots of people want dogs.'

'No, they don't.'

'I've heard them, they do.'

'There ain't no bloody dog man,' I said.

'Well there should be. There's demand.'

'Bloody hell.' I held a hand up to my forehead. 'You're as crazy as Jimmy. You know he was so blotto last night he went for a slash in my room.'

Duncan gave a nervous laugh. 'You serious?'

'Honest,' I replied. 'He was like a camel. He filled up an entire bucket.'

Duncan's face fixed into his boyish grin. 'Sounds like...Jimmy took the piss.'

I looked at him unimpressed. 'Don't wind me up. Just drink your tea.' I pointed at his mug. 'Look, you haven't touched it. I thought you said you wanted one?'

'I wanted a Julie.'

'That's what you got.'

He shook his head. 'You put sugar in it.'

'No I didn't.'

He waved it under my nose. 'Sniff it yourself.'

'C'mon. You can't *smell* the difference. Have you actually tasted it?'

'I don't need to taste it,' he drawled. 'I can smell it. It's got sugar in it.' He waved the mug at me. Reluctantly I grabbed it and swished some round my mouth. He was right.

'How the hell could you smell that?'

Duncan shrugged. 'I told you. I smell everything, I know when something is wrong.'

'Yeah, so you say,' I said sceptically. 'Here, I'll make you another.'

I grabbed his mug and went back to the "staff area".

Everyone has their quirks, and Duncan's thing is to sniff stuff. It's the first sense he puts to the test and he says his nose is never wrong. It's probably also worth mentioning that he thinks foxes can talk. But so far, whilst I've proved his fox theory is cobblers, I've never caught his nose out. I hadn't been trying to catch him out then, I just hadn't been paying attention. Sometimes though, when it's slow in the shop, I play little pranks on him just to see if his nose really is that keen, or if he's just putting me on with strange Kiwi humour I don't get. Once, I put a bit of egg sandwich in *Carry On Cleo* and hid it in the bargain bin. I didn't tell him I'd done it. He came back from a sit down in the "staff area" and sniffed it out in under two minutes before asking: 'Do you think the Egyptians would've liked egg sandwiches?'

- 8 -

NEWSPAPER

I flicked the kettle on again. I toyed with the idea of going for a cigarette but as I only had a few left I decided to hold out a bit longer. It wasn't even 10am yet. I wanted to at least make it to lunch before I had to go and buy more.

Whilst I waited for the water to boil I noticed a copy of the local newspaper sitting on the cistern. I picked it up and idly flicked through the pages. I don't know why I bothered. It was all the same news. The Olympics this. The Olympics that. They'd been rehashing the same stories for months. Probably years. Or at least as long as I'd lived there.

That day I remember I was reading a piece about a skydiving dog when another article caught my eye. It was about Casper Macvittee.

Casper Macvittee had become legendary round these parts. He was an amateur archaeologist who'd made some headlines a while back with his crackpot theories about the Olympic site. I don't recall the exact details but I think it had something to do with him saying the site was built on an ancient ley-line or meridian or something. King Arthur featured in his theory somewhere, but I didn't really bother trying to follow it. Nobody sensible did. And nobody sensible cared. After all, it wasn't like he was a qualified archaeologist or anything. He was a former chippie from East Ham who'd taken up archaeology at night school when he couldn't get work.

A lot of people say that's why he said the things he did. That he made all that stuff up just because he couldn't get work on the site. I don't know if I believe that. It's just what people say. Whatever his reasons the media seemed to love his eccentric ideas. Almost every week the local rag would run an EXCLUSIVE announcing "Casper's Latest Evidence!" to prevent construction workers desecrating what he called "holy land".

It was all a big joke. But, amazingly, he found supporters. Hippies, tree huggers and sandal wearers all rushed to his corner as well as the nimbys and other killjoys that didn't want the Olympics in London in the first place. Against odds and common sense a movement swelled behind Casper Macvittee and his quest to shut the Olympics down.

This was all becoming a bit of an embarrassment for the Olympic organisers and the harder they tried to silence him the more his supporters believed the Olympic site might actually hold some magical archaeological treasure belonging to King Arthur. In the end the organisers decided they'd had enough. They invited Casper to a special planning meeting, so he could make his case formally.

It was a press frenzy. It was the Goliath of the Government and the Olympic planning committee in one corner with a madcap East London amateur archaeologist in the other. Three days prior to the meeting, Casper Macvittee announced that once again he had "startling new and irrefutable evidence" that would bring the development to a halt once and for all. The committee welcomed this news. It played right into their hands. The more outlandish his theories, the easier they believed it would be for the public to see through him.

But the public never got to see through him. They never got to see him at all. On the day of his hearing, he disappeared. Vanished, like a puff of smoke, into thin air, just like that, gone. What do you make of that? I'll tell you what the press made of it, a three-course meal of whodunits and conspiracy theories, pointing the finger at a number of corporations and businesses that had reason to bump him off. It was flattering really to think that he and his nonsense theory about King Arthur and ley-lines actually stood a chance of disrupting the build, but police procedure was still followed and all contractors and businesses connected with the development were questioned, but no charges were pressed.

There was no foul play, they said. Casper Macvittee just vanished. And being a crackpot, it seemed that little more believable that a man who thought King Arthur had something to do with Stratford could just disappear like piss in a swimming pool.

That had happened just over a year ago. There'd been no sign of him since.

I returned to the shop, carrying the newspaper in one hand and Duncan's sugar-free mug of tea in the other. 'You see this about your mate?'

'My mate?'

'Yeah, Casper Macvittee.'

Duncan raised an eyebrow. 'Why'd you call him my mate? I've never met him.'

'Well, you believe in all the same tripe. King Arthur, ley-lines and all that.'

Duncan looked at me like I was crazy, which I felt was rich coming from a man who thought plants could read.

'Anyway,' I continued. 'You see the story about him in here?'

'I read it earlier,' said Duncan. 'They are selling his house.'

'What?'

'Serious, they are selling it.'

'Nah, they wouldn't dare.' I skim read the rest of the article. It was true. The council had found a way to acquire Casper's home so they could sell it to developers. It said something about "maximising the return for an occupant presumed dead". Something about "extenuating circumstances". I folded the paper up in disgust. It all sounded dirty to me. I told Duncan.

'That sounds dirty to me,' I said. 'Greed's got too much round here. He's only been missing a year. He's not even legally dead but they've still found a way to sell his house. Someone at the council or on the build must really hold a grudge.'

Duncan nodded. 'I wonder what Jaggers will make of it?'

I shrugged. 'Who knows? It must be legal or they wouldn't do it, but you've got to admit it's underhand. Everyone's out to make a killing on the Games. People are paying stupid prices for everything, trying to sell every last little bit of land. Maybe the Pearly King is right. Maybe the Olympics are a bad thing for this area.'

'Maybe.' Duncan sniffed his tea. Satisfied it didn't have any sugar in it he took a swig. 'This milk will go off tomorrow afternoon,' he said absently. He gave another sniff. 'Probably about 3.10pm.'

- 9 -

BUILDERS

'Oscar,' called Duncan. 'Can you lend me a hand?'

I returned from my third cigarette break to find the shop full of builders, all sporting high-vis jackets and with yellow hard-hats under their arms. All looking about with mouths agog, in amazement probably that a crappy little shop like ours was still standing.

A bloke with a five o'clock shadow and tartan undershirt tried to marshal everyone. 'No subtitles!' he barked. 'And no Polish films neither.'

Groans.

'No,' cried the tartan shirt. 'Fair's fair. Let's get something we can all watch.'

The builders turned their attention to the racks. I felt my stomach wobble. These animals wouldn't understand the subtleties of our genre splits. I could see myself spending the rest of the afternoon sorting out the *Welsh Blaxploitation* wall.

The tartan shirt leaned on the counter. 'What do you recommend? I've got to keep this lot entertained for the afternoon.'

'*The Pride and The Prejudice*,' called a Polish voice behind him, which was backed up by several shouts of approval.

'No!' spat the tartan shirt. 'I've told you, watch it in your own time.'

Duncan laughed nervously. 'What's wrong with *Pride and Prejudice*?'

The tartan shirt snorted. 'They'll pick up all sorts of bad language. I can't have my Polish plasterers talking like the Queen, can I?'

'How about *The Long Good Friday*?' I suggested. 'That's a good gangster film. And it's got the Olympics in it.'

The tartan shirt frowned. 'What makes you think I want to watch anything with the Olympics in it? I'm sick of it.'

'We're doing a special on *Police Academy* films at the moment,' drawled Duncan. 'Five for a pound.'

'And there's no fine if you don't bring them back,' I added.

'No,' said the tartan shirt. 'Just give me a Bond film or something.' He drew a crumpled fiver out of his pocket and threw it on the counter.

I began looking through the drawers for a Roger Moore. 'So how come you're renting films anyway? Shouldn't you all be working?'

'We'd love to mate, love to...but not today.'

'Not more delays?'

'I'm afraid so, guv.'

'You guys only delay so you get paid overtime,' said Duncan.

The tartan shirt's eyes narrowed. Some other builders stopped their searching and cracked knuckles. 'What was that? You calling me a liar?'

'No...' said Duncan, thinking quickly. 'I'm calling you an opportunist. It's how capitalism works. I read a book on it.'

'Listen,' said the tartan shirt. 'I'd love to work today, but it ain't happening. Some hippies got on the site and sabotaged all our gear.'

'What?' I said.

'Straight up,' said the tartan shirt. 'Someone's got in there and torn the place up. Tractors, diggers, materials, the whole lot. They've left it in a right two-and-eight.'

'But I heard the drills this morning,' I said.

'Not ours. Our site is closed till further notice.'

'So do you still get paid for today?' asked Duncan.

The tartan shirt laughed. 'You hear that lads? He wants to know if we still get paid for today?'

The place erupted in laughter, followed by a second wave as the joke was translated into Polish. I took that to mean they were more than quids in.

I popped the DVD in a bag and handed it over. As the tartan shirt turned to leave a thought hit me. 'Say, you don't fancy buying this one for the wife, do you?' I leaned over the counter and fished *The Three Amigos* out of the bargain bin. 'It's a classic.'

A short while later, Duncan was stacking some Portuguese dubbed Steven Seagal DVDs, shaking his head. 'It's a crime. You could go to prison.'

He was referring to the Polish builder who had left a short while ago believing *The Three Amigos* was based on a Jane Austen novel.

'I didn't lie to him,' I protested. 'I said it was *probably* based on a Jane Austen novel. "Probably" being the key word. Jaggers would call me innocent. And that's all that matters.'

I walked to the isle in the middle of the floor and removed *Cannibal Holocaust* from the Kids' section. I knew those builders would mix everything up.

'I've never heard of angry hippies,' said Duncan, changing the subject. 'You think hippies can get angry? They must have been pretty mad to attack the Olympic site like that.'

I shook my head. 'It weren't hippies.'

'No, I don't think so either,' said Duncan. 'I think it's a conspiracy of some kind... like *The Da Vinci Code*.' He suddenly got very excited. 'It could be Casper Macvittee!'

It was said that after Casper Macvittee disappeared some of his disciples would act in his name and seek to sabotage the Games. I don't know exactly where the rumour came from, or who was spreading it, but it sounded like nonsense to me. A far too convenient cover story to run whenever there were construction delays. They had their scapegoat, and they were wringing ever last drop out of it.

I scoffed. 'You really believe that rumour?'

Duncan looked down uncertainly. 'Erm, yeah. Why not?'

'That's precious. You reckon your mate has raised an army?'

'Hey, stop calling him my mate.'

I laughed. 'Look, Duncan, not everything is a conspiracy.'

'Then how'd you explain the sabotage stuff?'

'Easy,' I said. 'We live in the London borough of Newham, the roughest borough in the UK. Kids round here get up to all sorts.'

'You think it's kids?'

'No,' I said. 'I actually think it's an insurance scam or something. This close to the Olympics, someone's wanting to have a nice little claim up. It's obvious.'

- 10 -

OLYMPIC TALK

DI Ken Bludwyn stared at me from his chair. 'So far it sounds just like the other three times you've told this story.'

'You're the one wanting me to tell it again,' I protested. 'How many different ways can I tell the truth?'

'Well, we'll find out, won't we?' said Bludwyn, with an over-suggestive arch of an eyebrow. 'Now, the Pearly King wasn't the only one who wasn't a fan of the Olympics, was he?'

I smiled. 'I ain't coy about it either. I don't know what all the fuss is about with the Olympics. It is just going to be a load of doped up athletes trying to do things quicker and throw things further than anyone has done previously. So what? There's never any story to it. Never any real drama. The starting gun goes off, the action happens, someone wins. That's it. That's why sports films are so much better than the real thing. Take *Rocky* for instance, that feeling of elation, the power of a training montage. All completely redundant in real life...that's why sports are boring.'

'Boring!' said Slick. 'Sir, did you hear that? The man is clearly insane. Everyone knows the Olympics are the greatest sporting spectacle on Earth! What but a deranged mind could find that boring?'

'Alright,' I said. 'Let me put it like this...if I told you that in my spare time I enjoy nothing more than picking up a brick and throwing it from one end of the garden to the other, you'd call me *deranged*. But, if

I told you I were a shot-putter, you'd think nothing of it. If a Brit shot-putter wins Olympic gold they'll be a national hero with a guaranteed MBE from the Queen and a sponsorship deal for a cereal so high in fibre it's only good for making you run back and forth to the bog. Oh yeah, they'll be a hero to everyone in the land, that is everyone but me, because I will see them for what they are...a silly fool whose only achievement in life is to throw a brick further than the other prats who spend their lives throwing bricks...

'...*And*...the organisers are just as bad. Why don't they give the brick throwers something to aim for? Like bonus features or little wormholes that suck the brick in and shoot it out of a cannon in another country. *New shot-put record. One thousand miles.* Now that's a spectacle!'

Bludwyn studied me. The dark bags under his eyes seemed to spasm with loathing. I got a feeling we weren't going to go for drinks after this. I needed to endear myself to him. Give him the information he wanted. Do anything but annoy him.

'And,' I continued. 'If you can have the javelin as a sport, which is essentially a weapon of war, why not have the synchronised nuclear detonation? Or the fifty metre stab?'

Bludwyn waved me down. 'Okay Oscar, you've made your point. Now, tell us about that afternoon in the shop...'

- 11 -

COCKROACHES

That Saturday was so slow I'd taken four cigarette breaks already, and was now stood in the yard, puffing on my fifth.

The yard was small and grey and stank. It had a white line painted up the middle of it, marking out smoking and non-smoking areas. It was easy to tell which side was which. My side was carpeted in cigarette butts whilst Duncan's was covered in a mess of blue chalk lines. He seemed to think the Greenwich meridian ran through the yard, and had spent years trying to map it, believing that if he found it, standing on it would recharge his chi, or something. Which if that was his aim, he was going about it the wrong way. He should've started with the bins. They always stank. And were always overflowing. If he'd emptied them more often, standing in the yard might have made him feel better.

I sucked on my cigarette and let my thoughts drift. They never drift that far. Don't they say men think about sex every six seconds? Well, I have trouble making it last that long. My thoughts are always interrupted by cockroaches. And ways to kill them.

They must die.

You won't get it. You'll never understand how they torment you. How they infect your mind and haunt you day and night. How your ears jump at the sound of their heavy marching feet. How you start hallucinating thinking you can see one, but it's just a bit of fluff or a coin that dropped out of your pocket or something. The sudden waking up at night thinking they are on you. Constantly brushing yourself down, convinced they are climbing all over you.

You can try, you can say you sympathise, but you'll never understand. Not until you've had to suffer them. And it's unlikely you'll ever get to do that, unless you move into somewhere like my flat. You see, the conditions have got to be right. They like it hot and humid, like say a launderette. Anything less, they don't want to know. I doubt mine had even bothered to crawl next door.

I naively spent my first month moaning to Jimmy about the cockroaches. He was about as useful as a chair made of fog. He'd duck the subject, wave it off, ignore it, do whatever he had to do to stall me, and he'd been doing it ever since. So, I decided to take matters into my own hands.

I was five months into my guerrilla war at that point. Five months of running about like Rambo, booby trapping my room, trying weirder and more elaborate ways of killing them off: sticky traps, scented traps, poison traps, even rat traps. But nothing seemed to work.

So I decided to change my tactics and pursue "alternative" methods.

One day back in May, I was walking about the Stratford Shopping Centre when I stumbled across one of those esoteric hippy shops Duncan always bangs on about. You know the sort of place that sells wind-chimes, josticks, and strange books on the power of crystals, all that sort of guff. Against common sense I ended up buying a huge dream catcher thing. It was the size of a satellite dish. The shop owner said it was the best thing he had for warding off "evil spirits". Apparently it had been blessed by a high-druid from Glastonbury who, he had it on good authority, was a direct descendant of Charlemagne and second cousin to the drummer from Deep Purple.

I was assured that those were good things. I was also told results were "guaranteed". So, I took a punt.

I got results.

Bad ones.

As we ran into summer the cockroaches continued to overrun me. But what did I expect? I didn't buy the stupid dream catcher because I believed in any of the voodoo powers or pagan crap that was supposedly behind it all. Duncan might have believed that, but I wasn't fooled. I took a punt because when you've suffered as much as I have, and been driven mad by their loud marching, finding them in your sock drawer, under your pillow, staring you in the face when you wake up, everything is worth a shot. You'll consider everything and do anything to get rid of cockroaches. That's when I decided to quit messing about. I decided to go Chuck Norris on them. I took things to Def-Con 1.

* * *

Bludwyn leaned forward in his chair, 'Now we are getting somewhere, Oscar!'

His moustache could barely conceal his grin. Slick bounced up and down excitedly beside him. They knew what was coming next. So did I. I'd had have to tread just as carefully through this bit as I had done the previous three times I'd explained it to them. Perhaps I could stall them?

'Can I have another cup of tea?' I asked.

'No, Oscar,' smiled Bludwyn. 'I want to hear you explain again exactly how is it you came to be in possession of an illegal chemical weapon.'

- 12 -

THE PACKAGE

I returned from my cigarette. Duncan had a stack of DVDs on the counter and was marking them off.

'I've been thinking,' he said. 'It's long and narrow. You could definitely put one lane in there.'

'What?'

'Jimmy Strongbow's model shop. They'll have to turn it into a bowling alley.'

I tried to think of a reason why that was a stupid idea, but like a lot of Duncan's stupid ideas, I knew it shouldn't float but somehow I couldn't find a winning argument to make it sink.

'What do you reckon? It could be a bowling alley, right?'

'Maybe,' I replied. I didn't mean maybe, but sometimes that's the only way of avoiding the stupidest of discussions. We often had stupid discussions, that's the nature of two people working in a quiet shop with only each other for company. We'll talk about all sorts of crazy shit. Most of which centres around film. Or great unanswered questions such as: would you let Jesus touch you if he had poo on his hands?

That afternoon though, Duncan asked a very sensible question.

'What's that?' He pointed at the package under my arm. I smiled and placed it on the counter for him to get a better look. He studied the biohazard stickers whilst I told him what I hoped was inside.

'Junior Anthrax? Are you serious?'

I explained to him that I was deadly serious, and that if this "Junior Anthrax" only lived up to half the hype the box had given it, I'd be on to a winner. The cockroaches would be history.

'But, it's poisonous, right?'

'Oh, I hope so,' I said, tearing the box open.

'Where'd you get it?'

'eBay.' I explained that I'd bought it from a powerseller in Wyoming who called himself UncleSaddam01. And it looked like UncleSaddam had come up trumps. When I opened the package up I found the poison locked away in a hermetically sealed silver cylinder, like a thermos flask. I was impressed. It looked the real deal. I made a note to give him good feedback. Maybe even check out some of his other items.

I held up the cylinder in triumph. This was it. I finally had the one thing that would bring me peace and rid me of the evil cockroaches once and for all. It was at that point that Duncan said the most sensible thing he'd said since I'd known him.

'Oscar, shouldn't you be wearing gloves?'

- 13 -

FILM

Having found a pair of dirty marigolds in the "staff area", I spent the afternoon carefully reading the forty-four page instruction manual that came with the poison. It was full of long technical words I didn't understand, and scientific measurements I'd never heard of, to do with gases and air currents I couldn't pronounce, but I felt I got the gist of it – basically, avoid using it as mouthwash and you'll be safe. The notice about "for use in well ventilated areas only" seemed like an over precaution. I'd play it by ear and see how it went. If it killed me, so be it. Just as long as it killed the cockroaches too. At least then I'd die happy.

I was so engrossed in the instruction manual I hadn't really paid any attention to the film Duncan had put on.

We took turns, picking films for each other. We watched them on an old TV that was mounted on a bracket overlooking the counter. It wasn't like being in the cinema, but it helped pass the time when things were slow. That day the movie was *Dead Calm*, a suspense thriller from the late '80s with Sam Neill, Nicole Kidman and Billy Zane. Sam Neill was the reason Duncan had picked it. It was part of his "antipodean" season, which had been going on for five months now and basically meant any film with a Kiwi in it, or *Crowded House* on the soundtrack.

'You like it?' he asked at the closing credits.

'A tour-de-force,' I said, not looking up from the instruction manual.

'Great,' he grinned. 'Next up is a real gem.'

'Can't wait,' I lied.

He rummaged amongst some cases. 'Brace yourself for...*Jurassic Park.*'

I waved a marigold at him in protest. 'We've been through this before.'

'But it's a classic.'

'I don't care. I can't watch Spielberg. All his films are the same.'

'No, they're not.'

'I'm telling you. Have a look at his films. What have they got in common?'

'Erm...box office success?' suggested Duncan.

'Nazis.'

'Nazis?'

'Every film he's made,' I said. 'It's always about the Nazis.'

'*Jurassic Park* isn't about Nazis.'

I raised an eyebrow. 'You don't know about the T-Rex?'

'Know what?'

'He originally wanted to put a swastika on its leg.'

'No,' said Duncan in disbelief. 'That's not true.'

'Honest,' I said. 'But the studio said no. In the end they compromised and had a few shots where the T-rex gets a Hitler tash from some shadow. And what about the "sieg heil" it gives as it grips the fence?'

'Nah, that's not true. Sam Neill is one of New Zealand's greatest actors. He wouldn't agree to work with Nazi dinosaurs.'

I shrugged. 'Why don't we put on a decent film you haven't seen? Let's have English film season.'

'I've seen all the *Carry On* films.'

'Not *Carry On.*'

'A Bond film?'

'Not Bond.'

'I've seen *Lock Stock*—'

'Will you stop interrupting!' I said. 'There is more to British Cinema than *Carry On* films, Bond movies and *Lock Stock*. You need to watch some British musicals.'

'What?' said Duncan. 'Like *Bedknobs and Broomsticks*?'

'No, like *The Wicker Man*.'

'That's not a musical,' he replied. 'It's a horror.'

'C'mon Duncan, it's a musical, there's solos and dancing and it ends on a big sing-song!'

'Hey, is that why I keep finding it in *Musical*? You keep moving it?'

'Yup,' I beamed.

'But,' he spluttered. 'You can't put it in *Musical*. It'll be next to *The Wizard of Oz!*'

'Now that's a horror! That witch melting in glorious Technicolor is bit strong for kids.'

'But doesn't someone get burnt alive in *The Wicker Man?*'

I waved my hand unconcerned. 'Most of that happens off-screen. I'll put it on.'

I found the disc and fed it into the player. As the opening credits began I felt a warm wave come over me, like I was being greeted by an old friend.

UK cinema gets a rough ride. We've produced some fantastic films but people just think our sole output is limited to *Carry On* movies or the occasional gangster flick. There might be some truth in that, but if you look at the fuller picture, we've had much more to offer in almost every genre. The one film that stands head and shoulders above all others is *The Wicker Man*. It is an outstanding piece of film. I think you'd like it. A police officer goes to investigate the disappearance of a little girl on a remote Scottish island, only to find her disappearance may be linked to the religion of the island's inhabitants, all of which are pagan and believe in ritual sacrifice in order to appease their gods.

* * *

Bludwyn sniffed. 'Do the cops win in that one, Oscar?'

'I don't want to spoil it for you.'

'I'm only interested in endings where the bad guys lose.' Bludwyn looked down at his sheet and cleared his throat. 'Now, Oscar, we've asked you to tell us the story three times already. And every time you veer off and start talking about film.'

'Have you ever fancied your mother?' asked Peasworth.

'What?'

Bludwyn's hand crashed down on the desk. 'Slick! What the hell has his mother got to do with anything?!?'

'It's psycho-analysis, sir. It helps untangle the criminal mind. Shows us what they're really thinking. I did a sandwich course on it, at the academy.'

'Well, we'll have less of that,' said Bludwyn. 'Let him tell his story, all the pieces will come together, eventually.'

'Sorry, sir.'

I smirked. Peasworth's hunt for a promotion would have to start again.

'Now, Oscar,' began Bludwyn. 'Enough about film. What happened after you left work?'

- 14 -

HOME

I left work and walked straight home. No, tell a lie. I stopped on the way to buy a lighter. You can never have too many, can you? Oh, and I bought a set of marigolds, as I didn't think I had any indoors.

The launderette was shut. Berol had gone, so had the steam and the bags of dirty clothes in the hallway. I was pleased to discover that Jimmy had gone too, no longer comatose under a pile of clothes in my wardrobe. However, it took me a few minutes to realise that as the moment I opened my bedroom door, I was blinded.

The smell was evil.

Coughing and gasping I blundered to the window and threw it open. Car horns blew in from the street followed by a cooling breeze. The smell remained. It was so bad it stung my eyes. I kept them closed and turned to make my escape. That's when I kicked something that made a sloshing sound.

I stopped still and chanced opening a watery eye. The yellow bucket lay on its side. A dark damp oval spread between *Cape* and *Banana Republic*.

I growled.

Jimmy hadn't bothered to clean up after himself. Instead the dirty git had left his business there all day, letting it cook from the rising heat of the launderette. No wonder the place stank.

I perched on the edge of my bed and drew my cigarettes out of my pocket. I sparked one up, partly to calm me down but mostly to make the place smell better. I'd have been angrier, but knowing I was in possession of some cockroach killing weapons-grade poison, I stayed kind of mellow.

I picked up the box containing the Junior Anthrax and examined it. I grinned and took another drag on my cigarette. I didn't know if this stuff was going to change my life, but just having it made me feel good. Knowing that inside that metal container lay the end to my cockroach nightmare.

I glanced about my room to see if I could spot any of the bastards. As ever, they were hidden. You only see them when you're not looking. Out the corner of your eye something will crawl, but when you look, they've gone. They are sneaky like that.

Having re-read the instructions I'd decided it would be best to unleash the Junior Anthrax on a day I was well away from the flat, like tomorrow, which just happened to be Sunday. I quite liked that. There was something biblical in it. It's God's day of rest, apparently, which meant that whilst his back was turned I was going to unleash the apocalypse and wipe out every dirty little cockroach in a one-mile radius, according to the instructions. Although I took those with a pinch of salt. I'd be happy with a kilometre.

So, despite my shaky floorboards now dripping wet with my landlord's piss, things didn't look that bad. In fact I was feeling in such a good mood I felt like putting on a film.

Earlier in the day, whilst I was tidying the *Myths & Legends* section, Duncan and I had a chat about our favourite film cyclops. Duncan had banged on about Ray Harryhausen for ages. He loved all those old Technicolor stop-motion films like *Seven Voyages of Sinbad* and *Clash of the Titans* and all that jazz. I liked them too, but then, you'd have to be a noddy not to like them. To annoy him I tried not to be as predictable in picking mine, he was more than a little disappointed when I put a case forward for Kurt Russell in *Escape from New York*. This lead to a debate about how exactly you define a cyclops. Is it someone with just one working eye, or someone who has only ever had one eye? Is a blind cyclops still a cyclops? Or does he have his status revoked? See, put two blokes in a shop for long enough with just themselves for company they'll talk all kinds of crazy crap. If you think we're bad, imagine what the geezers on oil rigs talk about, or the astronauts on the space station, or scientists in Antarctica, or whatever.

So, my night was set. *Escape from New York* and a couple of drinks. I found the film in a stack of ex-rentals under my bed. The DVD menu repeated five or six times whilst I went hunting for the remote. I turned over cases, Laserdiscs, Mini DVs, when over by *Granny Smith*, something caught my nose and my eyes started to sting. I brushed a pile of VHS tapes aside to find a half eaten onion crawling with cockroaches.

'Bastards!' I stomped on the onion. But it didn't do any good. The cockroaches lazily walked away taking their stinky breath with them. As I bent down to inspect them something moved by my eye line. I looked up to see a cockroach scuttle into a stack of tapes.

'Die!' I yelled, jumping up and swinging a boot after it. Bad move. As the tapes crashed down cockroaches spilled out everywhere, hitting the deck like a bag of upended rice. They scurried for shade in all directions, disappearing quickly between the cracks in floorboards and hiding under DVD cases.

I stood up and tried to keep calm. I took a couple of deep breaths, but that only made things worse as my lungs filled with onion rich air. I decided to take decisive action. I grabbed my wallet and cigarettes and headed for the pub, yelling, 'The apocalypse is coming for you bastards!' as I slammed the door.

- 15 -

QUESTIONS ABOUT THE BLUE EEL

'The Eel,' said Bludwyn gruffly. 'The infamous Blue Eel.' He looked across at Slick, probably giving a signal that the rookie should take note, that his boss was about to pull off a bit of interrogation wizardry.

I yawned and waved my plastic cup at them both. 'Can I have some more tea now?'

'In a moment,' smiled Bludwyn. 'First, I want you to tell us everything you know about the pub. We want to know who you know, how it works and who got you in. We want every single detail.'

'Every single detail,' repeated Slick.

I raised an eyebrow. 'What about the special rules?'

'Stop stalling!' barked Bludwyn. 'Just tell us what you know.'

'But the last three times you said there were things I couldn't discuss. I thought I had diplomatic immunity of some kind?'

Bludwyn shifted awkwardly. 'Well...things change.'

I studied him. 'You still haven't got full jurisdiction, have you?'

Bludwyn looked down and shuffled his notes. 'It's only a matter of time.'

I grinned. 'I'd be very careful if I was you. You could lose your badge. You need proper jurisdiction to investigate an embassy, don't you?'

Bludwyn's cheeks flushed red. 'Oh c'mon, Oscar! You know as well as I do it's not an embassy! It's a public house!'

'Oh,' I said. 'Then how come the courts recognise it as an embassy?'

Bludwyn sighed. 'There is nothing special about The Blue Eel. It's a pub, nothing more. Given time the court ruling will be overturned.'

'No chance,' I replied. 'I'd be surprised if anyone can overturn what Jaggers did. You've got to admit he's a genius.'

Bludwyn gave a snort. 'Rest assured, he'll have his day.'

I laughed. 'You've got no hope. You can't use the law against him, he's too good.'

'We'll see,' said Bludwyn.

He seemed tense. I enjoyed winding him up. It made a change for the glove to be on the other fist for a bit.

'So, in your own words, Oscar. Forgetting what the newspapers say, can you tell us what The Blue Eel is really like?'

'Well,' I began, 'as you know, The Eel is a curious little haunt. I don't care what anybody says or thinks, the reason I chose to drink there was because it's local, and not because of its special status. I mean, it was just two streets from my flat. It couldn't be more local. In fact, that's the only reason I was ever allowed in there. The first time I went in the landlord barred me until I came back with a council tax form to prove I lived in the area. Can you believe that? It makes sense now obviously, but at the time I was offended. I don't think the locals liked me at first, but gradually they softened. Well...I think they did.'

- 16 -

THE PUB LANDLORD

I walked through The Eel's worn wooden doors into a thick cloud of smoke. It felt great. I was no more than two steps inside when I joined in. That first drag was the taste of freedom. You couldn't help but smile.

Everyone still talks of what The Eel was like for that first month of the smoking ban. Locals refer to it as the "dark age". Ask them about it and they'll shudder as they remember the smell: a mix between fried chicken and a rugby team's kit bag, apparently. I reckon people are smoking in there now as much for the enjoyment as they are to stop that smell ever coming back.

The Eel is what I'd call a proper pub. The ceiling's nicotine-stained and everything's wood panelled and covered in horse brass. The carpet is old and thick with an almost Persian patterning. My feet sighed into it as I strolled toward the bar.

A few old timers were in, two sat at the wonky wooden table in the corner, drinking Guinness and playing a game of crib, a few others were on the long benches enjoying a roll-up and a chat. The Pearly King was sat at the far end on his sofa. I couldn't actually see his face from the bar, but I could see two bright shiny knees poking out from behind a pillar.

Stood behind the bar, surveying his empire was the landlord, Big Mick, so named because he was the reason double-doors were invented.

Or so he said. Nobody argued with him. He was wider than he was tall. And everything was a muscle, or at least used to be. He'd been a bare-knuckle fighter in his youth, taking on all-comers, "from Bow, Billingsgate and beyond," and had all his trophies lined up behind the bar to prove it. They were dotted between the optics and served as reminders for punters to think twice before causing any trouble. Not that they needed reminding. The sight of a cannonball-headed landlord with his arms like wheelie bins should've been enough.

He didn't scare me though. I reckoned if push came to shove and shove came to punch, I'd outrun him before he and his legendary fists could reach me. Although, I didn't want to put that theory to the test.

Big Mick gave a theatrical crack of his knuckles as I pitched up on a bar stool. 'Allo Mockney. What can I get you?'

That was his name for me. Mockney. I hated it and he knew it. He knew what I drank too. I could live in the area a million years; he'd never see me as a local. Like Kent was another bloody planet or something.

'I'll have the usual,' I said, tapping ash into an overflowing ashtray.

Big Mick looked blank. 'What's that?'

'Y'know. Whisky and coke.'

'Oh right.' He turned and set to work. 'Lemon?'

'No.'

He nodded and carried my drink over, a big lemon floating in it. I don't think he could be any more obvious in the fact he didn't like me.

'You don't half look a prat in them sunglasses.'

I took my glasses off and looked at them. They'd gone dark. 'Mick, I've told you before, these are reactor lenses. They're supposed to go dark when the sun shines.'

'And I bet you think it shines out of your arse, donchya?'

'Ere, have your lemon back.' I fished it out and tossed it toward an ashtray. 'Do I get any change?'

Big Mick closed the till and, ignoring my open hand, dumped my change all over the counter.

'Thanks,' I said sarcastically.

'No respect, you youngsters,' he said, picking the lemon out of the ashtray. 'My dad fought the Germans so you could have lemons in your drink.' I watched him wipe the lemon clean on his apron before putting it back in a bowl behind the bar. 'You going to be here long?'

'I'll be in here for as long as it takes Jimmy to sort out my cockroach problem. It's his last chance. If he doesn't sort it today, I'm going to get serious.'

'What you going to do?' grinned Mick. 'Make 'em watch one of your films and bore 'em to death?'

I ignored him and sipped my drink. I noticed a copy of the local paper on the bar, laying half open by an empty glass. I nodded towards it. 'You heard the latest about Casper Macvittee?'

'I ain't read that rag in years. It's always the same stuff about the Olympics, innit?' Big Mick picked up one of his trophies, spat on it and started buffing it with his shirt sleeve. 'You know Mockney, I could've won an Olympic medal, if I hadn't hung up me gloves.'

I frowned. 'You fought bare-knuckle. You didn't have any gloves.'

'So I did.' He put the trophy down. ''Ere, did I ever tell you I was the reason they invented double-doors?'

I ignored him. 'You hear the council are going to sell that Casper's house off?'

Big Mick shook his cannonball head. 'Why can't we let the dead rest in peace, eh?'

'Who says Casper's dead? He's missing.'

'Oh come off it, Mockney. He ain't missing. And he ain't running some private army neither. He's dead as you like.'

'Oh, what makes you so sure of that?'

Big Mick shrugged. 'I know this area. A man goes missing round here for a year he's either doing a stretch or he's brown bread. I'll tell you now, he ain't doing a stretch in any clink I know.'

- 17 -

QUESTIONS ABOUT JAGGERS

Bludwyn scribbled something on the sheet in front of him. 'How many people drank in The Eel who weren't Cockneys?'

'Oh, that's a good question,' I rubbed my lip. 'I think there were just four of us. There was me, Duncan and Jaggers. We were regulars. And there was a bloke who was studying there.'

'Studying there?' said Bludwyn.

'Yeah, a geezer called Lionel. He was a student, doing research for his PhD on slang and the way language evolves or something. He reckoned a new word or meaning was coined every 2.3 seconds in East London. Apparently that's the highest hit rate in the northern hemisphere.'

'And the southern hemisphere?' asked Slick.

'I don't think that's relevant,' said Bludwyn. 'Please continue…'

'I sat on my own, nursing my drink and admiring the brass plaque above the bar. You know the one they always print in the newspapers? In big gilded letters it reads:

YOU ARE NOW IN THE EMBASSY OF

RUMBAGO

'There is a little flag next to it. Like the Scottish flag, only the white cross is over a black background.

'I took a sip of my drink and wondered if Jaggers was going to pop in that night. I could do with asking him about the legal implications of using a lower class chemical weapon in an inner city borough.

'How well did you know Jaggers?' asked Bludwyn.

'I wouldn't say I knew him well. I don't think anybody got to know him properly. Most of what anyone knew was from the newspapers really. I mean, everyone heard what he was like in court but in The Eel he was an extremely quiet man of few words. He was softly spoken but with dour calculating eyes. He had a lean sallow face and dark thin hair in a centre parting that he'd grown into jaw length curtains.

'I'd heard one newspaper say he was a second rate lawyer and that all he had going for him was his piercing stare. Like that was all that was needed to persuade a jury? It was hard to guess his age but I'd say he was somewhere above fifty, but definitely less than sixty-five.

'How'd you know that?' asked Bludwyn.

'He didn't qualify for pensioners' happy hour,' I replied. 'Which was a bit harsh considering what he'd done. I mean, c'mon, it was the only pub in the land to have got round the smoking ban! The bloke should've been knighted! But Big Mick still charged him full whack.'

Bludwyn leaned over and talked into a little microphone on the desk. 'It is to be noted that the issue the suspect is referring to is ongoing case number CC103A: The Crown versus the nation of Rumbago, with the Crown seeking to revoke The Blue Eel's status as a serving diplomatic headquarters and its structure being used as an embassy.'

I couldn't help smiling. 'You have to admit Jaggers was a clever bastard, please just admit that.'

Bludwyn waved it off. 'He displayed a certain resourcefulness, most criminals do.'

'Oh c'mon,' I said. 'I think you're like the rest of people who lose against Jaggers, you've just got sour satsumas. You set up this fail safe ruling that is a nationwide blanket smoking ban. The Lords go over it with a fine-tooth comb. The best barristers in the land vet it. It's bullet-proof. It's rolled out across the nation. And within a month, just one month, Jaggers finds an elegant loophole, and you can't touch him.'

'There is nothing elegant in breaking the law,' scoffed Slick.

Slick was wrong of course. Jaggers's plan had been masterful. Being an old naval lawyer he chased up some contacts overseas and found some tin-pot island no bigger than a tennis court out in the Caribbean, and for a sum of cash offered them The Blue Eel as an embassy. A deal was struck, papers signed, and smoking was once again allowed in the pub as it was now deemed to be foreign soil in the possession of the nation of Rumbago, an island whose population consisted of the occasional parrot and a self-appointed King, who put himself into exile due to the fact the principality was too small for a harbour and sea defences.

Because of this, Jaggers had acquired something of a Robin Hood status and was championed by smokers up and down the land. A keen smoker himself he enjoyed his Gauloise brand through a long thin cigarette holder that his bony fingers held between his thin grey lips. When it came to legal matters, there was nobody better than Jaggers.

- 18 -

JAGGERS

I returned from the gents to find Jaggers sat on one of the long benches, dressed in a black court gown. His face was emotionless, delicately sucking on his cigarette holder with a glass of rum in front of him. His heavy lids were looking up the table at the old boys playing crib.

'Alright, Jaggers?' I said as I pulled up a chair next to him.

'Good evening, Oscar,' he purred. 'What news?'

'Not a lot,' I lied, thinking it best to butter him up before I started yakking about chemical weapons. 'Work was fairly slow. Had a few builders in from the Olympic site, apparently they've had to shut shop — all their gear's been wrecked.'

'GOOD!' shouted someone.

I ignored it and continued. 'Yeah, they reckon it was hippies that did it this time. Got onto the site and caused havoc. Could be major setbacks.'

'GOOD!' came the shout again. I recognized the voice. It was the Pearly King. 'I'm happy about that.'

I turned round. 'I'm trying to have a private conversation here.'

'Well have it somewhere private then,' scoffed the Pearly. I couldn't see his face, just his pearly legs. The rest of him was out of view. I opened my mouth to say something but Jaggers gave a slow shake of the head, suggesting I should leave it. Somehow the Pearly sensed this because he shouted out.

'No, it's alright Jaggers, let him have a pop, he's too young to know.'

I hate that, when someone says you are too young. I really hate it. I looked at what I could see of the Pearly King. Those bejewelled legs beyond the pillar. Suddenly he leaned his chubby face forward. I took a drag on my cigarette and stared at him. He stared back, blankly. 'You want to smoke that somewhere else, son? You can.'

I dropped my gaze. Winding up a Pearly on his own manor simply weren't the way to go.

Jaggers shepherded me back into conversation. 'What filmic treats were screened today?'

'Oh, you know Duncan, always banging on about his "antipodean" season. We had another Sam Neill and then I forced him to watch *The Wicker Man*.'

Jaggers's thin lips curled into a smile. '*The Wicker Man?* An eighteen certificate, I believe. Hardly appropriate viewing matter for a public space. I put it to you that you were in breach of several laws there, particularly the BBFC Screenings Responsibility Act of 1988.'

'Not a case for you though,' I said. 'Not enough money in it.'

'No,' purred Jaggers. 'Perhaps not.' He sank back into his chair and took a sip of his rum.

I often wondered what was worth Jaggers's time? Nobody really knew. He'd taken a weird range of cases in the past. I mean, some people would have you believe he was instrumental in bringing the Olympics to Stratford. So you'd think he was pro-sports and healthy living, an advocate of peace. But he wasn't. After all, this was the same man who'd been a naval lawyer defending war criminals and court-martialled soldiers. But then he was also the same man who found a loophole in turning The Blue Eel into a smoking pub. It was hard to know exactly what Jaggers was about. The only thing anyone could be certain of was that in any case he took on, he invariably won. And that scared people.

* * *

Bludwyn smiled. 'He's not defending you though, is he Oscar?'

I looked back unimpressed. 'I'm not Sherlock Holmes, but I think it's pretty clear why he can't defend me.'

Bludwyn waved his arm dismissively. 'Continue...'

- 19 -

JIMMY STRONGBOW

The pub doors flew open with a loud *BANG* and in bowled my landlord. For someone who should have been horribly hungover Jimmy Strongbow beamed like a lighthouse having a hot flush. He had a grin from hairy ear to hairy ear. All of his dirty yellow chandelier teeth were on display.

'Lovely-ol'-job. Lovely-ol'-job. Sing up!' he cried as he made his way to the bar. A few people patted him on the back. I guess they knew about his windfall. He ordered a pint of Pride and shuffled across to join me and Jaggers.

'Shift up, Oscar. Room for a little 'un.'

I moved along the bench and looked at him. 'Feeling better now are we?'

'Tip top, me ol' china. Tip top.' He took a deep swig of his pint and licked the foam off his top lip.

I don't know how it happened but we soon fell into an argument. It wasn't as if there was anything to argue about. I mean, he'd only stormed into my flat uninvited, took a piss in one of my buckets, insulted me and dismissed the cockroach problem as a matter most trivial. We exchanged words. I called him a dirty money-grabbing bastard and a scam landlord, amongst other things.

'You want to be careful,' warned Jimmy. 'That's slanderous, ain't it, Jaggers?'

Jaggers nodded.

'But you are a bad landlord!' I listed all that he'd done wrong. He countered by going through his brief selective history of things he'd done right.

'Look Oscar, I fixed all your windows, tightened them up, didn't I?'

'Yeah, but—'

'And your door locks, put heavy-grade bolts on them too, just like you wanted. Your drum is tighter than the Queen's purse, me ol' son. Ain't no one getting in there.'

'Didn't stop you entering last night!'

'I was coming round to do repairs! I needed access.'

'It was midnight!'

Jimmy shrugged and picked up his pint. He looked over at Jaggers. 'Round the clock care, not many people have that nowadays.'

Jaggers nodded sympathetically.

'Forget all that!' I said, waving it off. 'I only care about the cockroaches. We need to sort this out once and for all.'

'Oh, have a day off.' Jimmy looked across at Jaggers and gave him a wink before turning back to me. 'These cockroaches, Oscar. Are you *plagued* by them?'

'What's wrong with your ears? Of course I'm bloody plagued by them!'

Jimmy laughed.

'What's so funny? Hey, are you taking the piss?'

Jimmy laughed some more. 'Jaggers, fill him in.'

'A *plague* is a biblical phrase,' said Jaggers solemnly. 'Therefore to be suffering from a plague is to be suffering from an act of God. Which means that Mr Strongbow is not culpable for the distress you are suffering at the hand of your chosen lord.'

'There you go, Oscar. You heard it from the horse's mouth. It's an act of God, and until he shines a light on you me ol' son, you're going to have to deal with it.'

'Fine,' I said. 'I will. I'll deal with it. I'll deal with it tomorrow. I was just giving you one last chance that's all. I won't be held responsible for what I do.'

'Oh yeah?' said Jimmy. 'What you going to do? Put on one of your films and bore 'em to death?'

'No, I've got some poison in. Real strong stuff. It will clear them out.' I turned to Jaggers. 'What are the legal implications of using a chemical weapon in a built-up area?'

Jimmy spat his pint out across the table. Jaggers, by contrast, didn't even blink. 'It depends entirely on the class of weapon. But, depending on previous convictions and other factors such as the who, what, where, when and why – those questions courts are so fond of asking – I'd say you're looking at a mandatory sentence for possession alone of between seven to fourteen years.'

'What about my diplomatic immunity?'

Jaggers's lips curled into a smile. 'As a diplomat of this embassy? Now that would be an interesting case.' He leant back and considered it. 'You could get off scot-free or, and this is the more likely outcome, they'll add years to your sentence for smuggling...terrorism...perhaps even war-mongering.'

'Ah,' I slumped. 'That's quite heavy.'

'And you'll lose your flat deposit,' added Jimmy.

'What for?'

'Damage to fixtures and fittings. Talking of which, I should have you banged up for smoking in my non-smoking property.'

Jaggers leaned forward slowly. His dull eyes surveyed mine. 'You may have a case to answer there,' he purred, not a drop of humour in his voice. It sent a chill through me. This man knew the law. It was a Swiss army knife to him, he could use it, bend it, brandish it, and slice the world up with it any way he wanted.

'I'm not smoking,' I lied.

'Pull the other one,' said Jimmy.

'I'm not!'

'No, Oscar. I can't hear any more of this.' Jimmy stood up and drained his glass.

'Oi!' I protested. 'Where you going?'

Jimmy yelled over to the bar. 'Yes please, Mick, same again.'

'Right you are, Jimmy!'

'Jaggers!' I pleaded. 'Help me out. Can't you get him done for contempt for leaving halfway through?'

'Leave it out,' said Jimmy. 'We're on international soil. Rules don't apply here. Besides, I need a piddle.'

I turned and looked earnestly at Jaggers. He considered my appeal, holding his long thin fingers to his lips in thought. 'Oscar, I can't deny a client their basic human rights,' he purred. 'If Mr Strongbow needs to use the toilet, he's legally obliged.'

'Lovely-ol'-job!' laughed Jimmy, ruffling my hair before strolling off to the bog.

I leant close to Jaggers. 'You're meant to be the best in the land,' I hissed. 'You do the impossible and make this place exempt from the smoking ban and yet you can't pin my landlord down about some cockroaches? You know, I'm serious about this chemical weapon thing.'

'Oscar, I work on a no-win, no-fee, basis. I fear that if I were to win this case for you, it will cost me more than if I lose. I daresay that you could afford but fifteen seconds of my time.'

'Huh.' I slumped back and grabbed my drink. 'Who can?'

'Only the guilty,' replied Jaggers, with a somewhat sinister smile. 'They always have the money.'

'But it's not just about money, right?' I asked. 'What about ethics? Principals?'

Jaggers smiled. 'Oscar, I take cases on a humanitarian basis. I'll offer my services for free if the case proves an interesting test.'

'My case is interesting.'

'To you perhaps,' remarked Jaggers, grabbing his rum. 'But not to me, dear fellow. Not to me.'

Jaggers was wrong, of course. He and everyone else in London would find my case very interesting when I opened the Junior Anthrax.

- 20 -

DUNCAN

A short while later Duncan turned up looking like he'd fallen through a Hollywood costume department. He had on his beaten leather jacket with brown combat trousers and a poorly pressed white shirt. He walked through the door with strides as uncertain as his dress sense.

He saw me waving at him and, after going to the bar, came over with a pint of Guinness. He sniffed it carefully before taking a sip. Satisfied, he addressed Jimmy. 'Hey, Oscar tells me you sold your model shop.'

'Certainly did, me ol' son.'

'Who'd you sell it to?'

'Pah! What are you? Old Bill?'

'I'm curious.'

'You're something,' crowed Jimmy. 'Doesn't matter who I sold it to.'

'BLOODY DOES!' came a shout from down the bar.

The pub fell into a tense silence.

Duncan oblivious, continued. 'Do you know what they are going to do with it?'

'What's it matter to you?'

'Are they going to make it into a bowling alley?'

Jimmy stared at Duncan. 'Are you serious?'

'Oh, he's serious,' I said over my drink.

Jimmy examined Duncan as if he were some museum curiosity. 'I know you're from New Zealand and all but the world can't be that backward where you're from. A bowling alley? You're off your rocker.'

'So, c'mon then,' I said. 'Who'd you sell it to?'

'Alright, if you must know, I sold it to a consortium. They made an offer. I had to take it. Had to. They were practically biting my arm off.'

'SELL OUT!' came a shout from down the bar.

Again a tense silence.

Again Duncan tried to puncture it. 'Jimmy, were you drinking Guinness last night?'

'Do what?'

I elbowed Duncan in the ribs before he had chance to repeat his question. Jimmy seemed to have forgotten that I'd lobbed an onion grenade at him the night before. With Jaggers in attendance I didn't want it brought up in case I could get done for something. Thankfully Duncan's fleeting mind moved on to another subject. 'Hey Jaggers, did you hear about the vandalism on the Olympic site?'

'Duncan reckons it's part of a conspiracy,' I mocked. 'Like *The Da Vinci Code*.'

'It might be,' said Duncan.

'No,' I said. 'It's an insurance job, plain and simple.'

'But what if it's Casper Macvittee's underground army?'

Jaggers tapped ash into a tray. 'Seems entirely plausible.'

'What?' I said. 'An underground army wanting to sack the Olympics?'

Jaggers's lips curled into a smile. 'There are many people whom do not want the Olympics. Some are sat closer than you think.' He nodded in the direction of the Pearly King. 'Some will stop at nothing to ensure the Games ever take place.'

- 21 -

JIMMY STRONGBOW
& THE PEARLY KING

Jimmy spent the night waltzing round the pub, his face in a wide grin, all his yellow teeth smiling. The Pearly King didn't seem impressed by it all. He sat alone on his sofa and spoke to no one. He and Jimmy were close. You'd have thought he'd have joined in celebrating the windfall.

'I can't believe it!' cried Jimmy, now stood by the bar, holding court with a group of locals round him. 'Ever since we've had that shop, we've done nothing with it. My great-granddad bought it for two-and-six back in the day, and never used it once. I think some bunting was tied to the front for VE Day but that was about all the action it had, and now I sell it for almost a million notes.' Jimmy laughed. 'The Olympics are the best thing that could happen to the East End.'

From the far end of the bar a glass smashed. 'Rubbish!'

The Eel went silent and watched as the Pearly King got up from his sofa and approached the bar, his face flushed red, his suit jingled. 'The Olympics are the worst thing that could happen to the East End, Jimmy. You mark my words, son.'

'Leave off,' retorted Jimmy. 'We're rolling in it now.'

'Rolling in it, are we?' said the Pearly encouragingly. 'Rolling in tom-tit is what we are!'

'Easy now!' The landlord cracked his knuckles, ready for trouble.

The Pearly continued unfazed. 'And how much more you going to sell off?'

'It's none of yours,' replied Jimmy.

'You going to sell your flats, your businesses?' The Pearly turned and pointed at Big Mick. 'And what about you? You going to sell your boozer?'

Big Mick dropped his cannonball head in shame. The Pearly continued. 'Yeah, I heard you'd been offered. Thinking about it, are you? Well, sell it! Sell it all! Sell off our heritage to the developers because, mark my words, when the last pie and mash shop falls, and they put up a McDonalds in its place, then you'll wonder if the Olympics were a good thing. Because by the time I finish my next pint another acre of our history could be gone. You keep selling and the dam will break. The soul of the East End will go, replaced by chrome wine bars and yuppies. You mark my words!'

'C'mon now,' Jimmy offered a consoling arm. 'Have a drink.'

'Gertcha!' The Pearly pulled his arm away. Gasps went round the pub. 'Don't you taint me with your money-grabbing mitts! I've got Pearly pride. Pearly heritage! This is the East End. This is the area of fruit markets, jellied eels, pie and mash, rag-and-bone men, horse and carriage funerals, and you want to sell that, sell it all down the river, just to make a few bob? You make me sick. This ain't no time to celebrate. You're selling off your birthright.'

'C'mon,' said Jimmy. 'You're overreacting.'

'History will be the judge.' The Pearly King straightened his cap and prepared to leave. 'The best of Pearly luck to you, Jimmy, but that won't mean much to you now, will it? You want to kill off the East End? It's bigger than you, Jimmy. You can't kill it, *it will kill you*.' And with that he left, slamming the door so hard a pensioner who'd fallen asleep on the piano woke up and instinctively started playing *Who's Sorry Now*.

* * *

Bludwyn looked at me. 'Those were his *exact* words? "You can't kill it, it will kill you."'

I nodded.

'Strange thing to say isn't it?'

'People say strange things when they are drunk. I had one bloke running down the street the other night yelling out that he shot Red Rum.'

'I see…but do you think he meant it?'

'He might…I don't know, how did Red Rum die?'

'No!' snapped Bludwyn. I smiled. It was nice to know I could annoy him. Telling the story four times over was tiresome. 'I mean, do you think he meant the threat?'

'I don't know…people say things, but they don't always do what they say. Sometimes it's so easy to say things, don't you agree?'

I couldn't help smiling. I was starting to find out just how easy it was to say things to Bludwyn. What would I say next? I wondered. The truth? Well, I'd give as much as they needed. I mean, they only needed enough to connect the dots, right? Who cared if they dots they were trying to connect were wrong? So long as it didn't get too close to the *actual* truth, nothing mattered.

- 22 -

WALKING HOME

I was not entirely happy when I left the pub, but I was entirely drunk. I staggered along the pavement like a bolt of pissed lightning. The roads were wet from a brief shower. Thankfully I'd been in the pub and missed it.

I hate being out in the rain. On film it looks great, normally heightening a dramatic scene or marking a significant turn of events in the plot, but in the real world it's just annoying. Rain's just Mother Nature's sweat anyway. Who wants to have that falling on them?

I found my way up to the crest of Water Lane and was crossing over to the foot of Leytonstone Road when my ears caught something strange. A long haunting drone rose and fell on the breeze. I stopped to listen. It sounded like a harmonica.

Curious and drunk, I took a drag on my cigarette and staggered off to investigate.

Leytonstone Road was still. No cars, no buses, no drunks, just the eerie note carrying through the night. I noticed a light was on above Jimmy's model shop. A silhouette was stood in the window. I followed the sound towards it.

I approached cautiously, or as cautiously as you can when you've had a session. My footsteps echoed down the street as the playing continued. As I drew closer I could see a new sign had been put up. It said: *Pirate Shop.*

I squinted, belched, and adjusted my glasses, thinking I'd read it wrong, but I hadn't. A Pirate Shop was going to open opposite my flat.

I had no idea what a Pirate Shop was, so I stumbled closer. I looked up at the silhouette. The harmonica playing stopped and a face leaned out of the window to examine me. It was rugged and old with a straggly grey beard. He looked like a tramp. The streetlight caught his arm and I could see he was covered in tattoos, the old green ones. And he was holding a pipe in one had, one of those corncob jobs that Popeye likes.

'Oi mate!' I yelled. 'What's a Pirate Shop?'

The man's eyes narrowed. He withdrew slowly.

'Oi mate!' I called after him. 'I was only asking a question. What's a Pirate Sho—' But I didn't get to chance to finish, because he returned and threw a pail of water over me with an almighty 'Y'arrgh!'

Soaked, I looked up at him. He gave a toothless grin. I looked at my sodden cigarette, now limp in my mouth, and threw it away. I knew when I was beaten. I crossed over the road and went straight to bed.

* * *

Bludwyn looked at me suspiciously. 'Doesn't make sense, Oscar,' he mused. 'You've just had a bucket of water thrown over you for no reason. You didn't retaliate?'

I smiled. 'Mr Bludwyn, in case it has escaped your attention, I live in Maryland Point. Just stopping someone for the time is enough to get you hospitalised. You tell me, how many murders have taken place near my flat?'

'Many,' said Bludwyn. 'But none caused such havoc and distress as what you were party too.'

'I wasn't party to anything,' I protested. 'I keep telling you. I'm the victim.'

'Of an unprovoked attack?' Bludwyn raised an eyebrow so high it nearly disappeared into his hairline. 'You ask a simple question and someone throws water over you? It just doesn't make sense.'

'You say you were drunk?' said Peasworth. 'Perhaps you said something abusive? Or threatening? You've admitted that you left the pub unhappy with the way Jimmy Strongbow had dismissed your cockroach problem. Perhaps, fuelled up on drink, you sought to take your aggression out on the nearest person, which happened to be this old pensioner enjoying a casual smoke out of his window.'

I grinned. 'You are trying to use reason to make sense of it all. And let me tell you, I learnt you can't reason with pirates.'

- 23 -

MORNING VISITOR

I awoke with a pounding hangover. The worst I'd ever had. Just repeated banging in my head until I realised it wasn't a hangover at all. Someone was knocking at my bedroom window.

I got out of bed and crossed the shadows of my room to investigate. As I opened the window the sound of the street punched me in the face, with one sound hitting me at point blank range.

'Morning, Oscar!'

I yawned. 'Morning, Danny.'

A toothy man in dungarees grinned back at me. Slim sort, with a face creased in a thousand places, like an unfolded bit of origami. 'Ere, ain't got a snout have ya?'

I fished a cigarette from my dressing gown and handed it to him. 'I weren't expecting you for another week,' I said, sparking one up myself.

'Olympics, innit?' said Danny. 'Got us working this patch overtime now. They reckon we'll be changing the boards every two hours when the Games are on. Ere, hold this a sec.' He thrust a bucket of wallpaper paste at me, some of it sloshed out and hit my chest with a splat.

'Thanks,' I said, unimpressed.

'I've got your videos here somewhere, hold on.' He searched a weathered satchel hanging from his shoulder.

I tried to lean past him and stare at the billboard on the side of the flat. 'What am I advertising now?' I squinted in the sunshine. 'Condoms?'

'*Olympic* condoms' beamed Danny, chuffing away. 'Gold Gentles, Silver Sensuals, and Bronze Barbs.'

'Barbs?'

'Yeah,' said Danny. 'Y'know, ribbed?'

'Bloody hell.' I blew out a cloud of smoke. 'Well, at least it's not tampons, eh?'

'Too bloody right!' he chimed. 'In fact, bring back that ad for cheese with that bird in the bra, that's what I say. I was a very happy man putting a 20ft pair of tits up against your wall, Oscar. Some of the best work I've done. The joins were seamless. *Seamless.*'

I looked out across Maryland Point. It was another cloudless day. Traffic grunted by below and I could hear people already shouting at each other in the street. There was a slight breeze. I couldn't feel it but I could see it was there. Across the road a flag flapped. It had a skull and crossbones on it and hung from the Pirate Shop window.

I pointed with my cigarette. 'Danny, you know anything about that place?'

'Nah. Nothing. Probably another takeaway, innit?'

Bloody takeaway. Danny had been sniffing too much wallpaper paste. I said goodbye and closed the window, throwing his returned tapes on the floor. The impact made a few cockroaches break cover and scuttle elsewhere for safety. I ignored them and lay back on my bed, thinking about the Pirate Shop. I shouldn't have bothered. I had bigger and better things to think about. After all, today was the apocalypse. Though strangely I didn't feel in an apocalyptic kind of mood. Perhaps that had something to do with last night and the seven-year sentence Jaggers said I could get just for being in possession of a chemical weapon. How many more years would I serve for actually using it in a built up area? Maybe I'd receive a knighthood or something from the government for services to the improvement of Newham borough?

Who was I kidding?

And anyway, was I really in possession of a chemical weapon? It had to be a hoax. Like those ghosts people buy in bottles. I'd been duped. I just didn't want to admit it. Even so, I was still wary of opening that silver flask and finding out what was actually inside. I mean, it looked too much like the real thing.

What was I talking about? Like I, a skint DVD rental shop worker, would know the real thing? Based on films I'd seen it looked like the real thing, which meant it was even more likely to be fake. I mean, thanks to Bond movies, for years I thought if you karate chopped someone on the back of the neck you'd knock them out cold, for hours. False. Duped. Lies. Just like the supposed "Junior Anthrax".

There was only one way to find out. I had to open it.

I got up from the bed. The flask stood on the floor by the collapsed remains of the wardrobe. I wrapped my hand around it but something felt wrong. Instead of feeling the smooth silver of the cylinder in my palm I felt a crunchy insect like lump.

I flinched and jumped back, kicking the flask over, ready to stamp an escaping cockroach into the next world. But there was no need. It was already dead.

Intrigued, I bent down and had a closer look. It was on its back with its legs all folded up. I sensed this was a ploy, so I jabbed it with my finger. Nothing. I flipped it over. Still nothing. It was as dead as Steve Guttenberg's acting career.

Curious, I picked up the flask and examined it. All the seals were intact. It was then I noticed another cockroach, laying just a few inches away. Dead.

A few moments later, I'd cleared a circular space round where the flask had been. I counted eight cockroaches. All dead.

I sat back on the bed and had a think. My money suddenly seemed well spent. I mean, all those dead cockroaches couldn't have been a coincidence. The poison had to be killing them, right? Which, if that were true, meant things were very serious. If this Junior Anthrax was the real deal, it meant I had weapons-grade chemicals in my room, traceable to me through my eBay account.

Oh boy.

But it wasn't the prospect of the seven-year stretch that scared me the most, it was the poison itself. I mean, if these chemicals were so strong they could kill cockroaches through a hermetically sealed flask, what had they already done to me? And what the hell would happen if I actually opened it?

- 24 -

DECONTAMINATION

Having made this discovery I took a very thorough shower. Usually, I'm never in the shower for long. It's on the blink. It keeps flipping from hot to cold to hot again every few seconds, and Jimmy's never bothered to work out why. That morning though, I showered properly. I used a whole bar of soap and a bottle of shower gel. And a bottle of washing-up liquid. I know it sounds silly, but I thought if it could shift stubborn stains off plates, it was worth a shot at shifting a chemical weapon off me. Although it left me smelling of lemons. All in all I must have spent thirty minutes in that poxy shower, which is some kind of record as I'm usually only in there long enough get washed and check for bum crumbs.

* * *

'No more lies!' interrupted Bludwyn.

'I'm not lying.'

'Really?' he raised an eyebrow. 'Then how come this is the fourth time we've discussed what happened, but it's the first time you've elected to mention these *bum crumbs*?'

'Oh c'mon, Inspector. Do you want the full story or not?'

'Of course! But these *bum crumbs* don't seem relevant.'

I sighed. 'Look, let me put it this way. You know when a DVD gets re-released there is usually an *extended* edition, then a *deluxe* edition, then a *collector's* edition?'

'What's your point?'

'Well,' I said. 'This is the fourth time I've told the same story. We're now up to the *ultimate* release. I'm throwing in all the extras, all the bonus features and behind-the-scenes stuff – I thought you wanted to get an absolute picture of what happened.'

Bludwyn closed his eyes and pinched the bridge of his nose. 'I do...I just don't see how your so-called *bum crumbs* are of any relevance to the crime that was committed.'

'I do,' chirped Peasworth. 'I think we should get the suspect to supply a stool sample. And then call in the boys at phrenology to read the bumps for clues. Might give us what we need to unlock this case.'

Bludwyn shook his head dumbfounded. 'Oscar, please continue...'

- 25 -

UNEXPECTED VISITORS

After my do-it-yourself decontamination, I got ready to leave for work. I trudged downstairs to the launderette. Amidst the steam there was shouting and a lot of commotion. Four men were in the hallway, each wearing sunglasses, black suits and ties. Two of them had Berol pinned against a wall.

'Oi!' she cried, trying to fight them off. 'Touch me like that again and I'll wallop you one in the jacobs!'

'Please calm down, mam.'

'What's going on?' I shouted.

One of them spun round. 'Who are you?'

'Who are you?' I replied.

'We ask the questions, pal.' The suit waved a badge in my face. 'FBI.'

Now, normally I wouldn't panic. Unlike Duncan I don't believe every word people say, because no matter how pure people reckon the truth is, it's often cut with salt and bullshit. In my experience everything in life is a tall tale, an exaggeration, or at worse a bare faced lie.

And that's what I would've normally thought when stopped by anyone claiming to be the FBI. But that day was different. For that day, I quite possibly had an illegal chemical weapon in my bedroom. As such, initials like F, B and I were not well received. In fact, those three little letters made me shiver with panic. It was one of those shivers that cause your ring to burp with fear. One of those burps that made me think Berol wouldn't look forward to cleaning my pants even if I pre-rinsed them. Because if this was *the* FBI and I really had a chemical weapon upstairs, then the game was up. They had me surrounded.

I looked at his ID. 'Where'd you get that, a joke shop?'

The suit grabbed me and pushed me back against the wall. 'Wise-guy, eh?'

I tried to push him away. 'What's this about?'

'I told you, pal,' said the suit. 'We ask the questions. And I'm going to ask you one last time. Who are you?'

'That's Barry Bunger,' cried Berol, still trying to boot her captors. 'He owns the video shop.'

'That's right,' I lied. 'I'm Barry Bunger. I own the video shop. What's all this about?'

'Barry Bunger, eh?' The suit let go of me and drew a pad from his pocket. He pointedly checked his notes before slamming it shut. 'Show me your hands.'

'What?'

The suit grabbed my hands, roughly. He took a moment to examine them before letting go. 'Scram, Bunger.'

'What?'

'You heard. Beat it.'

'Now, hang on a sec, what's all this about?'

'Didn't you hear me, buddy? I said go about your business.'

'And I said, what's this about?'

'You dumb schmuck, someone gethimouttahere!'

I was bundled out the back of the shop. During the bundling they read me *their* rights. It's sort of like when you read me my rights. You know that, "anything you say may be taken down in evidence," stuff.

Except they explained their jurisdiction. Which was rattled out at light-speed in the few seconds it took for two of them to pick me up and toss me into the yard: *'Maryland Point is a silent state of the United States in which the government of the USA has law enforcing powers in accordance with the ceding of the land parcel to...'*

I don't remember the rest. When I finally found my feet, I ran to work. And for the first time in my life…I was almost on time.

- 26 -

POLICE INTELLIGENCE

Bludwyn shuffled his papers. 'It's not good news, Oscar.'

'You amaze me.'

'As you know,' he continued, ignoring my sarcasm, 'we've been trying to contact our American friends to verify this part of your story, but so far we've drawn a blank. They will neither confirm nor deny they have ever had operatives in Maryland Point.'

'Oh the FBI were here alright,' I said. 'Trust me.'

'That's the problem,' said Bludwyn, 'We don't. And until you serve up ironclad proof they were here, we'll continue to believe that you're lying.'

'C'mon,' I said. 'What about Berol? Surely she says she saw them?'

Slick tutted. 'He knows the rules, sir. We can't talk to you about the other witnesses.'

'But she—'

'No,' said Bludwyn. 'We're not interested in her. We're just interested in you. *Extremely* interested. Please, continue.'

- 27 -

BUNGER'S VIDEO PALACE

The shop shutters were already up. I burst in through the front and wheezed into the darkness with my hands on my knees. 'Duncan?'

'You're not as late.'

'I need to get out of the country.'

A head poked up from beneath the counter. 'What?'

'I think I'm in big trouble...' I gasped, '...with the FBI.'

'The FBI? Serious?'

I began to explain just how serious I was. I told him about the dead cockroaches, the potency of the Junior Anthrax and that I'd been ambushed in the launderette by some blokes claiming to be the FBI. Duncan got so excited it took a few minutes to calm him down.

'A conspiracy! I knew it!'

'Never mind about that, do you reckon I should make a break for it?'

'A proper conspiracy!' Duncan shook his head in disbelief. 'I'd heard rumours, but I always felt that one was true.'

'What rumours?'

'The FBI rumours,' said Duncan. 'Y'know, that they operate in Maryland Point.'

'Don't wind me up.'

'I'm serious. It's been a rumour for years.'

'I've never heard it,' I said.

'You don't talk to the right people.' He began to tell me what he'd heard. I listened carefully and then I listened disbelievingly and then I listened thinking Duncan was talking out of his Kiwi-shaped hole.

'Let me get this straight,' I said. 'You're saying Maryland Point is named *after* Maryland in America?'

'Yeah.'

'How is that even possible?' I said. 'If the films I've watched are true, and I've watched more than my share of those crappy covered wagon westerns, the pilgrims left England *for* America. You've got your history arse about face.'

'No,' said Duncan. 'An early pilgrim didn't like America, so he came back to England and founded Maryland Point, right here,' he pointed at the floor, presumably for dramatic effect, 'but, he shouldn't have.'

'Oh?' I said. 'Why's that? Because the place rose up into this karzee?'

He shook his head. 'No, because of the American Constitution.'

'Are you pulling my peanut or what?'

'Serious, there's something in it that says any place named in honour of the motherland can be claimed as a state. The pilgrim that did it had dual citizenship. So, the minute he founded it as Maryland Point, it was like putting a flag in it and calling it yours. It was technically American soil. And it has been since, sort of.'

'"Sort of?" What's that supposed to mean?'

'Well, the rumour I heard was that it's a territorial dispute that's never been properly resolved. They say back in the 1920s the Americans tried drilling for oil, but when they found none they rolled over their claim on Maryland Point as an official *state*, but a loophole was never closed about legal jurisdiction and the responsibility for maintaining the peace. So, it's a silent state.'

I rubbed my chin and pondered it. 'Now you mention it, when they bundled me out of the launderette, they said something about jurisdiction and silent states.'

'See,' said Duncan. 'You laugh at my theories but I know what's going down around here.'

I gave him a slow handclap as thanks. 'That's great, Columbo, but you've solved nothing. I don't really care about their jurisdiction. I care about me. Should I make a break for it?' It was a poor state of affairs when a felon takes counsel from a man who thinks foxes can talk. I might as well have handed myself in there and then.

'You said you told them you were Mr Bunger?'

I nodded.

'Well, pretend to be Mr Bunger.'

'Duncan, he's Indian.'

'They don't know what he looks like,' he said. 'In fact, they can't know what you look like or they'd have arrested you, right?'

'I hadn't thought of that,' I said, suddenly feeling a bit stupid.

'Your eBay account doesn't need a photo or anything like that, does it?'

'No.'

'So, you're faceless. Mr Bunger is in India for another month. You can pretend to be him until he returns. And what better place to be him than in his shop? You can stay here. Lay low.'

I don't know how, but Duncan had some sort of point. So, with no better plan, I decided to lay low, literally. I spent the morning stretched out behind the counter reading DVD boxes, convinced the FBI would burst through the door any minute.

The shop bell rang.

I whispered to Duncan. 'Who is it?'

He kicked me in reply.

I nodded and stayed very still. There was a strange smell, really overpowering, like a napalm attack at a perfume counter. It was musky and burnt the nostrils. The smell was accompanied by the slow approach of footsteps. I couldn't see who they belonged to but from my position on the floor I could see Duncan and he looked terrified. His body was stiff but his arms were all over the place: folded, unfolded, rubbing his neck, his head, his face. This didn't look good. I closed my eyes.

'Hello…*big boy.*'

- 28 -

TALLULAH FUNBAGS

My eyes snapped open. Duncan flushed red and let out a nervous giggle. 'Hi…Miss Funbags.'

'Oh, you're so polite,' came a deep seductive purr. 'I could just gobble up *every single inch* of you.' I watched a feminine hand with long red nails reach across the counter and tweak Duncan's nose, which, given the sensitivity of that part of his anatomy, was equal to grabbing his crotch. As such, he let out an orgasmic sigh.

Duncan was always like this around Tallulah Funbags. He didn't carry a torch for her, he carried a mushroom cloud. Although he never did anything about it. He was too shy. Too nervous. Too…I dunno…Duncan about it, believing that she was out of his league. Which I found funny as it was common knowledge she was a Madame at the Stratford Tanning Depot, and for a few notes would probably have ridden him or anyone else like a Grand National winner.

Duncan refused to believe she was a prostitute though, thinking I was just trying to wind him up. He wanted proof, though I think the facts spoke for themselves. Any woman who goes about her day dressed up in zebra print, wobbling about in some twelve-inch stiletto boots and with a healthy half-inch coating of fake tan slapped on, might well be a law-abiding, church-going, tax-paying citizen. But when a woman does all that and seductively leans on the counter at every opportunity, pushing boobs between arms to increase an already monstrous cleavage, and starts licking her lips seductively and refers to you repeatedly as "big boy", then I think the game is up. Or in this case on. Or to put it more directly, she's on the game.

'I need you to fill my slot again…' she purred. '…just as good as last time.'

I went to sit up and take a closer look at things, but Duncan's foot quickly pinned me to the floor. 'S-s-sorry?' he stammered.

'My DVD slot,' she continued. The counter creaked, probably with the weight of her massive knockers leaning on it. 'You satisfied me for two solid hours with your last choice. Reckon you can please me again? I'm looking for something…*hard.*'

Duncan rubbed the back of his neck. Yeah, she was doing her cleavage thing alright. 'S-S-Sam Neill…' he spluttered. '…one of New Zealand's greatest actors…' And he began rifling through the drawers for a DVD. I tapped the foot that had me pinned to floor me and mouthed, 'Red list'. He ignored me and continued searching.

- 29 -

TALLULAH TALK

'She's not what you think she is,' said Duncan after Tallulah left the shop.

'Come off it, Duncan. You like a rumour. I could tell you a few "rumours" I've read about her on toilet doors.'

'You've got it wrong. She's a masseuse.'

'A masseuse who, according to the graffiti in the gents at The Eel, "gives a top wank."'

'Hey, that's not a nice thing to say.'

'Truth hurts.'

'You don't understand Tallulah.'

'You really think Tallulah Funbags is her real name?'

'It must be. It's the name she's registered her video card under.'

'Pfff...I bet if you pay enough you can call her what you want.'

'You shouldn't be nasty about her, she might be misunderstood. It could be like *Pretty Woman*.'

'*Carry On Up The Brothel* more like. Just don't let her play you, that's all. You grew up in New Zealand, you don't understand the East End.'

'Didn't you grow up in Kent?'

'Whatever,' I said. 'Anyway, you shouldn't have let her rent anything. She's on the red list. You know how much she owes.'

'Since when have you cared about the red list?' He stared at me. 'You know, since the FBI have been after you, you've become all uptight. She's nice. I like her. I like the way she smells. She has a very unique smell about her. Her perfume, I think. She smells amazing, like a spice caravan coming to trade from exotic lands.'

'No, she smells like the tide's out.'

'Well, she smells much better than you...' he stepped towards me and began sniffing. '...you smell of...lemons. Why do you smell of lemons?'

'Don't change the subject.'

'You do. You smell like...' sniff, '...washing up liquid.'

I pushed him away. 'You weirdo, I'm going for a snout.'

And I needed that cigarette.

I stood out the back of the shop, on the designated smoking side of course, puffing away and contemplating my existence, the way you do whenever you smoke a fag. It's like meditating, I imagine. You ponder life's strange twists and turns and why it is you haven't won the lottery yet. I knew why I hadn't won the lottery. I didn't play it. Mug's game. All gambling is. I'd bet my old man would tell you that, if you ever found him. You know he once tried to pawn his teeth to put on a bet? Can you believe that? It's not even as if his gnashers were made of gold. They were bog standard molars. But that's another story. Waste of space he was. Just like Maryland Point.

Just like my life.

I kicked an old Coke can toward the bins. It was rusty and covered in black crap, but it still gave a satisfying clatter. Although the satisfaction was short lived. As I looked down I could see most of the crap had transferred itself to my trainer. I swore and walked to the bin and began for looking some cardboard or something I could use to scrape it clean.

As I was rummaging I felt something. I don't know if the yard was overcome with a sudden stillness or what, but something didn't feel right. I felt eyes on me.

I froze.

A hand clapped on my shoulder. 'Thought you'd be here.'

- 30 -

INTELLIGENCE

'Jesus!' I cried, jumping up. 'You could've given me a bloody heart attack!'

'Don't be a tart,' said Berol. She pulled out a fag. 'Ere, got a light?'

I fished about in my pocket and handed one over.

'Cheers.' She puffed a couple of quick puffs and gestured at the bins. 'Cor, they chuck up don't they? Smells worse than your bog.'

'Forget that,' I said. 'What are you doing creeping up on me like that? Aren't you meant to be at the launderette?'

'Been shut down,' she replied, somewhat distracted by the blue chalk lines all over the yard. 'It's a crime scene apparently. Thought you'd want to know.'

'A crime scene?' I said. 'What crime?'

'I dunno.' She blew smoke skyward. 'They wouldn't tell me.'

'That's really helpful,' I said. 'You came here to tell me that?'

'Oi, don't get lippy. They did tell me something.' She scratched her head. 'They said it was part of a larger international investigation. Whatever that's supposed to mean.'

I had a reasonable idea what that might mean. And it didn't sound good. It sounded like trouble. In fact, it sounded like just the sort of thing they'd say if they were investigating the illegal purchase of a chemical weapon.

'Was that it? They didn't say any more?'

'Nah.'

'Nothing about weapons, chemicals, anything like that?'

'You what?'

'Chemical weapons. Did they say anything about them?'

'Nah.'

'You sure?'

'You mutton or summit?'

'I just want to make sure.'

'Bloody hell, Oscar. I'd remember if they'd asked me about the flippin' A-bomb.' She stamped her fag into the concrete. 'They asked me questions, y'know, about customers, that sort of thing. And then they took a load of washing off somewhere.'

'Washing?' Duncan poked his head out from the shop. 'I didn't know you did the FBI's washing.'

'No, you tart,' said Berol. 'Stop ear wigging.'

'Whose washing?' I said.

'Everybody's. I tried to stop them. You saw me kicking up a fuss, right? I had one of the Pearly's suits to clean special for today and those Yanks have had it away. The Pearly's going to do his nut when he finds out.'

'I wouldn't tell him if I were you.' Duncan had moved to his side of the yard and was now carefully positioning himself on one of his lines. 'He's in a bad mood. Last night in The Eel, he threatened to kill Jimmy.'

'He what?' cried Berol.

'No he never,' I said. 'Duncan makes everything up. He thinks foxes can talk.'

'Serious,' said Duncan, tip-toeing along as if he were on a high wire. 'You were there, Oscar. You heard how upset he was about Jimmy selling off his model shop.'

'Yeah,' I said. 'He was angry but he didn't say he was going to kill anyone.'

'He said to Jimmy, "You can't kill the East End, it will kill you."'

'To be honest, I don't give a toss about the Pearly,' I said. 'He talks a load of old toot.'

Berol gave me a hard stare. 'You don't want to be saying that.'

'He does though, don't he? He's bloody full of it, prancing about like a tit in all that,' I waved a hand up and down at my clothes, 'poncey Pearly stuff.'

Berol's eyes narrowed. I felt she was sizing up which foot to swing at me plums. 'I think you've said enough, Oscar. I'll be seeing you.'

She turned to leave.

'Ah, c'mon Berol. Don't be like that.'

'Got to get back to work, ain't I?' she said. 'Make sure the FBI ain't been too interested in the till. Know what I mean?'

I knew what she meant. She fiddled the books every week to be down exactly the price of two packs of fags.

'Berol...thanks.'

'What for?'

'For coming down here and telling us what's going on.'

'It's what Cockneys do,' she said. 'We take care of each other. And if you want people round here to take you in, you've got to start showing a bit more respect. Badmouthing the Pearly like that ain't a smart move. He's got plenty of clout round here. More than you ever will. Keep that in mind.'

'I will.'

'Be sure that you do.'

At that moment the shop bell went. I flashed Duncan a nervous look. He nodded and leapt off his blue chalk line to investigate. Berol went to follow him, but I called her back to the yard. As Columbo would say, I had just one more thing.

'Ere, why'd you tell them I was Mr Bunger?'

She grinned. 'Cockney tradition, ain't it? Giving old bill the run-around. If I'd given your real name they'd think I'd gone soft.'

- 31 -

BACK IN THE SHOP

After Berol left I stayed in the yard and lit another cigarette.

Something didn't feel right. Maybe it was the head-rush I was getting from having two fags so close together. Or maybe it was the weirdness of the last twenty-four hours, with my landlord breaking in dressed as Barry Manilow, a chemical weapon arriving at the flat, a Pearly King making public threats, pirate pensioners throwing water out of windows and with the FBI sniffing about. Whatever it was, there was something odd I couldn't put my finger on.

I stubbed out my fag with a foot and tip-toed back inside. I'd have another go "meditating" on things later. I stood out of sight and whispered. 'Duncan?'

'All clear,' he replied.

I let out a sigh of relief and bowled back into the shop. I found Duncan alone, sniffing the milk. 'I told you this was going to go off today, didn't I?'

'Nevermind that! Was it the Feds?'

'No, it was nobody. Just a pirate.'

I frowned. 'What do you mean "just a pirate"? What did he look like?'

'He was old, with a grey beard and he had lots of tattoos, the old green ones. And a cutlass.'

It sounded like a pirate alright. 'Let me guess, he had a pipe too? A corncob one, like Popeye?'

'Yeah,' said Duncan. 'Did you see him?'

I shook my head. 'I think I saw him last night. He sounds like the git who gave me a soaking.'

I proceeded to explain last night's attack, the walk home from The Eel, the water being thrown out of the window and all the seafaringness about the situation.

'A Pirate Shop?' said Duncan. 'That doesn't sound like a bowling alley.'

'Well, that's what it says in big letters out front. What do you reckon it means?'

Duncan shrugged. 'It's obvious. It means Jimmy's sold his shop to a load of pirates.'

'I don't think it's as obvious as that. Why would a load of pirates want that shop?'

Duncan thought about it. 'You'll find pirates where you find treasure.'

'Well done, Poirot. That's really helpful.'

'Serious,' said Duncan. 'Pirates always want treasure. That's what pirates live for.'

He had a point. In his head some twisted form of logic was making sense. 'Well, they're not great pirates.' I said. 'They are too far from the sea.'

He pondered it. 'Pirates bury treasure. Maybe there's treasure buried here somewhere?'

I laughed. 'What? Under Jimmy's shop?'

'Maybe,' said Duncan, getting excited. 'Perhaps they are after Casper Macvittee's treasure! The lost treasure of Albion!'

'Not that King Arthur cobblers again.'

'Leytonstone is built on an ancient ley-line.'

'So what if it is? That doesn't mean Long John Silver's moved in over the road to dig up some loot.'

'But they could be after the treasure, couldn't they?'

'Give it a rest, Duncan.' I did the only thing I could do in that situation to shut him up. I went to make him a tea. I came back holding two steaming mugs. One Julie. One Whoopi.

* * *

Bludwyn leaned forward. 'Oscar, who are these people?' He glanced at his notes, 'They keep turning up every time you drink tea. You mention Julie and...' he glanced again, '...Whoopi.'

I grinned. 'It's nothing. It's just what we call the teas. White, no sugar, is white with none. A white nun is Julie Andrews. So, it becomes a Julie, geddit?'

Bludwyn said nothing. I don't know if he understood or not. I continued. 'Black tea with no sugar is known as black, none. A black nun is Whoopi Goldberg. From *Sister Act*.'

'Bloody hell, Oscar!' Bludwyn furiously scribbled the names out of his pad. 'Convoluted is not the word. Can you see why we've been through this three times already? It's confusing for us. Continue.'

'Where was I?...Oh yeah, a white tea with one sugar, that's called a Westminster – because of the W1 postcode.'

'And a white tea with two sugars?' asked Slick.

'That's a Churchill,' I replied. 'WW2.'

'And a black tea with three and half sugars?' asked Slick.

'Stop this!' cried Bludwyn, banging a fist on the table. 'Get on with your story!'

- 32 -

RACE RELATIONS

The shop was a state. We were ankle deep in DVD cases and halfway through refreshing the most depressing part of the shop – the *Family* wall. I'd been putting the job off for weeks. I couldn't care less what we put out. All the films were the same.

I don't know what offended me most about *Family* films. The films themselves or the cases they came in. You know the type, with the crappy picture on the front of wide-eyed and panicked parents holding their hands to their heads whilst kids look down the barrel of the camera with precocious "I'm smarter than you think" looks on their faces. Crappy films, made for no other reason than to make money. Some say they are the lowest of the low. But there is one rung lower. A sub-section of this genre that really turns my stomach: family films involving animals.

You know the plot: a pet starts off as an outsider but finishes the film as a loved part of the family unit having saved one or all of the family members. Even the dad, who'd wanted to destroy the pet at the start of the movie, has been won over despite the pet destroying his car/house/career. They are so offensively formulaic. So bloody sweet. And always have a happy ending. The dog never has rabies or anything. That's the bit that stings the most.

As a kid, before I knew better, I watched films like this. I thought they were truthful, that somehow my life would be like it was on screen, all perfect and with a happy ending. That my dad might come back. That we'd be a happy family. I soon got wise to all that. By the time I was six I was watching *Robocop*. That felt closer to the truth. *Family* films were dangerous.

'I love *Family* films,' said Duncan, examining the case of *Bedknobs and Broomsticks*. 'I like the bit in this one where the humans play football with the animals.'

I didn't say anything, but I had a sudden inkling I knew what fed Duncan's belief that animals could talk.

As we sorted through the cases I kept an eye out for any banned titles. I don't mean video nasties or horror films, I mean films that were once acceptable but now, thanks to changing tastes and the wisdom of time, seem offensive and have no place in a video shop. You know, films like *The Italian Job*.

* * *

Bludwyn choked on his coffee. '*The Italian Job?*'

'We've got him bang to rights!' grinned Slick. 'Only the sickest and most twisted of terrorist minds would want to ban such a fine British film.'

'It's racist,' I said.

'It's nothing of the sort!' thundered Bludwyn. 'It celebrates the plucky adventuring spirit and camaraderie of the British character.'

I shook my head. 'It's racist.'

'But how can it be?' asked Bludwyn. 'There's a black man in it. He's part of their gang. He drives the bus.'

'Precisely,' I said. 'And what happens to the bus?'

'Oh, I know,' said Slick, excitedly. 'It ends up hanging over a cliff.'

'Spot on,' I said. 'Now, what sort of message is that? Michael Caine and his gang execute a brilliant heist. They are in the clear. Their plot only fails because of the careless driving of the black bus driver. So, subconsciously, the film is saying black people are useless.' I shook my head. 'One of the most racist things I've ever seen, and they call it a classic! Which, now we're on the subject of race, answer me this: how come I'm being interviewed by two white geezers anyway?'

'Interesting,' said Peasworth, writing something in his notepad. 'Would you prefer it if one of us was black?'

'Yes,' I replied. 'Yes, I would.'

'You're stuck with us whether you like it or not,' said Bludwyn.

I pointed at Peasworth. 'You could black-up.'

Peasworth shifted awkwardly in his chair. 'I'm afraid that's not politically correct.'

'It's an audio transcript. No-one will ever know.'

He considered it. 'Will it help you tell the truth?'

'It might,' I said, toying with him.

He shot a hopeful look across at his superior.

'Out of the question!' thundered Bludwyn.

'But, sir! He says it might help. And I'm willing to do anything that will help crack this case.'

I stifled a laugh.

Bludwyn seemed unimpressed. 'You really want to help crack this case, Slick?'

'Yes, sir.'

'Then stop asking stupid questions and bring us some biscuits.'

'Right away, sir.' Slick got up and left the room in an eager flash.

I leaned back in my chair and put my hands behind my head. 'Inspector Bludwyn, do you believe in positive discrimination?'

'I believe in truth, justice and upholding the law,' he replied, reviewing the case notes. 'Now, Oscar...' he looked up, '...what's this crap about *The Italian Job* and wanting Peasworth to "black-up"?'

I shrugged. 'I dunno. It's just, this is the fourth time I've told you this story…and the longer I sit in here, the more I want my money's worth. I want it to be more like *Lethal Weapon 2*.'

Bludwyn's eyes sparkled. 'Oh, so do I, Oscar, so do I.' He leaned over the table and fixed me with a piercing gaze. 'Because if there is one thing I know about those *Lethal Weapon* films – it's that the cops always win.' His tash gave a confident grin.

'Perhaps,' I sighed. 'But if Jaggers is right, you won't be able to pin a thing on me.'

'Oh, why's that?'

'Because,' I smiled. 'I'll have dip-lo-ma-tic-im-mu-nity.'

- 33 -

A CUNNING PLAN

I'd be intrigued to know what my horoscope said was going to happen that weekend. Not that I believe in any of that crap. I just read them to see how wrong those crystal ball numpties get it. I mean, their predictions are hardly far-fetched at the best of times: love wears clothes; luck is a number...and all that cobblers. Never anything specific, is it? Never anything like:

Your landlord will break in dressed as Barry Manilow; announce he's sold his model shop for a million notes before urinating in your bucket and passing out in your wardrobe. Fate comes in the shape of pirates. Luck brings you a chemical weapon. Danger circles the letters F, B and I. And Sunday's full moon brings change.

As it goes, there was change that Sunday night, and it appeared to be positive.

I was a bit on edge about going back to the flat. What with Berol telling me it was a crime scene and everything, I was worried the FBI were going to be waiting to pounce on me.

When I arrived at the launderette I took a moment to examine the shutters. They were down. Everything looked quiet. There was a large sign up that's said: CLOSED FOR REPAIRS.

I kicked the shutters hard and listened close for any sound of clicking guns or American voices saying 'Get him!', but there was nothing. I took that as sign that it was all clear. I popped round to the back and let myself in.

Inside it was dead. No sign of the FBI. No sign of Berol. No sign of any washing either. It was as if nothing had happened.

So far so good. I went to the first floor and up to my room, where I found, what my horoscope would've described as, "a surprise".

Dead cockroaches. Hundreds of them. All scattered within a metre of the Junior Anthrax. I didn't know if they were drawn to the poison or had just got caught in its tractor beam. To be honest, I didn't give a monkey's. It was killing the bastards. V for victory!

As I kicked them about a bit, just to make sure they were dead, I noticed a dark patch had appeared on the floor boards. It looked like a scorch mark and seemed to circle the cylinder. Wow...was this stuff strong enough to do that, unopened?

A filmic thrill went through me. It was as if the Junior Anthrax was the Ark of the Covenant, you know that scene in *Indiana Jones and the Raiders of the Lost Ark*, where the Nazis put it in a wooden box and it burns off the swastika? Powerful shit. Although, I didn't have the Ark of the Covenant in my room. I had something half as powerful and twice as real.

And I had to get rid of it.

Earlier in the shop I'd asked Duncan what he thought I should do. He said I should consult my horoscope. Adding that tonight was a full moon. As helpful as this advice wasn't, I decided to ignore him and think things out for myself.

I'd decided against doing a runner. There was no point. If the FBI had wanted me they'd have arrested me already. Which meant, they weren't on to me, yet. So, I was on borrowed time. They'd cotton on to me soon enough, I was sure, and when they did, I wanted to be squeaky clean and innocent.

So, no question, I had to get rid of the Junior Anthrax. But how?

I thought about flushing it down the toilet, but then as much as I hated Maryland Point, I didn't want to put it in the water system and be held responsible for massacring the entire borough of Newham. Even Jaggers probably couldn't get me off that.

I thought about burying it, but that seemed a stupid idea too. I was living in the middle of Britain's biggest building site. Over 40% of the country's cranes were currently in the area, so the papers said. There probably wasn't one inch of soil that wasn't going to be disturbed over the next couple of years.

So what the hell was I going to do?

I sparked up a cigarette and began pacing. Outside the street belched some noise. I went to the window to investigate. The sun was setting. The cranes stood motionless in the distance. The site still shut due to sabotage.

I looked down at the street. The usual chaos passed by. Cars crawling and honking. People shouting. A drunk pissing in a doorway. How was I going to get rid of a chemical weapon in this shit tip?

I drew on my fag and tried to think. If I couldn't dispose of the Junior Anthrax myself, I could always make it someone else's responsibility, couldn't I?

That didn't seem a bad idea.

I took another drag and stared over the road. The Jolly Roger flag flapped idly in the evening breeze.

A grin spread across my face. Yeah, making it someone else's responsibility didn't seem like a bad idea at all.

- 34 -

DRESSING GOWN

I lay in my dressing gown, lazily sucking the end out of a cigarette and watching *Rambo:First Blood.* All that bland family film talk earlier had put me in the mood for a meaty movie, something that skilfully stitched together murder, explosions, thrilling chase scenes and a close and deft examination of post-traumatic-stress syndrome through the barely comprehensible wailing of Sylvester Stallone.

My room was sauna hot. Despite it being around 8pm and with the sun on its last legs, the night was just refusing to cool. Normally, I would've put up with the heat, but seeing as the Junior Anthrax was now starting to burn the floorboards I decided a bit of ventilation might be a good idea. So, I opened my window. Wide.

Unchallenged, the insane din of Maryland Point poured in. It totally ruined the film. I mean, it's bad enough in the cinema when someone rustles a packet of sweets or something. But Maryland Point did background noise on a whole new level. There were shouts. Screams. Sirens. Helicopters. Occasional gunshots. Watching a film with the window open was like trying to hear a digital watch tick.

Watching sci-fi was the worst. It's hard to believe you are in deep space when you can hear someone throwing up at the bus stop. Watching the deluxe digitally restored extended edition of *2001: A Space Odyssey* was going to have to wait till I moved out.

* * *

'Please continue, Oscar,' pressed Bludwyn. 'Stop stalling.'

'Anyway, I don't like to pause a film. It doesn't seem right. The editor and director have conspired to serve you something in a single sitting, to take a break from it seems wrong somehow. It's like pausing a symphony and then coming back to it. You lose the tempo. So even though I needed a biblically desperate piss, I crossed my legs and waited for the credits. When they rolled I bolted downstairs to use the bog.'

Slick made a note on his pad. 'Your toilet is outside of your front door, correct?'

'Yeah, you have to leave the front door, go across the landing and then you're at the toilet. Stupid design really. Blame Jimmy for not changing it. Anyway, in my rush to take a piss I didn't bother to put my front door on the latch, and because I had my bedroom window wide open, a draft rushed through and slammed my flat door shut, locking me out.'

'Convenient, isn't it?' mused Bludwyn.

'No, a convenience,' I corrected.

Bludwyn raised an eyebrow 'Oh, so you admit it?'

I shrugged. 'Yeah, if you like. I mean, I call it a bog, but if you want to call it a convenience well—'

'No!' fumed Bludwyn. 'I mean, it's convenient that you happen to lock yourself out.'

I sighed. 'Mr Bludwyn, have you ever locked yourself out?'

'Yes.'

'Have you ever thought it was convenient?'

'No.'

'Then why ask me such a stupid question.'

'*Do you fancy your mother?*' asked Peasworth.

'*SLICK!*' Bludwyn held up a finger. 'I told you, no more psychological babble. I mean it. Oscar, please continue.'

'So, realising I'm locked out, I wonder what I should do. No phone. No keys. Worse still, no fags. I'm dressed in just a dressing gown, albeit a *Rocky* dressing gown. You know, the one he wears when he enters the ring – black with gold trim and the words "Italian Stallion" on the back?'

'Very nice,' said Slick. 'I've always wanted one of those.'

'You've got one of those,' I spat. 'You confiscated it as evidence.'

'So we did,' beamed Peasworth.

'Please continue,' urged Bludwyn.

'So, I weighed up my options. I remember thinking about forcing the door, but at my request a few months back Jimmy had seen to it that the locks were upped. It was the only job as landlord he'd actually done right. There was no way I was going to force my way back in. It would have been easier to break into the Bank of England.

'So, to my mind, there seemed only one solution. If I wanted to get back into my flat I needed a key. And there was only one man who had a spare. So I set out on a quest to find him. Not knowing where he lived, I decided a good place to start would be the place I saw Jimmy Strongbow most – the pub.'

- 35 -

THE BLUE EEL

I walked barefoot down Leytonstone Road with my dressing gown flapping about like a cloak. A few tramps heckled me, but I ignored them and kept walking, keeping focus on the pavement.

Walking the East End barefoot should be an Olympic sport. You've got chewing gum, broken glass, snapped plastic chip forks, half eaten kebabs, sticky sweet wrappers, used plasters, nail clippings, hair, dried pools of vomit. One wrong foot and you've got tetanus, rabies, Ebola. You deserve a gold medal for not catching anything.

It took mostly hop-scotch moves but I eventually made it to The Eel.

I threw open the heavy double-doors and bowled in, sighing as my feet sunk into the soft thick pub carpet, and savouring the smoke that rushed to tickle my nostrils. It was bliss.

I half expected some jeers for what I was wearing. But there were none. In fact the place seemed quiet. I could see the Pearly King was in, sat on his sofa at the back of the pub, his shiny knees poking out from behind a pillar. A few old boys were in the corner, drinking Guinness and playing crib. And Big Mick was behind the bar polishing his trophies, ignoring the overflowing ashtrays that surrounded him.

Here we go, I thought. If anyone's going to say something it will be Big Mick. He couldn't resist taking the piss, calling me a Mockney and putting the boot in every opportunity he could. I'd just served myself up on a plate walking in wearing a dressing gown that described me as an "Italian Stallion". He was going to rip me to shreds.

I watched Mick's grin widen as I approached the bar. 'Hello Oscar, what can I get you?'

I blinked. 'What's your game?'

'What?'

'Calling me Oscar,' I said.

'It's your name, ain't it?'

'Yeah, but you've never used it.'

'Course I have,' said Mick. 'What else would I call you?'

'Mockney,' I said. 'Sometimes even a Mockney bastard.'

Mick waved one of his large hands as if I was making an exaggeration. 'C'mon, less of that. Now, what can I get you? The usual?'

'The usual?!?' But before I could say anything he was already mixing my drink. He placed it on the bar, delicately. 'There you go…a whisky and coke. No lemon.'

'Cheers.' I took the glass and examined it cautiously. Something was up, but up in a good way, so I went with it and downed my drink.

'That's a fiver,' said Mick.

I sarcastically patted my dressing gown. 'Ain't got any cash on me.'

'No bread?'

'No, wallet's at home. I'm locked out. Sorry.' I waited for him to drop his nice-guy act and call me a no good Mockney son of a she-bitch.

'Locked out?' he sympathised. 'That's too bad. I'll pop it on the slate.'

'*Slate?!?* Since when have I had a slate?'

'You're right, Oscar. What am I talking about? It's on the house.'

'Are you ill?'

'No,' said Mick. 'Why, what you heard?'

'Nothing.'

'Good.' He poured me another drink. 'Keep it that way.'

I didn't know Mick well. And I definitely didn't know where all this sudden niceness was coming from. He'd seemingly hated me from the first time I'd walked in. I'm sure he only let me drink in there now because Jimmy sponsored me. So, why the sudden best mates routine? Had he found inner peace? Profound wisdom? Finally decided to welcome me into the inner Cockney circle? Or did he just fancy me in a dressing gown?

I cleared my throat. 'Say Mick, how'd you feel about *My Beautiful Launderette*?'

He grinned. 'I bloody love it!'

I downed my drink. In my whole time at Bunger's Video Palace we'd never rented *My Beautiful Launderette* out to anyone who didn't also rent *Wizard of Oz* and *The Rocky Horror Show.*

'That Berol's a sort,' he added.

'Excuse me?'

'At the launderette. I wouldn't mind putting her on a spin cycle, if you know what I mean!' He gave a wink and patted my shoulder with one his huge hands.

'Goodgood,' I said hurriedly, straightening out my spine, having nearly been sent through the floor. A change of subject was needed. 'Ere, you ain't seen Jimmy, have you?'

'Nah.' He picked up a rag to dirty some glasses. 'No sign of him today.'

'You expecting him in?'

Mick looked over his shoulder at an old clock on the wall. 'Well, if he's popping in he's usually here by now. You want another drink while you wait?'

'Erm...'

He leant over the bar. His eyes looked deep into mine. 'It's on the house, Oscar.'

I cleared my throat. 'Say...how'd you feel about *Brokeback Mountain*?'

- 36 -

JIMMY STRONGBOW

As the night wore on, Mick continued to ply me with free booze. I was suspicious at first, but the more I drank the less I worried. Having spent the evening questioning him on every film I could remember from our *Pink Pound* section, I'd come to the conclusion that he had no sordid designs on my body whatsoever. Which to be honest was a shame, as I could've done with a bed for the night.

I drained my drink and slid off my bar stool.

'You off?' asked Mick.

'Nah.' I waved an arm in the direction of the pool table. 'I'm gonna give him another bell.'

I swayed barefoot to the dark corner with the payphone, my dressing gown dragging behind me like a train.

I picked up the phone and dialled. Jimmy's number had been hard to get, but after some protest Mick had given in. I must have made a dozen or so reverse charge calls already. Every time, no answer.

I held the phone to my ear and listened to the dialling tone.

I don't know when the first reports started to come in. At first a few people said Jimmy was late. Then, that he was later than usual. And then, that nobody had seen or heard from him all day. He was missing, apparently. Which seemed a little convenient given my predicament. I felt I was the victim of some strange Cockney wind-up that Auslanders don't get. Just a ruse to keep me looking like a prat. "Jimmy's missing, yeah missing". Nudgenudgewinkwinkpassiton.

But the longer it dragged out, the more concerned everyone got.

A little earlier, a bloke known as Harry the Horse had phoned the pub. He was looking for Jimmy too. Apparently this Harry and Jimmy were meant to meet for lunch at the jellied eel stall in the Stratford Centre, but Jimmy was a no-show. Not even a call to say he was blowing it out. And that was unlike Jimmy, people said. That was, people said, highly unusual.

Talk in the pub soon turned to Jimmy's possible whereabouts and very quickly simple conjecture turned to full-blown conspiracy theory. Duncan would've loved it. Maybe he was pissed. Maybe he was sick. Maybe he was asleep. Maybe he was in hospital. This led to a flurry of debate as to the reasons why: kidney failure, alcohol poisoning, gout, car accident, superglued his pork-pie hat to his head. It got a bit silly. But people seemed worried. A few calls were put in, but there were no leads. Nobody had seen him anywhere.

Realising the phone was still ringing, I swore and hung up.

'Do you reckon I can break in?' I asked as I climbed back on my stool.

Big Mick sucked air through his teeth. 'Don't know about that. Jaggers would be your man.'

'Oh?' I brightened. 'What's he a cat burglar or something?'

'No, you tart. He's a lawyer ain't he? He'll know the rules. You want to speak to him before you try breaking back in.'

I raised an eyebrow. 'Is that right?'

'Property law is a strange thing. Jaggers is the expert.'

I looked up and down the bar. 'But Jaggers ain't in here tonight either, is he?'

'No.' Big Mick dirtied some glasses. 'Strange that. No sign of Jimmy tonight. And no sign of Jaggers either. I'd expect them both on a Sunday.'

'Maybe they are out together?' suggested someone. 'Gone to the dogs or something?'

'Nah,' said Mick. 'Jimmy would've said. He can't keep his trap shut about anything.'

That was true. Jimmy did like to talk. Most of the time he liked to talk "it". Whatever that meant. And he talked "it" a lot.

I waved my empty glass at Mick but he didn't see me. He was busy rubbing his bald head, looking into the middle distance, that space where answers often lay. 'Ere…he better not be in another boozer.'

'Doubt it,' I slurred, still waving my glass. 'He's probably done a bunk.'

'Nah! Not Jimmy!' cried someone.

'Where would he go?' asked someone else.

'Spain?' I mused. 'I mean he's just made a mint on his property. I'd go on a splurge, wouldn't you?'

This lead to a big debate, with everyone in the pub saying what they'd do with a million quid. All the usual answers were there. Buy a house. Buy a car. Open a pie and mash shop.

Mick finally saw me waving my empty glass and refilled it. As I gulped it down, I took a drunken look around. Throughout the whole evening the Pearly King had sat at his end of the pub behind his pillar, saying nothing.

- 37 -

THE PEARLY KING

A little while later the pub started to thin out. It was just me a few other barflies left. I wondered if now was the time that Jimmy would burst out of the birthday cake, as it were, and end this whole charade.

'I hope Jimmy's not come to grief,' said a voice.

I turned to find the Pearly King returning some glasses to the bar. I gave him a drunken look up and down. He seemed all present and correct. He was a big man, heavy-set, clean-shaven and with a double chin. The archetypal fat lad with a smooth potato head.

'You hope what?' I spat.

The Pearly narrowed his eyes. 'What, you mutton? I said, "I hope Jimmy's not come to grief."'

'Don't give me that old flannel.' I returned to my drink.

I felt a firm hand on my shoulder. The Pearly growled in my ear. 'Watch your lip, son. You're only welcome in here on our say so. Let's not fall out.'

'Fall out?' I said. 'You're one to talk. You hope Jimmy's alright? Yesterday you were running him out of town, now he goes missing you suddenly give a toss about him?'

'I do care,' said the Pearly defensively. 'I don't feel good about what was said.'

'Yeah, right,' I spat. 'You don't give a toss. You're more interested in your stupid outfit.'

Gasps shot round the bar. The Pearly King's eyes flashed with anger. 'A Pearly shouldn't talk to another Pearly like that.'

'What are you chatting about? I ain't no Pearly!'

'Too bloody right you're not! But Jimmy is!'

'Pull the other one,' I said. 'Jimmy's no Pearly. He doesn't go around in any of that...' I was about to say stupid Pearly shit but the anticipating frown of the Pearly King made me think twice. '...any of that traditional garb.'

'Do you have an idea how being a Pearly works, me ol' son? How it *really* works?' The Pearly King stared at me with hard East End eyes. The sort of eyes that say, "I'll fit you with concrete armbands and take you for a swim in the Thames, if you upset me".

'Let me tell you a story.' He drew up a bar stool and leant close to me. 'Jimmy Strongbow has been held in very high regard by Pearlys all over the land. You see, Jimmy was a Pearly Prince, but he could never be a Pearly King.'

'That's right,' nodded Mick, buffing a trophy.

'Why not?'

'Well...' continued the Pearly. 'During the Second World War, Jimmy's dad went to fight. You see, if you're a real Cockney, you have pride in who you are and where you're from, and you feel the same passion about other people, you embrace them and their heritage. Peaceful types, Cockneys. We've lived hand in hand and arm in arm with immigrants for centuries. All different kinds. We've welcomed 'em. Brothers and sisters one'n'all.'

'I'm not following you...' I said.

'Well, Jimmy's dad got conscripted. I mean he loved his country, loved his King, loved the Union Jack, but when it came to killing people, an eye for an eye and all that...seemed wrong.'

'So...I'm still not following...'

'Well, Jimmy's dad did a good job of avoiding action. He wanted to be a medic but he couldn't pass the exams. You see, you got to be smart to be medic. Don't need a good heart, just gotta be smart. Anyway, the time finally came when he could swerve active service no more, everyone was called up for the big push...D-day.

'Jimmy's dad had flat feet, he knew his number was up. He was going to get shot, either by his own side for desertion or by the enemy for being a soldier. But then he had an idea. If he was going to go for a burton, he knew what he wanted to be wearing. Gawd knows how he did it, but bless him, he smuggled his Pearly outfit onboard the landing craft and changed into it moments before they reached the beachhead. The doors went down. And as the enemy gunfire rang out, Jimmy's dad stormed the beach in his Pearly best.' The Pearly punched his fist into his hand. *'Have that Jerry!'*

'Wow!' I said, genuinely impressed with the image of a Pearly King taking on the Nazis, feeling there was perhaps a film in there somewhere. 'Did Jimmy's dad survive?'

'Course not!' snapped the Pearly King. 'He lasted less than twenty seconds.'

'He was shot?'

'Nah!' cried the Pearly, somewhat offended. 'He saved a bloke's life! He dived on top of a grenade and took it out. Apparently, his last words before it went bang were "Lovely-ol'-job". Cockney through and through that man.' The Pearly paused to wipe a tear from his eye. 'So you see, Jimmy couldn't become a Pearly because his dad didn't pass on the suit.'

'So...what?' I said, now totally confused by it all.

The Pearly King frowned. 'Tell him, Mick.'

'Pearlyism is hereditary. It's passed down from father to son. The power lays in the suit. The suit itself needs to be passed on.'

'That's right,' said the Pearly. 'There are few people who become Pearlys, my ol' son. *Very few*. It's a mark of pride to be one, and to miss out because of a noble act, well, it takes a big man not to get consumed by his father's shadow, and Jimmy has never once mentioned it. He's a Pearly to me, make no mistake…and when Pearlys go missing we bind together.'

He leaned forward and grabbed me roughly by the dressing gown collar. His face flushed with anger. 'Now…you Mockney prat, you better tell me where he is…because as far as I'm concerned you're responsible for him disappearing.'

'What? Why me?'

'You're an outsider,' said the Pearly. 'We don't turn on our own.'

'Pull the other one,' I said. 'Last night—'

'Forget last night.' The Pearly let go of me. 'You don't know what last night was about.'

'I think you'd better leave,' said Mick.

'Yeah,' I said to the Pearly. 'You better leave.'

'No, you,' said Mick, pointing at me with one of his abnormally large fingers. 'You've had enough for tonight. Go home.'

'Are you taking the piss?' I said. 'I'm locked out.'

'That's your problem,' said Mick. 'Sling your hook.'

I bit my lip. I didn't know what to do, but then a wonderful winning argument formed in my head, one to guarantee free drinks and a place to sleep. I opened my mouth and gave it to them.

- 38 -

OUTSIDE

As I stood shivering in the summer rain, I reflected that things could've gone better. With my dressing gown soaked and heavy, I cast what would probably be described as a longing look up at my bedroom window. I didn't know what I hoped to see. Jimmy perhaps, drunkenly waving a set of keys. Or maybe a troop of cockroaches employing *A-Team* ingenuity to help me out, making a battering-ram out of themselves to break down the door.

But there was no sign of life. All the lights were off and I was locked out in the freezing rain, drunk and looking like a tit.

I quickly weighed up my options. I could try Duncan. He could put me up, but he lived too far away. The tube had stopped for the night. It would take me the best part of an hour to get to him on a night bus, and if Jimmy amazingly decided to show up during that time I'd be screwed. No…I had to stay close.

I pondered opening up the video shop, and decided that was the best thing to do, until I realised that my keys were in the flat. I hate it when your brain misfires like that. Like trying to turn on the TV during a power cut because you are bored. I blamed the booze.

I began shuffling away from the flat, still trying to think of a plan. All the pubs were shut or about to close. Maryland Point was going into stasis. Sure, pissheads and nutters would still stagger through hollering loudly, but I didn't want to be in their sights when they did. I needed a refuge, but where the hell was I going to find one at gone midnight?

Across the road a red neon sign flashed at me. It said: **Stratford Tanning Depot. Open 24 hours.**

- 39 -

STRATFORD TANNING DEPOT

I didn't really know if what I was about to do was a good idea. Having recently got hold of a chemical weapon through eBay, perhaps I was no longer in a position to judge exactly what a good idea was anymore, but I'm sure drunkenly bursting into a brothel in the middle of the night, wearing nothing but a dressing gown and asking for a place to kip wasn't the smartest of ideas. Especially when I didn't have a penny on me. And especially when the dressing gown declared me an "Italian Stallion."

So why did I do it?

Simple, I was desperate. They say it's desperation that forces girls onto the streets. And that night it was desperation that forced me from the streets into the Stratford Tanning Depot.

I crossed the road and headed for the neon sign. It was above a heavy steel door that bore several dents and boot prints. There was a small strip of masking tape above a peep-hole. Written on it in marker pen were the words: PRESS BUZZER.

I did as instructed. The peep-hole slid back. Two haggard female eyes peered out. 'Yes, darling?'

'Hi…look…love, I live over the road and I'm locked out and I was wondering—'

The eyes rolled. 'First time here?'

'Yeah, but listen to me, I'm locked out and—'

'Save the chat for later.' She unbolted the door and waved me inside. My glasses steamed up on entry. But once they had cleared I discovered that the haggard eyes were perfectly in keeping with her body. She was ropier than the exam for a Cub Scouts knot badge. If she was the shop window I worried about what I'd find inside.

'Bit busy tonight, darling.' She swung the heavy steel door shut. 'You'll have to be patient.'

'No, look love, I'm locked out and—'

She put a haggard finger to my lips. 'Sssh…I told you, save the chat for later.'

'But—'

She pressed her finger harder. 'No buts, it's first time nerves is all. Relax.'

She was right. I did have nerves. For a start I didn't know where that finger had been, and I can't say I liked the smell of it. But before I had time to find out exactly how she planned to help me "relax", I was saved by a knock at the front door.

'Use the bloody buzzer!' she barked. I was waved away. 'Just go down the corridor, darling. Take a seat and someone will see to you.'

The buzzer sounded. She turned to answer it. And I turned to get away from her, quickly, wiping her fingerprint off my lips as I went.

- 40 -

WAITING

I walked down a brightly lit corridor and came to a waiting room. It was a bit like a doctor's surgery. There were rows of plastic chairs filled with bored looking blokes, arms crossed, yawning and all that, completely disinterred in the old copies of *Angling Times* and *Daltons Weekly* scattered on a coffee table in front of them.

My arrival caused a few to glance up, but only momentarily. I guess I wasn't what they were after. There was an old TV mounted on a bracket in the corner. It was showing a *Carry On* film, but nobody paid any attention. Everyone seemed more interested in a number counter above a beaded doorway. It read: NOW SERVING CUSTOMER: 87

A gruff voice came from behind me. 'Ere, you going to take it?'

I turned to face an old man with a ruddy face and a nose like a potato. He looked to be one social rung above a tramp and was soaked from head to foot. I guessed this was the customer who failed to use the buzzer.

'Take what?'

'What do you think?' said the potato nose.

'I don't know, Morse, that's why I asked.'

'The number.' He pointed at a ticket dispenser under the NOW SERVING sign. 'House rules. No queue jumping.' He shook his head, like it was a very bad thing. 'No queue jumping here, son, make no mistake.'

'No, I'm alright,' I said. 'I just want to wait.'

'You can't wait without a number,' said a bloke sat doing a crossword.

'Says who?'

'Says me,' came a deep menacing voice. Which was appropriate as I soon discovered it belonged to a menacing-looking bloke sat at the back of the room on a high stool, like a lifeguard. He wore a smile and a high-vis jacket emblazoned with the words CUSTOMER RELATIONS OFFICER. He also had a truncheon, that he slapped into an open palm, and it looked like he wanted to test it out on someone, very much, very brutally.

I noticed a nametag hanging from his vest. It read: Malcolm.

'Alright, Malcolm,' I said, trying to play things down. 'I'll take a number.' I walked towards the dispenser with my best bowl, snatched my ticket and strolled back, cool as a snowman's cool bits. I'd play along. Just to stay out of the rain. And it wasn't all bad. After all, there was a *Carry On* film to watch.

I propped against the wall and looked down. I was number 123.

From somewhere a klaxon sounded. The counter changed: NOW SERVING CUSTOMER: 89

- 41 -

THINGS YOU LEARN

'How long's this going to take?' moaned the potato nose.

'New beds, innit,' said Malcolm, the scary customer relations officer. 'We've got the freshest springs in London. Word gets round quick.'

'Yeah, but—' the potato nose continued to moan. I ignored him. Luckily, I'd managed to get a seat, and was now sort of engrossed in watching *Carry On Camping*. It was coming up to the bit where Barbara Windsor's bra flies off. I remember that being a highlight when I was a kid.

'If you knew it was going to be busy – how come Tallulah's taken on a group booking?' asked someone.

My ears pricked up. Tallulah? Tallulah Funbags? Could this be the same Tallulah that Duncan pined for? The same misunderstood masseuse? Was this question proof that she really was a brass? And not only that, a brass that takes on group bookings? Duncan would be mortified. I'd have to tell him.

'Who says Tallulah's taking on a group?' said Malcolm.

'It will be those bloody builders again,' said someone. 'They spend more time in here than on site. If there were a gold medal for shagging, they'd win it.'

'Nah,' said someone else. 'It's not builders. They've packed up for a week.'

'Packed up?' said another. 'But the stadium's not finished.'

'Ain't you heard?' piped up a new voice. 'They can't do any work. Casper Macvittee's army's done them up like a kipper. All the gear's been sabotaged. Everyone's on paid leave till it's fixed.'

'There's no army,' said someone.

'Who's doing it then?' said someone else. 'Who's putting up all that graffiti that says "Viva Casper"?'

'Kids, innit?'

'You don't half talk it,' said another. 'That site is surrounded by security guards with CCTV and all that cobblers. You saying kids can smart their way round that?'

'I'm just saying, it's kids, innit. Not some bloody army.'

'Anyway, getting back to the point,' said the potato nose. 'Who's booked Tallulah out for the night if she ain't got the builders in?'

'Maybe she's got the decorators in!' quipped someone, which cracked everyone up.

'I thought she was doing a stag party,' said a bloke in a blue cardigan. 'Y'know for those fellas that came in dressed as pirates.'

My ears went positively sonar at this point. I abandoned *Carry on Camping* to join in. 'What do you mean pirates?'

The cardigan pointed at me. 'Yeah, you know what I mean. They're your mates, ain't they?'

'Eh?'

'Fancy dress thing, ain't it?' The cardigan gestured at my dressing gown. 'They're pirates and you've come as, whatsit...' he snapped his fingers trying to think. '...Rocky?'

I waved him off. 'I ain't nothing to do with any pirates.'

'Then why are you dressed like a twat?' said someone.

'I'm locked out!'

'Yeah, me too,' scoffed someone.

'And me,' said another.

'I'm locked out and so's my wife,' added the bloke who made the earlier quip about the decorators, only this time nobody laughed.

'So where'd these pirates come from then?' I asked.

'I don't bloody know,' said the cardigan. 'I didn't ask questions. They just turned up looking like pirates, you know with sailor trousers and beards and cutlasses and tri-corn hats, parrots and the like.'

In my limited knowledge, that sounded like the pirates alright.

I wanted answers, but I didn't know what exactly I wanted answers to, so I left it. Perhaps the less I knew about the pirates the better. After all, I had plans to make them scapegoats for the Junior Anthrax. That's if I could ever get back into my flat to plant it on them.

'Nevermind who they are, I want to know why they are getting special treatment,' moaned the potato nose.

'Down with Thatcher!' cried someone.

'And why ain't you using those Olympic condoms!' moaned someone else.

Malcolm waved everyone down. 'Alright, that's enough noise.'

'It's true though, right?' asked someone. 'Tallulah's taking on a group booking?'

'I can't discuss it,' said Malcolm. 'Client confidentiality. You know the rules.'

'Balls to the rules,' moaned the potato nose. 'I've been here over two hours now.'

'All I can say...' said Malcolm, '...is that a late booking was made, for a party of gents, and she couldn't turn it down.'

'But some of us are regulars,' said a bloke, waving what I think was a loyalty card.

'Take it up with Tallulah,' said Malcolm.

I smirked. I imagined quite a few people were here because of things they wanted to take right up with Tallulah.

'Something funny, Rocky?' said Malcolm.

'No,' I said. 'Ere, is Tallulah Funbags her real name?'

- 42 -

A QUESTION ANSWERED

Well, bugger me.

- 43 -

NUMBER CALLED

I looked nervously at the pink ticket in my hand. The counter was currently hovering on 121. If the two blokes in front of me were premature I could be seen within a minute. At this point I felt perhaps I should have tried harder to explain myself, but there seemed no point. The best bet was to just stay out of the rain for as long as possible, watch the movie, and hopefully talk to the prostitute and see if I could reason with her in getting a bed for the night.

Pffffff.

I wasn't happy with the idea of talking to a prostitute. You hear stories about blokes who go to them, just to talk. Were they all locked out like me? Would anyone believe a bloke if they said that? I'd soon find out.

The klaxon sounded, twice. I froze.

'That's you!' said potato nose, waving his ticket. 'You're in front of me.'

'No, it's okay,' I faltered. 'I just want to watch the film.'

'Hurry up!' cried someone.

'Bloody first-timer!' added someone else.

A consoling hand clapped on my shoulder from somewhere. 'We're all nervous our first time, son.'

'It's not your fault you're that ugly,' added another.

'You go through that door, she'll make you feel better,' said someone else.

I stood up to get away from them. 'No, I'm really okay,' but my protests fell on deaf ears and I was pretty much pushed through the beaded curtain into a darkened corridor lined with white wooden doors. I noticed one at the far end was ajar. Red light bled out from inside. I figured that was the room for me.

- 44 -

SEX TOURISM

I pushed open the door to find a fat lad in Bermuda shorts, smoking a cigarette. He was sat at a computer, some porno picture on his screen. He held out a podgy hand. 'Number.'

'What?'

He rolled his eyes and snatched my ticket. '123,' he read aloud. 'You've not been done yet. Come back afterwards.'

'Back for what?'

'Souvenir photo.' He handed back my ticket back and turned to his screen. He was zoomed in close on some bloke's hairy back.

'Souvenir photo?'

'Sex tourism,' he said matter-of-factly. 'Can't be a tourist without taking a photo.'

'A photo of what?'

He gave me a wink and nodded at his screen. 'Being on the job.'

I looked and could see the hairy back now had a border round it with the words: "I had a ride at the Stratford Tanning Depot."

'You mean photos like when you're at a theme-park?'

'Yeah, that's it,' he said. 'Your climax face on camera for a fiver. Get your girl to put it on your bill. As an extra, like. It's all the rage. All the rage on the continent.'

'Right,' I said uncertainly.

'And...' he leaned close and whispered behind his hand '...if you want anything photoshopped. Y'know, bits and pieces downstairs made a little longer...' he glanced at my groin. 'Y'know...a pick me up. We can do that too. At a good price.'

'Right,' I said, wanting to get away from him. 'Where do I go to...'

He pointed to the corridor. 'Just wait out there and one of the girls will call you in a sec.'

- 45 -

TALLULAH & HER GROUP BOOKING

I stood in the corridor, tapping my bare feet impatiently on the lino, wondering what was going to happen to me next in this perverted fun-house. The sounds coming from the various rooms didn't give me much encouragement. I heard whips cracking, battery powered devices whizzing and blokes groaning as they jumped the final fence. One sound however caught my attention. It was a harmonica, blowing a sea shanty of some kind. A chorus of male voices crowed along in a drunken mess that was occasionally punctured by a girly giggle.

Curious, I edged toward the door for a closer listen. Red light pulsed from behind it, blindingly bright one moment and dim the next. What is it with knocking shops and red lights? I mean, how much more cliché can you get?

'Ooh, Captain!' said a girly voice, possibly Tallulah's. 'Your ring is...so... so...*BIG!*'

There was laughter.

'More rum!' cried someone. 'More rum, me hearties!'

'Aye-aye, Cap'n!'

'This be a glorious day!'

'Oh, you saucy bunch,' said the girly voice. 'You saucy bunch of *BIG* seadogs.'

'We'll be rich!' cried someone. 'Rich, Cap'n! Viva Casper Macvittee!'

There was a loud *BANG*. It sounded like a gunshot, and was so loud it loosened crumbs of ceiling plaster around me. It caught me so off-guard, I couldn't help but jump back in shock and yell *'Shitting-Christ!'*

The room fell silent.

I froze in fear, thinking I'd given myself away. I held my breath and listened.

Silence, then a chorus of raucous laughter. The harmonica blew back up as if nothing had happened, and the pirates continued singing their shanties.

I let out a relieved breath and moved back to the door. I noticed there was now a smoking bullet hole in it. With drunken judgement, I decided to have a look through it and see what was going on.

The room was dark and there was lots of smoke. It might have looked like a disco, but the pulsing red-light had stopped. A midget sat on a barrel by the far wall, swigging from a tankard. A few other pirates were sat on a dirty chaise-longue, slapping their thighs in time with the music. I could see Tallulah, sitting on a pirate's lap, her bosoms bouncing in his face as she waved a tankard about with gusto. She seemed to be having a good time.

A tall thin pirate stood nearest the door with his back to me. He had sparrow like legs, a tri-corn hat and was dressed entirely in black. He seemed to be surveying the room. 'Wench!' he clicked his fingers, 'Away! Bring more rum.'

'Certainly, *Captain Big Boy*.' Tallulah made eye flutterings and bosom heavings as she rose. She said something else, a crappy double-entendre involving either "walking someone's plank" or loving their "spanker", before leaving through a side door, much to the pirates' upset.

The figure in black waved the room down for quiet. I noticed at this point he had a smoking pistol in his hand. I can only assume it was he that fired and made my rather convenient peep-hole.

'Me hearties,' he waved the pistol, somewhat theatrically. 'No more careless talk when strangers be present.'

'Cap'n, I only said "Viva Casper",' said a sheepish-sounding pirate. 'It was a toast in your honour.'

'Aye, be that as it may, we are too close to the booty to jeopardise our good work. And ye be wanting that booty, donchya?'

'Y'arrgh!' cried the room.

'That's what I thought,' said the Captain, nodding to himself. 'In less than twenty-four hours the greatest treasure in the world will be ours!'

'Y'arrgh!' cried the room excitedly.

'And yet,' said the Captain, examining his gun. 'And yet, some of you, I think doubted me.'

'Never!'

'A captain knows when his crew been talking of mutiny.'

The room became a nervous shuffling of feet and bowed heads.

The Captain nodded. 'Aye, I thought so, that's why it's time to settle a few scores before sun up tomorrow.'

The pirates yelped as the Captain cocked his gun and began waving it about the room. 'Now, I'll swab the slate clean. Who here still thinks we should've worn disguises?' The Captain examined the faces in front of him. 'No-one? Not one of you? I thought I heard talk about disguises? Are you saying I'm deaf as well as stupid? Boatswain, am I stupid?'

'No, Cap'n,' replied the midget.

'Aye, then what's been all this talk?'

'Nothing Cap'n,' said the Boatswain. 'It's just that…'

'Yes?'

'It's just that…'

'Spit it out!'

The Boatswain scratched the back of his small head nervously. 'Erm…we don't understand everything.'

'Y'arrgh!' cried the Captain. 'What do you mean? Be more specific.'

'Well…we want to know why we, being pirates and all, are not in disguise. But you, being who you are and all, wear a disguise when you're with us.'

Murmurs of 'Aye,' circled round the room.

'You wretched fools!' cried the Captain. 'I should keelhaul all of you for your stupidity. Do you know how many years I've been living in this area? How many years I've spent living on this stinking scrap of Terra Firma, masterminding the whole thing? I've built up a reputation round these parts. People love me round here.' The Captain laughed to himself and scratched his forehead with the muzzle of his gun. 'And little do they know what we are planning. Little do they know that by tomorrow night, all this will be gone, just like us, me hearties, for we'll sack London, set this city bright with flame as we escape down the Thames, victorious.' The Captain picked up a glass. 'To victory!'

'To victory!' cried the pirates in unison.

'To you Cap'n!' added one.

'Viva Casper Macvittee!' said another.

And with that they all raised their glasses and drank.

I drew back from the door.

Treasure? Fire? Sacking London? I'd discount such cobblers at the best of times, but when a group of men dressed up as pirates say it, then it's absolute cobblers. These pirates were crazy fantasists who seemed to have no respect for the law.

I grinned. They were perfect.

I mean, who better to plant a chemical weapon on? The police wouldn't think twice. Especially as they had all these pistols on them already. I was going to get off scot-free, just as soon as I could plant it on them. Which meant, just as soon as I could get hold of Jimmy and could get back into my sodding flat.

Down the corridor something creaked. A door near the end stood open. Muted light spilled out.

'123,' called a female voice.

- 46 -

LADY OF THE NIGHT

I walked into the room. It was lit, but not brilliantly, and smelt of jos-ticks. There was a bed in the corner and large mirrors on the wall and ceiling. But no sign of a prostitute.

Result, I thought to myself. A bed for the night was all I wanted. I went over to it and lay down. I jumped up again as a wetness pressed through my dressing gown. I looked down at the mattress suspiciously.

I heard the door close behind me. 'Alright darling,' whined a voice. 'You looking for a good time?'

I turned round to find a horror wrapped in fishnets that looked too briny even for Captain Birdseye.

I cleared my throat. 'Look love, I just need somewhere to sleep.'

'Well, you can sleep with me, for a score.'

'No chance!' I said. 'I've thrown out steak in better nick than you!'

She raised a sharply pencilled eyebrow. 'You ain't no oil painting yourself, love. I reckon we do this with the lights off.'

'I'm not here to dip my wick.'

'Oh right,' she said, brightening. 'You're a taker?' She pulled a monster black rubber strap-on out of an old sports bag. 'Please, put yourself in the stirrups.'

'Now hang about! Look…can we talk or something?'

'Oh, you're one of those.'

'I'm not one of anything,' I protested. 'I just want to talk for a minute.'

'You want to talk, it's a ton.'

'A ton?' I cried. 'You've got some front. How comes talking costs more?'

'Because thinking is harder than fucking, darling, so it's extra.' She held out her hand for the money.

I stepped back. 'I've been locked out of my flat, I'm waiting for my landlord to turn up, can you just let me stay here, or sleep here, till he arrives?'

'Look, darling, if this is some role-play game, I don't know it.'

'No,' I said, edging toward the door. 'Forget about it, look I just wanted somewhere to stay out of the rain, it's pissing down out there. I—'

'MALCOLM!'

And just then I felt my eyes start to sting, there was the smell of onions and then everything went black.

- 47 -

KICKED OUT

As my body flew through the air it struck me as something of an irony that whilst prozzers will indulge a punter in almost any kinky activity, the one kind of punter they won't indulge is a time waster.

I crashed into some bin bags before gravity finally brought me to a folded halt. I looked up through stinging eyes to see Malcolm standing in the doorway, probably surveying the distance he'd thrown me, and whether or not it merited him looking into taking up the shot-put. He gave an exaggerated wipe clean of his hands and barked an unnecessary 'Don't come back!' before slamming the door, leaving me shut out in the rain.

And it was still raining hard. The water didn't so much as slap, but punched down on cardboard boxes around me. I would've got up, but with nowhere to go, I just lay in the darkness and planned my next move, but considering all I'd seen and suffered that evening, I was a little short on ideas. So I lay down a while longer and took in the surroundings.

The alley was dark and narrow, it seemed to run behind the parade of shops. I'd never been down it before. Which was no surprise really. It looked like it only existed for running boxes from the street to the store rooms; taking deliveries on sack barrows, that sort of thing.

The rain forced me to my feet. I brushed myself down and took a look about. A large metal bin stood a little way along. My feet splashed in puddles as I made my way over to it. I'm not a gambling man, but I felt confident, given my circumstances, I'd make it to work early for once. The sooner I was indoors with one of Duncan's brews, the better. And those were words I never thought I'd say.

I opened the bin and had a look inside. It was empty, and didn't smell that bad. Well, why not? I thought. It's a few hours shelter at least. I clambered inside and tried to get some sleep.

I was just nodding off when I was awoken by laughter. Well, it was more like cackling really. I pushed the lid of the bin open a little to see what was going on.

The pirates piled out the back of the Stratford Tanning Depot. All happy, full of song and drink. They shuffled along one by one, cawing sea shanties and saying "y'arrgh" and all that.

A pirate at the back of the group stopped suddenly and walked over to a shadowy nook. I thought he was going to take a piss but was surprised to see him pull a spray can from his trousers. Giggling to himself, he stepped up to the wall. A few moments later he stepped back and admired his handiwork. He gave a satisfied smile and then shuffled off, still giggling.

I stared at the wall in disbelief. In fact I remember blinking several times because what I saw didn't make any sense. But there it was, in large red letters, the words: VIVA CASPER!

The pirates were writing Casper Macvittee's graffiti.

Which could only mean one thing...*the pirates* were Casper Macvittee's army.

Which meant, the Pirate Captain was none other than Casper Macvittee himself!

- 48 -

BLUDWYN & PEASWORTH

'Oscar, let's face facts,' said Bludwyn. 'You didn't see a Pirate Captain in that room, did you?'

I frowned. 'I just told you I did.'

Bludwyn shook his head. 'No, Oscar. Admit it, you were with the pirates that night. You were in that room with them as they hatched their plan, only you weren't listening, because you were doing the talking. You are the real leader of Casper Macvittee's army.'

'Are you high?'

Bludwyn ignored me and continued. 'You thought your disguises would throw people off the scent, that nobody would ever know the real nature of your plan, to destroy the Olympic Park, not for treasure, but as part of a sick campaign of terror.'

'You want proof it wasn't me? Raid the brothel, see if any of those sex-tourist photos are still there. Y'know, the ones the fat lad was developing? They'll show I'm not the Pirate Captain.'

'Oscar, you know we can't do that,' said Bludwyn. 'The computer was stolen.'

'Well, find it!' I crossed my arms and leaned back. This seat was really starting to numb my arse. 'How many more pages of this have we got?'

'Your case notes point to a troubled childhood,' said Peasworth.

'The only trouble I had was with my old man. When he went things were fine.'

'What about when you were fifteen?' asked Bludwyn, looking at his notes. 'When you went on a crime spree.'

'It wasn't a spree. It was two incidences...or maybe three, I can't remember. I was a kid.'

Bludwyn looked closer at his notes. 'You set fire to a Fiat Panda.'

'*Abandoned* Fiat Panda,' I said. 'That car had been rotting at the end of the road for years. Nobody would come to the estate to collect it. It was a write-off.'

'You still set fire to it,' said Peasworth. 'And then there was the graffiti.'

'Graffiti is a human right, everyone knows that. Even cavemen did it. It's in our nature, just like fire. Anyway, that was years ago. One incident of arson. One of graffiti or "public defacement" or whatever you call it. Never got an ASBO, did I? Never went in front of a judge. Cautioned, both times. Moved on and learnt me lesson. I'm a changed man now.'

'Are you?' said Slick. 'You wouldn't commit arson again?'

'Never.'

Slick reached into his blazer and reintroduced the pack of cigarettes. 'I think you'd like to commit a few acts of arson with these though, wouldn't you?'

'*I...quit,*' I said, through gritted teeth. 'Didn't you hear me? I'm never smoking again.'

'We will see,' said Slick, returning the cigarettes to his pocket. 'We will see.'

- 49 -

WAKING UP IN PARADISE

That morning was like so many others. I came round to complete darkness, a horrid smell, and cooing. Only things were different somehow. The darkness blacker. The cooing louder. And the air tasting that much more like a shot-putter's armpit.

For a second I wondered why that might be. And then, as all my senses clicked back together, I remembered I was in a bin.

The pigeons didn't know what hit them. They took to the air in shitting panic as I burst out like a jack-in-a-box, coughing and gasping for fresh air.

I'd just spent the night in a bin. Which, given that my life had been an encyclopaedia of lows, seemed like a new personal worst. Right down there with having watched more than two Macaulay Culkin movies at the cinema.

I ran a hand through my hair, it felt greasy, but not in a way that costs you five pound a pot. I looked down into the bin. My feet were hidden beneath a grey syrup of rotting veg. With disgust I raised a big toe. It poked its pruned head above the goo, whispered "kill me" and then sank back to the bottom.

As Mondays go, it wasn't getting off to the best of starts. There was a bright side though, literally. The rain had stopped. I looked up from the shadows to see a strip of clear blue sky between the buildings.

I clambered out of the bin and brushed myself down, flicking a banana skin off my shoulder.

The alleyway was quiet. There was no sign of the pirates. Although there was a pirate sign. In runny red ink the words: VIVA CASPER! punched out from the opposite wall.

What did that mean? I had no idea. Whether these pirates were Casper Macvittee's army or not, didn't matter. The only thing on my mind, aside from having a thorough wash and round of booster jabs, was getting back into my flat and getting rid of the Junior Anthrax. Nothing else mattered.

And the more I learnt about these pirates the more it seemed right that I should plant the Junior Anthrax on them and let them take the rap. I mean, they were up to no good from the start, right? Who knows what crimes they were plotting, best the FBI collar them before they do any real harm, right?

Problem was, even if I got back into my gaff, my plan for planting it on them was a tad ballsy. The only way I could see myself doing it would be to walk out into Leytonstone Road, bold as brass, and try to lob it through their open window.

Don't get me wrong, stranger, weirder and more violent things happen every day on my road. Even the Avon lady will greet you with a Molotov cocktail round here. But I'd sooner a more stealth-like method if I could. Which is why I was rubbing my chin, looking up and down the alleyway with cunning thought.

What if the Pirate Shop had a back door? That would make things easier. I could break in tonight unseen whilst they were all out doing their treasure hunt. They'd come back and be swooped on by the Feds following an "anonymous" tip-off.

I pulled my dressing gown round me and paced up the alleyway. The Pirate Shop was easy to find. There was a skull and crossbones painted on the back door with the words "Ye no be enterin!" underneath it.

I tried the handle. It was locked.

I decided to give the door a test with my shoulder. I only gave a little nudge but the wooden frame replied with a loud crack. I began whistling and started to walk away. With a bit more effort I felt that door would give. I reached the end of the alleyway and turned into the main road with a wide smile.

Everything was coming to plan.

- 50 -

WORK

I thought my earlier-than-normal arrival might impress Duncan, that my sudden and unexpected promptness would earn praise, a pat on the back and a cracking "well done" cup of tea brewed in my honour.

'You stink.' He poked his head up from behind the counter and pointed at his watch. 'And you're late.'

I ignored him. I was somewhat disappointed by the fact that I'd slept in a bin and still managed a lie-in. I walked towards the till.

'Why are you in a dressing gown,' he asked. 'Hey, are you sick?'

I ignored him and opened the till.

'Is it dress down day?' he asked. 'I wasn't told it was dress down day.'

I took a twenty out, closed the till and turned to leave the shop.

'Hey, what you doing?'

'Fags,' I said. 'After the night I've had, I need a smoke.'

- 51 -

FIVE MINUTES LATER

Five minutes later I was stood in the yard, smoking my third cigarette in as many minutes, whilst Duncan stood on one of his chalk ley-lines, scratching his curly brown bird's nest of hair, trying to understand everything I'd told him.

The Junior Anthrax scorching my boards – he went for that. The being locked out bit and going to The Eel to find my landlord – that was fine. Jimmy Strongbow being missing – that interested him. My adventures in the Stratford Tanning Depot – he didn't really go a bundle on that, choosing to ignore my comments about Tallulah Funbags, though he did brighten at the prospect of a conspiracy. And I think he must have ruined his pants when I told him about the possibility of Casper Macvittee being alive and running a pirate army.

'Serious?' he drawled. 'Casper Macvittee has an army of pirates?'

'Absolutely,' I said, sucking hurriedly on my fag. 'There he was, as bold as brass, bragging about treasure and all sorts. The papers were right. That geezer's a fruitcake.'

Duncan grinned his boyish grin. 'So there is treasure on the Olympic site after all?'

'Whoa!' I said. 'Hold up, Poirot, how'd you work that out?'

'You just told me,' said Duncan, confused. 'You just said that Casper said there was treasure on the site.'

'It says baked beans on the side of buses, don't mean they sell them.'

'Eh?'

'You believe what that muppet says is actually true?' I said, tapping ash onto the concrete. 'Bearing in mind he's dressed up like a pirate and got some goons to dress up and play pirates with him, even going so far as opening up a Pirate Shop to divert attention from their pirating skulduggery treasure hunting nonsense.'

'It must be true,' said Duncan. 'He wouldn't do all that if he didn't think it's true.'

'Ah, that's the point though, isn't it? Just 'cos he thinks it's true, doesn't mean it *is* true. You think foxes can talk.'

'I didn't say that,' said Duncan. 'I said I didn't *discount* it.'

'Whatever,' I waved him off. 'I'm not having that argument again. You know where I slept last night?'

'Yeah,' said Duncan. 'I could smell you a street away this morning.'

'Yeah, right.'

'Serious,' he said. 'My nose was twitching. It hurts standing this close to you now.'

I blew some smoke at him. 'That better?'

He waved it towards him and took a sniff. 'Not much. Hey, I know what will make you feel better. Stand here.' He pointed to a spot on his side of the yard.

'I'm not standing over there.' I said.

'It's good for you,' said Duncan. 'A ley-line can restore your chi. I stand out here everyday. I feel it working.'

'Leave it out.'

'Serious, try it.'

Begrudgingly, I went over to his side and stood there. I sighed, 'What do I have to do?'

'Just stand on this line here,' he said, positioning me. 'Keep your legs together and your back straight…and you'll feel it.'

'I feel like a prat.'

'Sssh.'

'This is stup—' I felt something, in my toes. 'Duncan...' I whispered. 'Duncan, I can feel something.'

His face brightened. 'You can?'

'Yeah,' I said. 'Cramp.'

- 52 -

SPRUCED

I rooted around the "staff area", looking for anything that might resemble a change of clothes, a towel, a bar of soap, some aftershave, deodorant – anything that could make me feel fresher and smell better.

I called out to Duncan. 'What happened to the samples?'

'Samples?'

'Y'know, the stuff we get through the door. Little tubes of toothpaste and samples of stink.'

'Try the fridge.'

'The fridge?'

'Yeah, to keep it cool.'

Duncan's logic would never make sense to me. It must be the whole other hemisphere thing. Thinking backwards. Upside down. Inside out. I wondered if I seemed as crazy to him.

I opened the fridge and after a bit of a rummage, pulled out a carrier bag. It was a disappointing haul, the best of the bunch being a Magic Tree air freshener and some lemon scented hand wipes from a fried chicken place. I washed my face with the wipes and hung the tree round me like a necklace. It was better than nothing. The dressing gown would have to stay, for now.

'I think we should investigate,' said Duncan, as I returned carrying two teas.

'Investigate what?'

'These pirates.' He took his mug and gave it a sniff. 'They're up to something. I think we should go back and spy on them. Take pictures. Evidence.'

'Duncan, haven't you heard a thing I've said? They are a load of day release patients playing pirates. Playing, I should point out, with real guns. Your mate Casper nearly shot my face off.'

'Don't you think it's suspicious though?' he said. 'These pirates turn up and buy Jimmy's shop. And then Jimmy goes missing.' He tapped his lips. 'Maybe they've kidnapped him.'

'No, it's probably something simple. Jimmy's probably just had another heavy night out, celebrating being a millionaire.'

'What if he's not a millionaire?' said Duncan.

'What?'

'How could these pirates afford to pay a million?'

'How should I know?' I said. 'But if I had a million I wouldn't blow it on some crappy little shop in East London. I'd retire.'

Duncan went very stiff all of a sudden. 'Maybe they don't have the money. Maybe Jimmy found out. Maybe they killed him!'

'Can your imagination give it a rest?'

'It's a conspiracy, I'm telling you. We should go to the police.'

'Whoa!' I cried. 'We don't need the rozzers.'

'But Jimmy's missing, he could be dead.'

'Duncan, I've got a bloody chemical weapon sitting in my flat and the FBI sniffing about asking questions. I'm looking at a serious stretch if I'm caught. The last thing I need is to draw any more attention on me by marching into a police station and saying, "hold up plod, I think pirates have kidnapped my landlord."'

'You can be selfish sometimes,' drawled Duncan. 'Sam Neill would go to the police.'

'No, Sam Neill would get rid of the Junior Anthrax. Which is exactly what I'm gonna do once I've broken back into my flat.'

'The only way you'll get back into your flat is with Jimmy,' said Duncan. 'Or some dynamite.' His eyes brightened. 'Hey maybe the pirates—'

'No, Duncan.'

'They might have some.'

'No, Duncan.'

'Or a cannon.'

'No, Duncan.'

'There's only one way to find out,' he said. 'We'll have to go to the Pirate Shop and investigate.'

Before I had chance to tell Duncan where he could shove that plan, the shop bell rang.

- 53 -

CUSTOMER

I couldn't help but smirk as the kid put the DVD on the counter.

'What you smiling at?' he spat.

'How old are you?'

'What? You a paedo or something?'

'You want to rent this? I need to see some proof of age.'

'Here's the proof,' he said gesturing to himself. 'I'm eighteen.'

'Are you?' I leant over the counter and sized him up. He was baby-faced, all dimples and freckles. He stood on tiptoes, thinking height makes age. Like a dwarf can't be old. Idiot. And if further proof was needed of his idiocy I clocked he had biro'd on some stubble on his top lip. The lengths these kids go to. And for what? The DVD he'd picked wasn't a video nasty or anything. It was a Russ Meyer, *Beneath the Valley of Ultravixens*, which is like an American version of the *Carry On* films, except tone down the laughs, pump up the titties and throw in a dose of the surreal and you're about there. They are probably a revered form of cinema somewhere, but round here it's only kids who've got internet blocks at home that rent them, wanting a quick fix of largely ungraphic celluloid sex. I quite like them for their off-centre dialogue.

'C'mon you nonce, you gonna let me rent it or not?'

I put the DVD back down on the counter and looked at the kid. 'It's Monday, shouldn't you be at school?'

'Don't go to school. I'm eighteen.'

'Does your mum know you're here?'

'Don't dick about,' he said. 'I'm double parked outside.'

He had some pluck and was trying every trick. I felt for him. The best thing that ever happened to me was seeing *Total Recall* when I was eight. It's about the bloodiest, goriest, most violent film of the 1980s. There's guns, girls, double-crosses, kung-fu, mutants. There's even triple titted aliens! That film blew my mind. I doubt it would have been so good had I watched it at the age of eighteen as the certificate insisted.

'Alright,' I said. 'You can rent it.'

'Immense!' cried the kid. He reached deep into his pocket and dumped two pounds on the counter, in brown shrapnel.

'But it's a tenner.'

'I don't have a tenner!'

I leant toward him and cupped my hand. 'Look,' I whispered. 'I'll do you a favour. I'll set it aside for you until you get your next bit of pocket money, okay?'

'But that's not till next week!'

'Gotchya!' I whisked the DVD away. 'You're not eighteen. The Family section's by the front door.'

The kid moaned. 'Can't you take a joke you gown-wearing ballbag? I was only pulling your pisser.'

'Whatever,' I said. 'Come back when you've got ID.'

The kid huffed, picked up his rucksack and left the shop, kicking the Documentary section on the way out. *Marching With Penguins* nearly marched out the front door.

'You little git!' I cried. But it was no good. He'd gone.

* * *

Bludwyn looked down at his charge sheet. 'Very good, Oscar. Threatening a minor.'

I shrugged. 'What would you have done?'

'Well, the law states that—'

'Quiet, Slick,' said Bludwyn. 'Now, that child identifies you as being the man responsible for everything.'

I snorted. 'Of course he does. He's got a grudge. Week in, week out, he or one of his mates come in and try and rent something they ain't supposed to. If you asked him, he'd tell you I was the bastard that shot Bambi's mum.'

'Bambi's mum,' said Slick, making a note on his pad. 'You want me to follow that up, sir?'

'No,' said Bludwyn. 'We've got plenty to occupy us already.' He leaned back in his chair and considered me. 'So, you're saying our star witness is mistaken?'

'He's not mistaken, he's lying. He can't have seen a thing. It was past his bedtime when it happened.'

'But he does see you entering the property.'

'I can't deny that, I've told you already that's what I did, whether the kid saw me or not.'

Bludwyn looked at me. 'Okay, Oscar, what happened next?'

- 54 -

JAGGERS

The shop bell went. I looked up expecting the kid to come back and have another pop at me, but to my surprise it wasn't him, it was someone I'd never seen in the shop before, and judging by the spooked expression on his gaunt features it seemed unlikely he was here to open an account.

'Jaggers?' I said. 'What you doing here?'

'Hey, you want to buy *Kramer versus Kramer*?' asked Duncan, fishing it out of the bargain bin.

Jaggers shook his head. 'Gentlemen, I'm here on business. *A personal matter.*' He drew up to the counter, his black gown swishing around him. He gave a cautious look over his shoulder then leaned toward us and, in a barely audible whisper, said: *'I fear we are all in great danger. Is there somewhere safe we can talk?'*

I raised an eyebrow and looked at Duncan. He raised one back.

Within a few moments the shop was shut and the three of us stood huddled in the "staff area". We were in such a tight huddle our shoulders kept touching. Which was annoying as Duncan's were rather pointy, and kept knocking into my glasses.

In a manner much like Marlon Brando in *Apocalypse Now*, Jaggers's wrinkled features leaned forward and caught the pallid light of the nearby window. His eyes were normally docile but today they had a panicked sparkle about them.

'Are you on any new medication?' I asked.

Jaggers shook his head. 'Listen carefully,' he whispered, 'because you are the only people I can trust. I think something terrible is about to happen.'

'It's about the smoking ban, isn't it?' I said, guessing at the only thing that could spook Jaggers enough to have him come running here. 'They've finally found a way to close the embassy loophole?'

'No,' said Jaggers. 'It's worse than that. I fear I'm soon to be murdered.'

'Murdered?'

'Serious?' said Duncan.

'Who'd want to murder you?' I asked.

Jaggers's eyes developed a new seriousness. He took a deep measured breath. 'The Pearly King...' he said, in barely more than a whisper. 'I believe the Pearly King wants to murder me.'

- 55 -

JAGGERS TELLS HIS TALE

Duncan and I listened closely as Jaggers told his tale. His voice kept its usual composure, never deviating from his deep measured purr, but his eyes betrayed him. They flitted about like a frightened animal, constantly looking over his shoulder and shooting worried glances out the window into the yard.

Naturally, I wanted to interrupt him as he told his tale. I wanted to ask a thousand questions, kick off a volley of debate and generally issue a flurry of interruptions, but I felt Jaggers, being the man he was, and having the reputation he did, was not someone who was known for talking a load of old cod, and that I should hold back and hear him out.

'Murdered?' I said. 'What load of old cod is this?'

'Fishy business indeed, but not cod, I assure you. I've had my suspicions for months now about the Pearly King. Have you noticed he's become increasingly hostile towards anybody who endorses the Olympiad? I fear his anger and rage have finally boiled over, which is bad news for us all.'

'What?' I scoffed. 'You're scared of that posing numpty doing you in? Pull the other one.'

'The Pearly King has every reason to kill me,' said Jaggers. 'Don't forget, my efforts played a large part in helping bring the Olympiad to East London. The Pearly King has never forgiven me for that. I feel he now seeks retribution.'

'Serious?' said Duncan.

'No, it's not bloody serious,' I said. 'Jaggers, nobody's going to kill you. You're a local hero. So, you helped bring the Olympics here? You also worked your magic and helped overturn the smoking ban at The Eel, surely that makes you better than even?'

Jaggers shook his head sadly. 'Small recompense, Oscar. Would the Pearly King rather have a kingdom?' he threw his spindly arms out, 'or a bunker? For that's all The Eel has become, a smoke-filled bunker in which he hides from an ever-changing world. In confidence, I only ever sought to overturn the smoking ban to appease his anger, but it didn't work. As more and more people have sold properties to the developers, the more bitter he's become. You don't understand what it means for him to keep this area Cockney. It is a cause he'd die for. It's a cause he'd let other people die for. It's a cause I believe he has already killed for.'

'You what?' I said.

'Serious?' said Duncan.

'Gravely,' nodded Jaggers. 'Jimmy Strongbow was due to meet me last night. He telephoned to request an urgent meeting at my chambers. I waited but he never arrived. He sounded troubled. I believe he knew the Pearly King was coming for him. I put it to you that the Pearly King killed him.'

'Where's your proof?' I said.

'I have no proof,' said Jaggers. 'Just well reasoned suspicion.'

'Well, I put it to you...' I said, '...that your suspicion is wide of the mark. Alright, Jimmy and The Pearly King didn't see eye to eye about the sale of the model shop, but murder...'

'May I put it to you...' said Jaggers, '...that Pearlyism is a fanaticism, and to preserve his realm the Pearly King will stop at nothing. Consider the model shop. Who do you think would offer the exorbitant sum of one million pounds for such a sorry piece of property? A legitimate developer? Or someone who knew it was an offer Jimmy couldn't refuse?'

Duncan frowned. 'What are you saying?'

'I'm saying...' said Jaggers, '...that the Pearly King tabled a dishonest bid for the model shop in a desperate attempt to keep the area safe from redevelopment, and that Jimmy had no clue as to the bidder's true identity or intentions until last night, when he discovered the bid was bogus and that the Pearly King was behind it. A confrontation would have certainly taken place, based on the episode in The Eel the other night we can assume it was hostile. Maybe Jimmy threatened to go to the police. Or perhaps he rejected the idea that he was betraying the East End. Either way, there was only one outcome: when the Pearly King didn't get his way, he killed him.'

Duncan's jaw had pretty much hit the floor at this point. He was in conspiracy heaven, lapping up every single word that fell from Jaggers's thin lips. However, I on the other hand, was having a lot of trouble swallowing it because of a good old thing called evidence. There was none of it. Not a shred. Plus, I knew something Jaggers didn't. I knew about the pirates.

'Jaggers,' I said. 'You're talking out of your trumpet. And here's why...'

Jaggers listened thoughtfully as I explained all I knew about the true identity of the shop's new owners. The throwing of the water. The "Viva Casper!" graffiti. I even explained the bit I didn't fully believe, namely, that a load of pirates led by a crazy local archaeologist were, for reasons unclear, going to sack London.

Jaggers gasped. 'You saw Casper Macvittee? He's alive?'

'Yeah,' I said, feeling smug about going toe-to-toe with the lawyer and winning.

'How did he look?'

'What?'

'Casper Macvittee,' said Jaggers. 'How did he look?'

I shrugged. 'Alright I suppose. I only saw him from the back.'

'But you're sure it was him?'

'Yeah,' I said. 'The pirates were toasting him, saying "Viva Casper!"'

Jaggers stroked his gaunt cheeks in thought. 'Pirates? Most interesting.'

'So, Jimmy's not been murdered by the Pearly King?' said Duncan. 'He's been murdered by pirates?'

'Wait a minute,' I said. 'You don't know he's been murdered by anyone. No body. No evidence. No case, right?'

'Normally I'd agree with you,' said Jaggers. 'But, something is definitely afoot. This all requires further investigation. Jimmy is missing...that is the absolute fact. And there is plenty of evidence, albeit circumstantial, that suggests he's come to harm, either at the hands of the Pearly King, or at the hands of these pirates. I warn you, if *real* pirates have control of that shop we are in grave trouble, for take it from me, a naval lawyer with many years experience of dealing with these land-hating lubbers – pirates are ruthless. It's often best to think the worst and act first.' Jaggers collected himself, patting down his robes. 'And that's exactly what I intend to do. I'm off to the town hall, to see what I can dig up in the archives.'

'Archives?' I said.

'Yes,' said Jaggers. 'I want to get to the bottom of who really bought that shop. We need more information before we can act.'

'Perhaps we should go to the shop to investigate,' said Duncan.

'Good idea,' said Jaggers. 'See what you can sniff out.'

'Forget it,' I said. 'If they are murderers, do you really want to go snooping about?'

'I leave your actions to your consciences,' said Jaggers. 'But please don't breathe a word of this to any living soul. You are the only people I can trust.'

'What?' I said, looking at Jaggers as if he were an idiot. 'Why us?'

'Neither of you are Cockneys. You pretend to be, Oscar—'

'I don't pretend!'

'Oh you do, my dear fellow, you do, but deep down in your heart of hearts you know as well as I do that we three outsiders will never be fully accepted into the Pearly King's kingdom, which means I know you're not involved. Whatever is going on, I fear Jimmy's paid with his life already, and I fear more people will yet pay with theirs.'

Jaggers stepped out of the "staff area" and made to leave the shop. Duncan and I followed, unlocking the front door.

'We shall reconvene later.' Jaggers shook both our hands. 'Stay vigilant.'

And with that and a fearful look over his shoulder, he left.

- 56 -

ALLEY

'I can't believe you talked me into this.'

'Where is it?' said Duncan.

'Just up here.' I waved my cigarette up ahead at the dark alleyway between the shops. He nodded and walked on. I trailed behind him, without enthusiasm.

All Jaggers's talk of conspiracies and my talk of pirates had overexcited Duncan a little and as the longest serving member of staff he'd pulled rank and made something of an "Executive Decision". We were to close the shop for lunch and go and investigate. Investigate what exactly? To connect the crazy dots in Duncan's head or confirm I was telling the truth? Like I'd make it up? If that doesn't prove Duncan's not the brightest light in the street I don't know what does. So I told him, as far as I was concerned, he could shove his "Executive Decision". I was in no mood to go traipsing about Maryland Point in my dressing gown, giving him a guided tour of the newly discovered briny nightlife. Not happening. End of. Never.

'Oscar, I'll get you some cigarettes.'

As such, my services were easily bought. Jesus, now I look back on it I see what a fall from grace I had in just twenty-four-hours. I spent one night in a brothel and the next day I was prostituting myself for a pack of fags. If I'd known then what I know now, I would have asked for a whole lot more. Or better still, given up smoking altogether.

Duncan's gangly figure disappeared amongst the alleyway shadows. I followed a short distance behind. As we walked further into the darkness the noise of the street deserted us. I kept my eyes on the ground and tried to avoid trampling my bare feet into torn bin bags and sodden newspapers.

'Where is it?' he whispered.

'You can't miss it. Just keep walking.'

The dirty walls drew in around us. Duncan stopped a short way ahead. He put his hands on his hips and cocked his head. He had a curious look on his face. I knew he'd found what he was looking for.

'Viva Casper,' he said, reading aloud. He stepped closer to the wall. I thought he was going to touch it but instead he placed his face close and traced the graffiti with his nose. 'Smells fresh.'

'Should do,' I said. 'They only painted it last night. Look,' I pointed, 'you can see how the rain mixed with it.'

The red letters had run slightly, but the words were still strikingly clear.

Duncan stepped back from the wall, scratching his messy hair. 'Viva Casper,' he mumbled to himself, as if repeating it out loud would solve anything, like "open sesame" or something. 'Are you sure pirates did this?'

'I told you, didn't I?'

Duncan stepped forward and gave the wall another sniff. 'It's just...it doesn't smell like pirates.'

I threw my fag on the floor. 'Sorry, Lassie! I'll get you a stronger scent next time! How the bloody hell do you know what a pirate smells like?'

Duncan shrugged. 'I don't know...it's just...this doesn't smell right.'

'You sure you're not smelling me?' I reached for the Magic Tree medallion hanging round my neck and waved it at him.

Duncan considered it and shook his head. 'No, it's not you.' He turned back to the graffiti. 'It's this wall. Something just doesn't smell quite right.'

'What? Smells like pie and mash? Smells like the Pearly King?'

'I'm not sure,' said Duncan.

'The Pearly is not involved, I'll tell you that now. Jaggers didn't see what I saw last night. He's got it wrong. Yeah the Pearly has been a bit off recently, but this has nothing to do with him, right?'

Duncan shrugged, 'Maybe.' He turned back to the wall and continued sniffing.

- 57 -

BLUDWYN & PEASWORTH

A short while ago Peasworth had left the interrogation room, presumably to follow up on some of my leads, corroborate some evidence and generally get on with proving my unquestionable innocence. So, when he came back fifteen minutes later with nothing more than a plate of pink French fancies, I was a little cheesed off.

'Seconded from the canteen, sir,' he grinned. 'Your favourite.'

I sat back in my chair with arms folded and watched as Bludwyn shovelled the cakes through his tash whilst Slick licked clean his thin promotion-hungry fingers. It was disgusting. No wonder they're called pigs.

'Thought it was doughnuts for you lot?'

'That's regular force,' said Peasworth with a mouthful of cake. 'We're Special Branch.'

Special seemed about right.

'Now, Oscar,' began Bludwyn, with pink crumbs flying from his mouth. 'Something seems very odd about all this.'

'You don't say,' I said sarcastically.

'You say it was Duncan who wanted to investigate the alley?'

'Yup.'

'Doesn't that strike you as odd?'

'Everything about Duncan strikes me as odd. He once told me he thought dolphins were harder than steel.'

'I see,' said Bludwyn, who didn't really see. 'What I mean is, you describe Duncan as someone with a very open mind, prone to believing far-fetched theories and conspiracies, yet he had trouble swallowing yours. He needed proof.'

I shrugged. 'It's different when it's on your doorstep.'

'How so?'

'Well...' I leaned back in my chair and tried to think of a way to make them understand. '...if you tell me a bloke that lives up a mountain in China has got the longest fingernails in the world, then I won't really give a toss. I'll just take your word for it. But if you told me the bloke with the longest fingernails in London was waiting for a bus outside my bedroom window, then I'd get up and a have a look. Not because I care, but because I can.'

'I see,' said Bludwyn, who was seeing even less. 'But in this case, your colleague, a man whom by your own admission believes foxes can talk, had trouble swallowing the lie you spun about pirates and underground armies.'

'It wasn't a lie!' I protested. 'And it wasn't just me! Jaggers was now feeding his ear too. Duncan was drowning in conspiracy theories. He was like a baby in a barrel of tits. He didn't know which one to suck on first.'

'As happy as he may have been, he still wanted to go and investigate,' said Bludwyn. 'He didn't believe it all.'

'Can you blame him?' I sat up in my chair. 'I mean, I've given you the facts three times already and still you can't handle the truth.' Given the circumstances I was disappointed not to have been more Jack Nicholson in giving that line. I decided to keep the interview interesting by slipping in film quotes whenever I could.

'Oscar,' began Bludwyn.

I smiled. 'Call me...Snake.'

'Snake?' said Peasworth. 'Is that your pirate alias?'

'Are you talking to me? *Are you talking to me?*'

'Of course we are,' said Bludwyn. 'You are our chief suspect.'

'Well, frankly my dear, I don't give a damn.'

'Well, frankly, we do,' said Bludwyn. 'Now, get back on with your story. You were in the alleyway with Duncan…'

- 58 -

DOORS

'Are you sure this is the right door?' questioned Duncan. 'I thought you said—'

'I know what I said,' I replied, 'I'm telling you. It wasn't like this a couple of hours ago.'

I examined the rear of the Pirate Shop in puzzlement. Where this morning stood a door so shoddy it wouldn't have stopped an ant's fart, now stood a door made of shimmering steel that would've stopped the farts of Superman's older, more super, brother.

Duncan leaned forward and gave it a sniff.

'Anything?' I asked.

'No,' he replied. Another sniff. 'Nothing.'

I reached into my dressing gown and drew out a cigarette. 'Right, can we go now?'

Duncan stepped back from the door, wearing a frown. 'Why would they change it?'

I shrugged and blew a smoke ring up to the sky. 'I dunno, Poirot, maybe they want to keep people out.'

'Or keep something in?'

I looked at the weight of the door. 'Like what? King Kong?'

'They're hiding something,' said Duncan. 'Why else would they change it?'

'Why'd you think I had Jimmy up the locks at the flat?' I replied. 'Maryland Point is bandit country. People want security. I mean, look at this door, nobody's getting through it. It could stop a bomb.'

Bad choice of words, for no sooner had I said them Duncan's eyes suddenly brightened. 'A bomb?' He looked back at the door excitedly. 'Do you reckon that's what they've got in there?'

'Is everyone in New Zealand as mental as you?'

'You said they were talking about sacking London. Maybe they've got a bomb. Maybe this is their bunker to survive it.'

I blew out smoke. 'Maybe. Tell you what, I'll add that "maybe" to your growing list of "maybes", which includes, "maybe" they've got Jimmy, "maybe" they've killed him, "maybe" foxes can talk.'

'Hey,' said Duncan. 'Can you stop going on about that. I only said it once.'

'Whatever.' I blew out a cloud of smoke. 'I'm going now. You can stay here and cook up more of your crazy theories.' I turned for the main road. This had been a big waste of time. I had better things to do than prat about down alleyways in my dressing gown.

From behind me there came a sound. It was squeaky and sounded like a hinge opening. I turned round to find Duncan kneeling at the foot of the steel door. He was prodding something with his finger.

'Can a bunker have a cat flap?'

'Eh?' I took a few steps back to have a closer look. And there, to my amazement, in a door as imposing as any bank vault, was a small steel cat flap.

- 59 -

INTO THE UNKNOWN

Duncan prodded the cat flap with a long cautious finger.

'What you doing?' I said.

'I want to know more about these pirates.' He leant forward and gave the cat flap a sniff.

'Let me guess,' I said. 'Smells of cats?'

'No,' said Duncan. He began sniffing quickly, like an excited police dog. 'It smells…familiar.'

'You sniff a lot of cats' arses?'

He didn't reply, too engrossed in finding a scent.

'Nevermind what you can smell,' I said. 'What can you see? Is Jimmy in there bound and gagged with Lord Lucan or what?'

'I can't see anything,' he said, peering in through the flap. 'It's too dark. Hang on.' He reached inside. 'I think something's in the way.'

Duncan had the tongue problem. You know when people start doing tricky things with their hands or whatever and their tongue pops out of their mouth and lamely explores its pathetic reach, thinking it can actually be of some use when in actual fact it's as helpful as a spanner made of butter. It's called phantom limb syndrome apparently. And Duncan had it bad. Which made the situation weird. Me, in a dressing gown, stood over a bloke in a back alley, his arm in a cat flap, his tongue writhing about. I'm surprised one of the things I'm not charged with yet is solicitation.

'Will you stop pratting about,' I said. 'C'mon, let's go before we get caught and they chop your arm off and give you a hook or whatever.'

'Got it!' Duncan withdrew his arm. Clenched tightly in his fist was a ball of black fabric, it was covered in shiny buttons and rhinestones. He looked up at me nervously. 'Oscar!' he gasped, waving the fabric at me. 'You know what this is? This is the Pearly King's jacket!'

- 60 -

INTELLIGENCE

Before you could say *Jaws 4: This time it's personal*, Duncan was crouched looking through that cat flap the same way I used to try and peer into the girls changing room at school. Flicking his head back and forth, peering up and down, excitedly trying to find something, anything, that could fuel the inferno of conspiracies undoubtedly rolling round his head.

'It's too dark,' he moaned.

'Use your phone.'

'To call the police?'

'No, you noddy, to take a picture.'

'A picture of what?'

'Inside the room,' I said. 'Turn your flash on, slap your hand inside, take a picture, bosh.'

'Or a video!' he cried. He pulled out his phone and went to put it through the cat flap, but stopped.

'What's the matter?' I whispered.

'What if we find something?'

'You've already found something.'

'No, what if the Pearly King's body is in there? What if Casper and his pirates are in there?'

'Wouldn't you be able to smell all that?' I mocked.

Duncan started to get up. 'No, we should go to the police.'

'You heard what Jaggers said – don't tell another soul.'

'But we've got evidence now,' said Duncan. 'Jimmy's missing...you've heard pirates talking about destroying London...and now we've found this!' He waved the Pearly King's jacket about.

I quickly dismissed his worries. 'Missing person: presumed pissed and in a wardrobe somewhere. Day-pass mental patients talking cobblers, and some lost property. Hardly the gunpowder plot, is it?'

'You just don't want to call the police because of your Junior Anthrax.'

'Oh, that's cheap,' I said. 'I'll tell you what. Turn your camera on, slide your hand through and take a pic. If it comes out looking like a scene from *The Shining*, we'll tell Jaggers and then we'll go to the police.'

'Serious?'

'Serious.'

Duncan nodded and then took several deep breaths.

'What you doing?'

'*AWOOGA!*' he cried, punching himself in the chest. '*AWOOGA!*'

'Shut up!' I hissed. 'What are you playing at?'

'I'm nervous,' he said breathlessly. 'I'm doing a Haka to psych myself up. *AWOOGA!*'

I slapped him on the back. 'Nevermind that, just shove your hand through.'

Duncan knelt down and slipped his arm inside. At this point I took a cautionary glance up and down the alleyway, as you do. All seemed as it should be, apart from the face peering round a building from the far end. It had dark glasses and an earpiece and slick side parted black hair. On seeing that I'd spotted him, the face disappeared.

I kicked Duncan.

'Hey! What was that for?'

'We're being watched,' I whispered.

No sooner had the words left my mouth when the face reappeared, only this time his suited body came with him. He began walking down the alley towards us, mumbling into his cuff.

'Duncan, leg it!' I shouted. 'It's the Feds!'

- 61 -

BUNGER'S VIDEO PALACE

I stood in darkness. My heartbeat was painful. It was like a pneumatic drill on my chest. With a trembling hand I approached the front door and tried to find the bottle to open a gap in the shutters and peer outside. I had been too caught up in legging it to look over my shoulder and see if they were closing on us. For all I knew there were now hundreds of Feds stood outside the shop waiting to bust me, just like at the end of *The Blues Brothers*.

I'm not scared of plod, never have been, but the FBI are something different altogether. I've seen enough films to know they don't mess about.

When the FBI turn up, all the regular cops brick it and get out of the way. I was bricking it too because I knew I was bang to rights on the charge of possessing a chemical weapon. And if they arrested me, by the time I'd served my sentence everyone would be going about in flying cars and living like *The Jetsons*. And that's *if* they let me out. It was more than likely I'd never be a free man again. I'd spend the rest of my life in a small grey cell. Although, given the state of my so-called "penthouse", a cell was probably a move up the property ladder.

You get TV in prison now, right? I could serve a life sentence in front of the box, no probs. It's just the commercial breaks that would drive me crazy. A film is a work of art. The thought of having scenes interrupted by an advert for diarrhoea tablets and toothpaste was just too much. I wasn't going to prison to be tortured like that.

I called out, 'I'm not going down without a fight!' which I guess was somewhat ironic as I was still wearing my *Rocky* dressing gown. But I didn't see it like that at the time. Instead I stood still, listening carefully for any sound beyond the shutters: footsteps, guns being cocked, whispers – but I heard nothing.

I took a deep breath and delicately parted the shutters.

The alleyway was empty.

The only thing that stared at me was the brick wall opposite. I pushed my face to the glass and tried to look further along.

'It's going to be a long night,' I whispered. 'This is the last stand. I won't name you. It's me they are after. You can go if you want. Leave me here.'

I expected some heartfelt comments. Some gratitude. Some reassurance maybe, but instead all I got was silence. I turned round to find Duncan stood behind the counter playing with his phone, completely oblivious to the news that he was now standing in the Alamo. 'Oi!' I cried. 'Have you even been listening to me?'

'What?' Duncan looked up. 'Hey, why are the shutters still closed? Flip the sign round. We're open.'

'Open?' I spat. 'The FBI could turn up any minute.'

'Cool,' he said. 'Hey, reckon they'll want to rent those *Police Academys*?'

'No!' I said. 'I reckon they'll want to nick me for having an illegal chemical weapon sitting in my sodding flat!' Just then, there were footsteps outside. I gasped and drew back. 'They're here! Hide!'

- 62 -

IDENTITY

I stood in the shop drinking a tea so strong it didn't have a name. It was so black it made a Whoopi look like a Julie. And it was my second in ten minutes. I needed it. I probably needed more. With a guilty conscience and a bad night's sleep, the paranoia was starting to bite, hard.

'I'm telling you,' I said. 'I heard footsteps.'

'I didn't hear anything.' Duncan pointed a heavy remote control up at the TV. The screen flickered. A Sam Neill came on. *Event Horizon.* A jumpy horror from the '90s that scared the crap out of me as a kid. Cupping my tea I drifted out to the Chevy Chase section to see if I could find something a little calmer. One thing that had already calmed me down a little was remembering who I was. Or rather, remembering who the FBI thought I was.

You see, to the FBI, I wasn't Oscar Hume. I was Mr Bunger, owner of Bunger's Video Palace, as identified by Berol. Which meant I was kind of hiding in the right place. I mean, where else would Mr Bunger be but at his video shop?

Yeah, it was a flimsy cover. I didn't know how long it would last, but it's all I had. And I had to cling to it, just for a little longer. Just till I could get back in the flat, grab the Junior Anthrax and dump it on the pirates. Then I'd be a free man. And we could all do the tango.

'Can we open up now?' asked Duncan.

'No we bloody can't.'

'But I'm the boss. I should decide.'

'No, I'm *your* boss,' I said. 'I'm Mr Bunger and Mr Bunger says...that door stays locked all afternoon.'

'Hey, if you're Mr Bunger, can I talk to you about a promotion?'

'No.'

'How about complaints? Oscar's always late for work.'

'Don't get smart.'

'He takes too many smoking breaks,' continued Duncan. 'It affects productivity.'

'You want to talk about being productive?' I said. 'Show me what you managed to film in the Pirate Shop. Let me see if your "Executive Decision" was a good one.'

Duncan handed me his phone. It was heavy and took two hands to hold it properly. 'Jesus! How old is this thing?'

Duncan shrugged. 'Five years, maybe. It's from New Zealand.'

'How do I make it play?'

'It is playing.'

'Bloody hell!' The video was a horrible grainy mess made up of blacks, browns and greys. I held the screen close to my face, but it didn't make any difference. 'You can't see a thing. You'd have been better off taking a brass rubbing!'

'I wonder what the Pearly King's jacket was doing there?' Duncan pulled it out from under the counter and gave it a sniff. Why he had to run away from the scene of the crime holding it, I'll never know. But you do all sorts of strange things when you believe you're about to be arrested. I should know.

'Do you reckon it's like Jaggers says?' asked Duncan. 'Do you think the Pearly King is in on it?'

It was a loaded question. Whatever my answer, Duncan probably already had the next step of the conspiracy mapped out in his head.

'How the hell should I know if he's in on it?' I said. 'I don't even know what "it" is.'

'Casper's plan to sack London and the Olympics. The Pearly King would be up for that, wouldn't he?'

'Nah,' I said. 'He hates the Olympics, but not enough to blow London up as well. He loves the city too much for that.'

'Well, what about this jacket?'

I shrugged. 'I don't know. You put your hand somewhere you shouldn't and found something you don't understand. There could be any number of rational reasons for it being there.'

'Yeah,' nodded Duncan. 'The pirates have killed him too!'

'No,' I said. 'It's not always your crazy theories. It could be something simple.'

'Like what?'

'Like...up until two days ago that model shop had been in Jimmy's family for over a hundred years or something, right? Who knows what crap got stored in it? I mean, listen to this, I found out yesterday Jimmy is a Pearly Prince. What's to say this suit isn't his? And that he likes dressing up behind closed doors like a tranny or something?'

'That doesn't make any sense,' said Duncan.

'Makes more sense than him teaming up with a load of pirates to sack London.'

Duncan turned his attention back to his phone. Trying to angle it one way or another to catch the light and pick out some detail. His busy brain flitted off somewhere else. 'Hey, if you did hear someone outside earlier...why didn't they knock?' No sooner had the words left his mouth when there was a sharp rap at the front door.

Duncan and I looked at each other.

'I think we should run,' I mumbled, rejecting the idea of a last stand. I never did have much sticking power.

'But it might be a customer.'

'Don't be a prat!' I hissed. 'It's the Feds!' They've sussed my cover.'
I started to pull Duncan toward the back door. 'C'mon! Let's go!'

Duncan refused to budge. 'Who's there?' he called out.

'You Kiwi prat!' I hissed, pushing past him. 'What did you do that for?'

From outside came a voice. Its tone flat and even. 'Nothing to fear. It is I, Jaggers.'

- 63 -

JAGGERS'S DISCOVERY

'Jesus, Jaggers,' I said as I unlocked the door. 'You nearly gave me a coronary.'

He pushed past me, clutching a bundle of paperwork under his arm. 'We've no time to lose,' he said. He opened his mouth to say something else, but stopped dead as he caught sight of Duncan. He pointed excitedly, 'Is that—?'

'The Pearly King's jacket,' replied Duncan, waving it. 'We discovered it at the Pirate Shop. You were right.'

'Oh how I wish I were wrong,' moaned Jaggers, holding a hand to his wrinkled forehead. 'I had hoped you would find nothing. This proves that things are so much worse than I feared.'

At Jaggers's insistence we retired to the safety of the "staff area". We huddled together and he proceeded to explain where he'd been and what he'd found out. He started with the pirates. Being a former naval lawyer, he called up an old friend at the Admiralty and asked if they were trailing a radical terrorist cell in London of the pirate persuasion.

'My enquiry was roundly laughed at,' said Jaggers, bitterly. 'I was told that in most instances they could neither confirm nor deny a line of enquiry, but in this case they'd make an exception and tell me directly they were absolutely not trailing Long John Silver or any of his crew.'

However, Jaggers refused to give up. He went to the library and searched the local newspaper archives but found nothing, not a sausage, save for a small story about some pirates turning up at a fancy dress fun run in Mile End, but Jaggers dismissed that as coincidence, and probably nothing to do with the seemingly bloodthirsty terrorists we were trailing.

So he changed tact, and putting his legal contacts to good use, spoke to a notorious grass in Newham called Terry Ten-Tongues.

This time he struck gold. This Terry had heard some rumours going around last summer about a bunch of pirates operating in the East End, touting their services as mercenaries. Jaggers asked why the pirates had come looking for adventure here. Terry was unsure. One rumour he heard said they were diversifying their pirating portfolio. Another, that since the boom of the internet, the bottom had fallen out of traditional pirating. Whatever their motives, one thing was clear: for the right price, you could hire them as your own private army.

'I put it to you...' began Jaggers, '...that Casper Macvittee's profile roused attention. His talk of treasure being buried on the Olympic site piqued the interests of these pirates, so much so that they approached him and brokered a deal so favourable that Casper decided to abandon his plans to confront the Olympic committee head-on and instead sought subversion as his approach to undermine the Games.'

'Why?' I said. 'Why would he do that?'

'A motive?' said Jaggers, tapping his lips. 'How novel. Let's say, vanity. A man dismissed as a fool wants his day as a king. Many people mocked Casper Macvittee. Derided him. And still do. Who's to say how that makes someone feel? How much propellant it gives them to prove everyone wrong?'

'Okay,' I said. 'But I still don't get how the Pearly King figures in all of this.'

'Oscar, there is a phrase that says the art of good business is connecting people,' Jaggers raised an eyebrow, 'whom do you think is the most connected man in the area?'

'The Pearly King!' answered Duncan, unnecessarily.

'Exactly,' nodded Jaggers.

'So, what?' I said. 'You're saying the Pearly introduced the pirates to Casper, and they struck a deal?'

'Not at all,' said Jaggers. 'We can only theorise, but I'd say the deal was struck before they even met.'

'What?' said Duncan. 'Are you saying the pirates are psychic?'

'No,' scoffed Jaggers. 'I put it to you that the Pearly King paid the pirates for their services and set them up with Casper Macvittee as a cover.'

'Why?' I asked.

'Motivesmotivesmotives,' said Jaggers to himself, tapping his lips. 'In order to work out *"why"* you must first work out *"what."*'

'What?'

'Exactly,' purred Jaggers. 'What do each of them want?'

'Pirates want treasure,' offered Duncan. 'That's what pirates lives for. And Casper says there is treasure under the Olympic site.'

'Very good,' said Jaggers. 'But the treasure Casper speaks of is mythical. I mean, who really believes King Arthur has anything to do with the East End of London?'

Duncan opened his mouth to say something, but I shook my head to tell him no. Now wasn't the time to get into that.

Jaggers continued. 'The pirates are mercenaries for hire to the highest bidder. They are not going to work for a slice of treasure they are unsure even exists. That's Casper's prize. Their prize is money. And the Pearly King's prize is having the Olympics wiped out. He's bankrolling it all, to get what he wants.'

'But he doesn't want to destroy London, surely?'

Jaggers smiled. 'No, Oscar, far from it. But we don't know how they are planning to destroy the Olympic site. Maybe there is no way to restrict the damage. I did ask my contact at the Admiralty if any nuclear warheads had been lost recently. I'm afraid he could neither confirm nor deny that.'

'What about the model shop?' said Duncan.

'Yeah,' I said. 'What's that got to do with anything?'

'I don't know yet,' said Jaggers. 'But I intend to find out.'

Duncan brightened. 'You're going to break in?'

Jaggers grinned. 'Me? Break the law? I think not.'

'So, what are you going to do?' I asked.

'Tonight at The Eel, I will question the Pearly King, discreetly. I'll need you both to be there as witnesses. My prosecution will tie him up in so many knots, he'll confess everything.'

'Why be discreet?' I said. 'Just ask him straight.'

Jaggers went pale. 'Are you mad? A man who can get hot pie and mash out of hours is not to be trifled with. Maryland Point is his manor. Accusing him directly of murder could tip him over the edge. If he doesn't want to kill me already for all I've done to bring the Olympics here, questioning him directly could well cost me my life.'

'This sounds serious,' said Duncan. 'Shouldn't we go to the police?'

'Now let's not be hasty,' I said, recalling the chemical weapon sitting in my bedroom.

'I hope I'm wrong,' said Jaggers. 'And that Jimmy is alive and the Pearly King is not bitter enough to team up with a deranged Casper Macvittee and a mob of hired pirates in order to lay waste to the Olympiad. It is possible, despite the evidence, and my revered record as a lawyer, that I may have got the wrong end of the gavel with all this.'

'No,' said Duncan. 'You never get anything wrong.'

Jaggers's lips twisted into a smile. 'That's kind of you to say. But I fear that if we went to the police now they'd arrest us for time wasting, such is the tallness of our tale.'

And, let's face it, he wasn't wrong. Here I am telling it to you for the fourth time and still you can't get your head around it.

'We need firm evidence,' purred Jaggers. 'And tonight I intend to get it.'

'Duncan, listen to him, the man is an expert. Let him do it his way.'

Jaggers studied me. His eyes sparkled. 'Oh Oscar, believe me, I shall.'

- 64 -

SOLVING THE VIDEO

After Jaggers left the shop, Duncan and I opened up again. I don't know why we bothered. No one was going to rent anything in this heat. The weather was just too perfect. Surely anyone who wasn't at work was sunbathing in a park somewhere or standing round a barbecue giving it chat about knowing the best way to light it.

Stuck in the shadowy gloom of the shop we spent the afternoon watching *Highlander*. Well, I was watching it. Duncan was still playing with his phone, trying to see something in the pointless surveillance video he'd recorded. He was now trying to pause it frame by frame, making notes as he went on what he could see. Or what he thought he could see.

'You better hurry up,' I said, not looking away from the TV. 'Those muppets reckon they'll sack London tonight.'

'I'm trying,' said Duncan. 'But it's hard.'

'How many seconds you done?'

'Four.'

'Four? You've been doing it for over an hour!'

'I had to keep starting again.'

'Why?'

'I thought I saw something.'

'It's pointless. It's pretty much a black screen. You'll see what you want to see.' I drifted over to look at the pad he'd been scribbling on. 'What's that say?' I pointed at his spidery handwriting. 'Pony farting?'

'Penny farthing,' he corrected.

I looked up at him. He was serious.

'I need a cigarette,' I said. I went over to the till to get my lighter. As I reached out to grab it my hand passed under one of the few lights Bunger insisted we always keep on. Under the ultra-violet bulb of the fraud note checker, my hand glowed a strange purple and my nails lit up like Christmas trees.

It gave me an idea.

'Duncan, give me your phone a sec.' I held the screen under the violet light and began playing the video back.

'What you doing?' he asked.

'Here, have a butcher's at this!'

Duncan peered over my shoulder and we looked once more at the now not so impenetrably black footage. Shapes and objects started to present themselves, but they were still vague.

'That *is* a penny farthing,' he chimed.

'Probably their getaway car.'

Duncan looked at me seriously.

'I'm pulling your leg.' The camera made a clumsy pan of the darkened room. A few things emerged from the shadows. In one corner stood a large piece of stone, like a head from Easter Island, you know with stern lips and a frown, only it was more like something from a Punch and Judy show, with a big hooked nose and creepy grin. Around it were totem poles made up of the same sort of faces. If I was asked to coin a name for it, I'd describe it as Aztec Cockney. It was bloody bizarre.

'There you go,' I said. 'No bodies. Just knick-knacks and weird tribal shit. Your theory is sunk, son.'

The screen then filled with what previously had been a dark blur, but violet light exposed more detail. The blur was a beard. The white smudge behind it a broken smile. Its owner…a pirate, staring down into the lens with crazy eyes.

'Ah…' I said. 'That could be a bit of a problem.'

- 65 -

AFTER WORK

After work I trudged home to have one final go at breaking in. I didn't want to spend another night in a bin, or in a brothel. Amazingly, I'd prefer to kip in my cockroach-infested "penthouse". Though, how infested was it? I wondered. A whole twenty-four hours had passed with the Junior Anthrax unchecked. Maybe it was fine. Or maybe a chemical supernova had gone off in there, with bright light streaking out of the metal container, zapping every evil cockroach in the room and melting them, just like that bit at the end of *Raiders of the Lost Ark*.

I had no way of telling.

Though, if the demise of the cockroaches had been as cinematic as that, I was sorry I'd missed it. I'm still not convinced Spielberg directed that bit of the film anyway. He's made a career out of being pedestrian and all of a sudden he comes over all video nasty in a PG certificate. If he could do it then, why not in *Hook*? That film was crying out for the entire cast to have their heads melted in the first reel.

Anyway, Spielberg aside, I felt certain that if I didn't break back in to my flat soon, the FBI would. Time was short. I could sense it. There was only so long I could pretend to be Mr Bunger, and very soon the FBI would realise that the real Mr Bunger was quite a bit more bald, middle-aged and Indian than me.

But, what choice did I have? I mean, what would you do? Spend the rest of your days hiding in the video shop? Or would you try and take charge of the situation and get rid of the Junior Anthrax as soon as possible and put your name in the clear?

Yeah, I thought so.

That evening was a scorcher on Maryland Point. I could have lit a cigarette off the pavement, it was that hot. My bare feet were burning. I hopped, skipped and jumped about like a water boatman in a kettle, trying to stay in the shadows. A difficult job made harder by the fact I was trying to smoke at the time. And trying to make sense of everything Jaggers had said.

I don't know if I was now in the realms of being so tired I'd believe anything, but as far-fetched as it seemed, Jaggers had made sense, mostly. I mean, I'd seen a lot of it with my own eyes, right? In The Eel the other day, the Pearly King had threatened Jimmy, in front of the whole pub. I'd seen Casper Macvittee alive and well in a Maryland Point knocking shop. Heard him and some pirates talk about the Olympics, sacking London and finding treasure. And, Duncan and I had found the Pearly King's jacket *in* the Pirate Shop. It all stacked up. Although nobody had a scooby as to what it actually stacked up to.

But, did I really care?

I mean, you learn pretty quick round here not to put your bugle in where it's not wanted, and this pirate business definitely had nothing to do with me. I mean, really, I should've been jumping for joy about it all. My landlord out of the picture would mean free rent. I should probably have got myself an eye-patch or whatever and joined their motley crew, firing one of them old pistols in the air and saying "yee-hah" or whatever it is pirates say.

I arrived outside the Pirate Shop. Aside from the Jolly Roger flapping in the sweaty evening breeze the place looked as quiet as it had been for the last hundred years. I noticed all the windows were shut. I guessed they'd left already. Gone off to do whatever it was they were supposed to do. Although judging by what was around me, the sacking London bit didn't seem to be going too well.

Traffic crawled past. Motorists cursed buses pulling out. Buses cursed motorists pinning them in. Cyclists cursed everyone. And everyone cursed them back. Maryland Point was its normal, dirty, gridlocked self.

Pedestrians, on the other hand, didn't do any cursing. They just ignored each other. Boob tubes ignored burkhas. Turbans ignored tattoos. Denim jackets and mullets ignored saris and sarongs. And everyone ignored my dressing gown, apart from some tramps who wanted to reach out and touch it, although they might have just been asking for change.

Yup, there was definitely no sacking happening here. Which made me feel that my suspicions were correct: Jaggers had done a Duncan and connected all the facts to cook up a conspiracy feast, when the likely truth was that these pirates were just some escapee mental patients on a bender, like in *One Flew Over the Cuckoo's Nest*.

Whatever the truth, I was looking forward to seeing Jaggers turn the heat up on the Pearly King. See how he liked it when someone was bossing him about.

I flicked my cigarette into the gutter and crossed over the road to the launderette. The shutters were still down. The "CLOSED FOR REPAIRS" sign was still in place.

I walked round the back to the yard, hoping to find an envelope with my name on it taped to the door, a little key tucked inside. Or even better, to find the door kicked in and discover I'd been burgled. Yeah, that would've been funny. Have something in my flat I want to get rid of only to have burglars steal it. Perhaps that was the best way to get rid of it? Slip a note in through the Pirate Shop telling them there was treasure in my flat. Quicker than you could say "shiver me timbers" they'd have looted the place.

I could dream.

I stood there for a bit, stupidly scratching my head, looking up at the back of my flat, trying to suss any other way I could get in. I examined the rooftop with its broken tiles. Pigeons cooed at me from the chimney. My eyes traced down, along the peeling paint and chipped brickwork, down past the dirty closed windows of the second and third floors to the ground and the edge of the parade of shops. A head was peering out at the end of the row. It wore sunglasses and a side-parting. Sensing an FBI ambush I began whistling and coolly turned in the direction of The Blue Eel.

'Mr Bunger,' called a voice.

I ignored it and walked on, quicker. Whistled a bit louder.

'Mr Bunger!'

I gave up on the whistling and broke into a run. Footsteps fell in pursuit. I bombed it out from behind the parade of shops and onto Leytonstone Road. Within moments I was up and over the crest of the hill and into Water Lane. The awning of the pub loomed ahead. Already wheezing I tried to find more pace. My bare feet smacked down onto the hot pavement in agony. The footsteps behind me grew louder. I reached for the front door, and dashed inside.

- 66 -

THE BLUE EEL

The pub was heaving. People were hurrying about in all directions carrying clipboards with orders being shouted above their heads. A dozen blokes were sat round a wallpaper pasting table answering a bank of red Commissioner Gordon style phones. It was like a WAR room.

I turned back and peered out of a window. I could see my pursuer, pacing back and forth on the pavement, talking into his cuff. I wondered what he was doing. Was he calling for back up? Or was he going to come in and collar me himself? I hoped he was telling his boss he was simply "too old for this shit."

Over the pub chatter came a shout. 'Mockney! Get over here!'

I ducked behind a table and looked about. Were the FBI already inside? Through the swarm of bodies I could just about see the bar with Big Mick stood behind it. He waved me towards him with one of his giant hands. Still crouching I squeezed forward.

'Didn't think you could get any shorter,' said Big Mick.

'I'm hiding.'

'Don't blame you with a face like that.'

'Could you be any nastier?'

'You still look a prat in them sunglasses.'

'They ain't sunglasses!'

'Whatever,' said Mick. 'You're here now, and that's all that matters.' He leaned over the counter and pressed something against my chest. 'Here you go. Now join in.'

I looked down to see I was now sporting a big black rosette. It had Jimmy's face on it and the words: "Seen this geezer's boat?"

'What the hell is this?' I cried. 'Since when has Jimmy owned a boat?'

'No you prat,' said Big Mick. 'Boat race...face. *Have you seen this geezer's face?'*

I gave him a blank look.

He shook his cannonball head. "You're not a very good Mockney, are you?"

'Nevermind that,' I said, over the din. 'What's going on?'

Big Mick threw his arms wide, nearly knocking over some of his trophies. 'Welcome to headquarters.'

'Headquarters?'

'For the *official* "Find Jimmy Appeal",' he beamed. 'And not the *unofficial* one they are doing over at the Coach and Horses.'

'"Find Jimmy Appeal?"'

'You betchya!' said Big Mick, collecting a few empty glasses off the bar. 'He's been missing for over twenty-four hours now. Nobody can find him. And we're not going to rest till we do.'

'HearHear!' cried a few sozzled locals propped at the bar.

'But—'

Big Mick waved me down with one of his giant hands. 'I know, Mockney, I know. No need to thank me. It *is* very generous of me, isn't it? And I appreciate you saying so. But you won't understand. I'm not doing this for money. I'm doing it because I'm a Cockney, which makes Jimmy like a brother to me.' Big Mick held a giant hand to his heart and fluttered his moistening eyelids. 'Now, what can I get you?'

'The usual,' I said.

'What's that?'

'What I had yesterday.'

He shot me a bemused look.

I reminded him. 'A whisky and coke, no lemon,'

'Oh right.' He began making the drink. 'That's a score.'

'How much?!?'

'Prices have gone up, to raise money for the appeal. My hands are tied.'

'Yeah and your wallet's bursting, I bet.'

'Watch it, Mockney,' warned a barfly.

'Whatever,' I said. 'Put it on my slate.'

'Your slate's been liquidated.'

'Funny that, being that it was made of liquids.'

'You watch your lip, son,' warned a local.

'Mockney bastard,' said another. 'I don't know why we let him in 'ere.'

I ignored them. Big Mick pulled a chalkboard from beneath the counter and examined it. 'I've been meaning to talk to you about your slate, actually. You owe a couple of monkeys.'

'Monkeys?' I said. 'What's this? Noah's Ark?'

'He don't know what a monkey is!' scoffed a barfly.

'What do they teach in schools these days?' asked another, concerned.

'Just talk English!' I said. 'What you on about?'

'You owe a bag of sand,' answered Big Mick.

I looked blank.

'A grand,' he said.

'A thousand pound?' I cried. 'I only had a dozen drinks at most!'

'You had eight drinks, actually,' said Big Mick, checking his board.

'That's never a grand.'

'I've had to charge interest, for the appeal.'

'Shove your appeal,' I said, and walked away.

'Ungrateful sod,' muttered someone.

Appeal or not, there was no way Big Mick was going to stripe me for a grand, I'd see to that.

I went back to the window. The FBI agent was now sat on the kerb, looking directly at the pub. As stakeouts go, he was making it kind of obvious. I guessed nothing was going to happen for a while. I'd only really start to panic if The Eel suddenly lost power. That's something the FBI do before they storm a building. I saw them do it in *Die Hard*.

But what would I do if that happened? I had no idea. I needed to think of a plan.

I dipped into my robe, fished out a cigarette and went hunting for somewhere to sit. The pub was packed, mostly with faces I'd never seen before. Who were all these people? I thought as I weaved past them. Were they here to help find their mate Jimmy? Or to help find a millionaire in the hope he'd slip them a few bob?

I edged past the pool table. It was covered over with a wooden board. People were stood around, pointing at a large map laid over it of Newham. Pensioners took instruction from nearby people on phones and pushed small Subbuteo men across the map with their walking sticks. Three darts stuck Jimmy's smiling face to the dartboard. "Seen this geezer's boat?"

I sidled round to the other end of the pub. All the benches were full. Everyone squidged up, elbows tucked in, all talking about where Jimmy could be. I pushed past and got up to the far end by the Pearly King's sofa.

It was empty.

That was weird. I stopped for a moment and looked about. Wasn't it a cardinal sin to sit in his chair? Well, waste not want not, it seemed as good a place to sit as any. I turned and went to slump on the sofa when a hand grabbed me roughly by the shoulder and pulled me back up.

- 67 -

BEROL

'Ere, you mental or summit?' Berol looked at me like I'd been lobotomised.

'Nono,' I said. 'I was just sitting down.'

'That's the Pearly's throne, innit? No one parks their 'arris on it but him.'

I looked about. 'Where is he? Taking a slash?'

Berol shrugged. 'Gawd knows. He was here earlier, but he bolted.'

'Bolted?'

'Yeah, he got up and just went out.'

'Did he?' I said, my brain already working back through what Jaggers had told us. The plot. The mischief. The pirates. The conspiracy. 'Did he say why he was leaving?'

'Nah.'

'You ask him?'

'You ain't the brightest light in the street are you, Oscar? I told you, you don't ask a Pearly questions. They are the dons round here. I leave him and his business well alone. Whatever made him go, I'm sure he's got his reasons.'

I bet he has, I thought.

I stood with Berol for a bit. She bought me a drink, hers were still normal price, plus ladies discount. I asked how long the launderette was going to be shut. She said the FBI wouldn't tell her. It was to stay closed until they'd finished their investigations.

'They ask any more questions about me?' I said.

'Nah, not a dicky bird.' She tapped ash into an overflowing tray. 'Why? You got something to hide?'

'No,' I lied. 'Nothing. It's just that I had one chase me to the pub just now.' I stood on tip toes trying to find a window. 'He's still outside, I think.'

'Well he can't come in here.'

'Eh?'

'Jurisdiction or something. The Eel ain't Maryland is it? It's international land cos it's the Embassy of Rum—' she waved her hand trying to find the word. '—that island out in the Caribbean.'

I couldn't believe it. I'd spent the last however many hours thinking I could be arrested and carted off to Guantanamo Bay, when all I had to do to obtain diplomatic immunity was go to the pub. If I'd thought about it, I'd have come to the pub a whole lot sooner.

I slapped my head in anger. 'Buggering ball bags!'

'Ere, don't start swearing at me!' said Berol, picking up an empty glass. 'I'll do ya!'

I quickly apologised. There was a noise at the bar. I looked up to see Big Mick laughing and joking, showing off one of his trophies to the barflies, probably talking them through one of his greatest bare-knuckle fights. I pondered being nicer to him. Maybe he'd let me sleep in the pub for a few nights until Jimmy returned? I could even man the phones or something to pay my way. Anything to keep the FBI away from me.

I noticed Berol looking me up and down. 'So, you got roped into the fancy dress fundraising then?'

'This ain't fancy dress! It's a dressing gown!' I quickly explained the whole locked out business minus the chemical weapon bit.

Berol rattled out a raspy machine gun laugh. 'Ha! You better hope Jimmy turns up for your sake. Ain't nothing going to be able to take those locks off your doors. They were made for the Bank of England.'

I blew out smoke. 'You don't half talk it.'

'Straight up. Minted especially for London vaults, they were.'

'And how'd you know that?'

'Cos my dad, gawd bless his soul, worked at the factory that made them. They're from the sixties, they are. Before everything went digital and all that.'

'Oh right,' I said. 'And how'd Jimmy get hold of 'em? Fell off the back of a lorry I suppose?'

'Don't everything?' grinned Berol. 'Especially in the sixties. And especially when my dad was about. Gawd bless him.'

Just then, out of the scribble of noise, a few words drifted toward me that I didn't like the sound of. 'Who you looking for? The Mockney?'

I looked up to find Big Mick pointing in my direction. 'He's over there,' he said, giving me a wink.

- 68 -

A WANTED MAN

'Oscar!' came a cry.

I ducked behind Berol.

'What you playing at?' she rasped. 'Ere, get your hands off me.'

'If anyone asks, my name ain't Oscar,' I whispered. 'I'm Mr Bunger!'

With my heart doing a rumba I peered round the blue and white check of Berol's apron and scanned the pub.

'Oscar!' A thin arm emerged above the crowd like a shark's fin. I watched as it cut a path towards me. As the arm got closer I could see it was attached to the body of a very thin man in dungarees, chuffing away on a roll up through his mostly toothless smile.

I got up from behind Berol and tried to look casual, like I hadn't been hiding, like I crouch behind launderette workers in pubs all the time. 'Danny? What you doing in here? This ain't your local.'

'Jaggers told me to meet you here,' he said, squeezing past the last few people to reach us. He greeted Berol with a nod. She gave him the same nod back.

'Jaggers?'

'Yeah. He said you needed my help?'

'I do?'

Danny looked me up and down. 'Well, it's not my place to say, Oscar, but I reckon you could do with it, unless you want to walk round dressed like a tit the whole time.'

Berol laughed. 'He don't half look a prat in that gown, don't he?'

'Don't you start,' I said.

'Berol!' came a cry. I looked up to see Big Mick waving her over to the bar. 'Someone on the dog for ya.'

As she left us, I pulled Danny close. I shot a glance over both my shoulders. 'So, Jaggers sent you? Did he say anything about the pirates?'

Danny looked blank. 'What pirates?'

I studied him, trying to understand why Jaggers would send him to help me. Surely about the pirates? Perhaps Danny was speaking in code. I cupped my hand and, standing on tiptoes, whispered in his ear. 'Is this a test?'

'It's testing my patience.' Danny looked me in the face. 'Listen, I'm doing you a favour being here. I'm meant to be putting new boards up in Mile End at midnight. Jaggers said it was urgent. You need my cherry picker. Something about a window?'

My mouth fell open as he explained. Jaggers had found a way for me to get back into my flat. My bedroom window was open, on the street side. It was what caused the whole being locked out thing in the first place. Jaggers concluded that I could regain entry to my flat if I could just get to that window. The problem being that it was three storeys up. Suddenly, remembering the billboard mounted on the side of my flat advertising Olympic condoms, he realised an ad-man's cherry picker was all that was required.

It was at that point I knew Jaggers was a genius. I'd been stuck on the problem for almost two days, he'd solved it as part of a teatime teaser in and around this pirate business. I made a mental note to buy him a drink, though probably after The Eel's fundraising had finished.

I slapped my hands together excitedly, 'Right, let's go!'

'Not yet,' said Danny. 'Cherry picker ain't free till eleven. Mate at the depot is dropping it off here. I'm buying him a pint and then taking it to Mile End via yours.'

'Lovely,' I said. 'Just give me a shout when you're ready.'

'Will do.' And with that Danny turned to go to the bar.

'Ere,' I said, calling him back. 'Did Jaggers say what time he was popping in?'

'Yeah. He said he'd be here bang on eight. And to tell you he'd definitely be here.'

I nodded thanks. Danny went in search of a drink, and I did a little shimmy, fighting the urge to break into a full-blown tango. And I had every right to. After all, I had diplomatic immunity and a cast-iron way of breaking back in to my flat. Before midnight I'd have my hands back on the Junior Anthrax and would be dashing across to the Pirate Shop to stuff it through their cat flap. Call the police. Mention pirates. Use the word "terrorists" and they'd swoop on the place in a matter of seconds. Everyone gets banged up. And I'd be off the hook. Bosh.

I drifted barwards wondering who'd buy me a pre-victory drink, when the front door of the pub slammed. A sudden hush descended. I got caught up in the crowd as it parted to make way for the Pearly King. He trudged to the back of the pub and slumped exhaustedly into his throne. He took off his pearly hat and ran a hand down his chubby cheeks. The pub stared at him in silence.

'No news?' he asked.

Big Mick shook his head. 'None. You?'

The Pearly gave a glum shake of his head. Murmurs went round the pub and very soon it bubbled back to life. I watched as Big Mick carried over a pint of London Pride. He carefully set it down in front of the Pearly, who ignored it, continuing his sad stare into the carpet.

I felt my blood boiling. What an act. Forty-eight hours before the Pearly had threatened Jimmy with murder. And now he was moping about like his favourite puppy was missing. He was playing the pub like a cheap bassoon, I was sure of it. And that made it so much sweeter knowing Jaggers was going to turn up and grill him. He'd cut down his house of cards in a few skilful blows. Then everyone would see the Pearly King for what he really is, for what I'd always known him to be, a jumped up bully in fancy dress. An odds-on murderer who'd bumped off his closest mate to get what he wanted.

Oh yes, Jaggers was going to take him to the cleaners and I was going to love every second of it. Could my day possibly get any better?

- 69 -

COCKNEY-OKE

Now, for the sake of smoking indoors, I could stomach pretty much everything about The Eel. The rude landlord, the constant piss-takes from the locals, the fact the whisky was watered down and the way the gents always smelt of cheese and onion crisps. But I drew the line at Big Mick's latest fund-raising idea. 'C'mon everyone! Let's have a knees-up for Jimmy and raise a bit of bunce!'

Only this "knees-up" wasn't your normal Friday night Cockney-Oke car crash. Given the fact that one of their favourite locals was missing, Big Mick had ramped the idea up and declared, 'Twenty-four hour, round-the-clock, non-stop Cockney-Oke!'

Cheers went round the pub whilst I repeatedly head-butted the wall in an attempt to knock myself out. With the FBI still outside I couldn't run. I couldn't even dull the pain with booze. Not at the prices Big Mick wanted to charge me.

No, I had to suffer it. Sober.

You might think I'm overreacting, but you really have to experience Cockney-Oke first hand to know just how painful it is. The locals aren't a tuneful bunch. Half squawk like seagulls, the other half grunt like seals, and they all sing together in one horrible, tortured mess.

It wouldn't be so bad if there were an actual karaoke machine, you know with the poor synth versions of popular hits and the crappy ball bouncing lyrics, but no, that was too expensive for Big Mick. And too fancy for The Blue Eel faithful. They liked their Cockney-Oke the way it had been for generations, namely a bloke belting out a narrow range of hits on a poorly tuned piano.

The piano in question was a sorry looking job. The black veneer was heavily scratched and covered with cigarette burns. It had been wheeled out on squeaky wheels and set up as close to the bar as possible. For acoustics, apparently. And nothing to do with the fact the pianist could reach across and serve himself a pint whenever he wanted. Which he seemed to do with all the grace of a long distance runner, reaching out mid tune, leaning over and pulling a pint with one hand whilst tickling the ivories with the other.

At that moment, one pissed up pensioner in a flat-cap was having the time of his life, wailing his way through *The Lambeth Walk*. Twice I thought he'd put his hip out, throwing a leg up high as if he were doing a Cockney can-can.

I mopped the sweat off my face. I didn't know how much more I could take. Every song made a chat with the FBI that bit more appealing. They'd be no Cockney-Oke in Guantanamo Bay, I felt certain of that.

Thankfully Duncan saved me from a coma. He arrived dressed in his dusty leather jacket that was far too short in the sleeves and looked about the pub in puzzlement, no doubt confused by all the goings on, especially with the pool table being covered with Subbuteo men.

I stood up and waved him towards me. I'd managed to bag a short stool by the fruit machine. Normally this seat would've been taken by one of the many locals who liked a flutter, but Big Mick had worked his fund-raising magic on the machine too and now nobody would touch it, not at ten pound a spin. The banner tied to it, announcing that it was the appeal's *official* fruit machine, was fooling no-one.

'Wow, new fruit machine,' said Duncan, his eyes caught in the dance of flashing lights.

'It's not new,' I said. 'It's the same one. Mick's just tarted it up, that's all.'

Duncan bent down and examined the reels. 'Hey, looks like it's going to pay. All you need is three nudges and you'll have four lemons.'

'You're a lemon,' I said. 'It's a tenner a spin.'

'Serious?'

I blew out smoke and nodded. 'If you think that's steep I hope you ain't thirsty.'

Despite my warnings of rip-off prices, Duncan went in search of a drink. As he stood by the bar, I wondered if Jaggers had got it all wrong somehow. I mean, it's police procedure, innit? Working out who stands to profit from a crime. Well, Big Mick wasn't so much profiting from Jimmy's disappearance as raking it in. Punters were waving cash at him quicker than he could pocket it. In fact, I fancied that, more likely than not, Jimmy Strongbow hadn't fallen victim to some crazy plot involving pirates and treasure, but that instead the beloved pork-pie wearing Pearly Prince was bound and gagged in the pub basement in some scam to make Big Mick more money. In fact, maybe he wasn't even gagged. Maybe he was down there with one of his mates playing crib or something and taking a cut of the till.

Knowing Jimmy, if that had turned out to be the truth it wouldn't have surprised me at all.

Duncan returned from the bar with a Guinness for himself and whisky and coke for me. 'It's happy hour,' he drawled. 'Mick said Kiwis pay normal price.'

I shook my head. 'That's racism or something. Just because I come from Kent, he's trying to shaft me.' I took my drink and raised it. 'Cheers.'

Duncan stood up and took a couple of long sniffs. He started looking about the pub. 'Jaggers not here yet?'

I checked the clock above the bar. 'No, it's still early. He said he'd be here bang on eight.'

Eight o'clock came and went but there was still no sign of Jaggers. And it wasn't long before his absence was noticed. Gossip started to float about the pub, passing like a cloud from table to table. It turned out that a few people were booked to see him that night for one of his free legal surgeries, always popular with the locals who seemed to think being Cockney made them somehow tax exempt.

'He's never late,' said someone.

'Always sticks to his word, that man,' said someone else.

'What am I going to do about my boundary dispute?' said another.

'Stuff your boundary dispute,' came a reply. 'Jaggers could be missing.'

'What? You reckon someone's done Jaggers in n'all?'

The pub was shocked into silence by the sound of a glass smashing against a wall. The Pearly was on his feet. His face flushed red with rage. 'Shut your noise!' he thundered. 'I've had enough of this chat! Nobody's done anybody in, you hear me? If you want to gossip, sling your hook and drink somewhere else. I only want people in here who want to help find Jimmy. You understand?' His eyes were full of anger, scanning the pub, looking for someone to challenge him. That was all the proof I needed. It was clear he was coming apart with the stress of what he'd done.

With nobody challenging him, he sat back down. The pub was silent for a few moments before the volume crept back up. Cockney-Oke resumed. Another half hour dragged by, but there was still no sign of Jaggers. There was no gossip either. Though I reckoned I knew what was on everybody's mind.

I whispered to Duncan, 'Something's not right. He should've been here by now.'

'I wonder what's happened to him?'

'I dunno.' I nodded discreetly towards the Pearly King. 'But I swear he knows more than he's letting on.'

The Pearly King sat on his sofa, staring his thoughts into the intricate patterning of the pub carpet, a miserable look on his face.

'In fact,' I said. 'If Jaggers doesn't show up, I'll do it for him.'

'Do what?' said Duncan.

'Have it out with the Pearly,' I said. 'I'm going to ask him straight if he killed Jimmy.'

'You can't!' hissed Duncan. 'You've got to leave it to Jaggers! He's the professional!'

I waved him off. 'You don't need a degree to confront someone.'

'But he's had training.'

'But he ain't here. Which means it's up to us.' I drained my drink and got to my feet. 'Now, back me up.'

- 70 -

DUTCH COURAGE

Duncan grabbed me by the shoulder and pulled me back. 'Are you serious?' he hissed. 'You can't question the Pearly King! We have to let Jaggers do it!'

'It's too late,' I replied. 'He's picking people off one by one. If we don't do anything, it could be us killed next.'

Duncan frowned. 'Who'd want to kill us?'

'Think about it,' I said. 'We reckon the Pearly is involved with whatever's happened to Jimmy, right?'

Duncan nodded.

'And we don't know yet, but what if he's bumped off Jaggers, too?'

'Because of what he knew?' said Duncan, getting excited. 'Because of the conspiracy?'

'Right,' I replied. 'And we know what Jaggers knows. At the shop earlier he told us everything. How the Pearly was involved with the pirates, probably paying them. And sure enough we found the Pearly's jacket at the Pirate Shop, right? And a few days back, when the Pearly and Jimmy had a bust-up in here, he said the East End would kill him. I mean, I'll be the first to admit it's far-fetched, but it adds up. I mean, when is Jaggers ever wrong?'

'Never wrong,' said Duncan.

'Right. So, if you found out the greatest lawyer in the country was closing in on you, what would you do?'

'Run?'

'What if you can't run?'

Duncan looked confused. 'Taxi?'

'No, you plum.'

'Boat?'

'No...you fight back. First form of defence, innit? And I reckon the Pearly will do anything to defend what he's planning. Something big is going down. Big enough to start getting rid of people to keep it all a secret. And not just any people. We're talking faces like Jimmy and Jaggers. If they can be bumped off with ease, what chance have you and I got? And if they've already got to Jaggers, then they may already know what he told us. We can't wait for them to strike first. We have to act...fast.'

'Okay,' drawled Duncan. 'What do we do?'

I looked around the bar. 'This place is like a wild west saloon. You can't come in here and kick the no-good sheriff out of town just like that. You've got to humiliate him first. Turn everyone against him.'

'How'd you know this?'

'Have you never seen a western?'

'Sam Neill doesn't do westerns.'

'Nevermind that,' I said. 'I've got a plan. Just back me up.'

I slipped away and headed over to the Cockney-Oke desk. It was manned by an old lady with a blue rinse and a face like a walnut. 'Oh, bless ya, Mockney,' she smiled. 'You want to sing for Jimmy?'

'I sure do, Mrs,' I lied. 'He's like a father to me.'

'Oh, bless your cottons,' she flashed a set of ill-fitting dentures. I tried not to wince. 'That's a fiver.'

I winced. 'Five quid?'

'Everyone's paying a fiver a song. Even us pensioners.' She rattled a plastic bucket on the desk. 'It's all for the appeal. The *official* appeal.'

I cleared my throat. 'Erm...I'll be back in a sec.'

Having scammed a fiver from Duncan I returned to the table and tried to pick a tune. Unsurprisingly, there was little to choose from, and even less that I knew. In the end I picked a tune, much like a person picks a horse for the Grand National, taking a punt on an appropriate name. I settled on *Rabbit*. I don't know if it was a good one or not. I just liked the idea that I was going to pull the rabbit out of the hat, as it were.

'Oh, that's a good one,' said the pensioner, noting my selection. 'A Chas and Dave, we like them.'

I grinned. 'You're gonna love my interpretation of it.'

I returned to the fruit machine, trying hard to keep a straight face. 'All done,' I said.

Duncan nodded. 'When are you on?'

'Don't know. We'll just have to wait.'

'Will you sing your song before you attack him?'

'Leave it out.'

'What are you going to say?'

I curled my lip and looked over at the Pearly King. 'Don't worry. I'll think of something.' My brain began racing, a wonderful winning speech was forming. The Pearly King was about to go down in flames.

- 71 -

BLUDWYN & PEASWORTH

'It didn't exactly go to plan though did it, Oscar?' said Bludwyn.

I shrugged. 'I suppose it could've gone better.'

Peasworth's irritatingly narrow head grinned at me. 'They banished you, didn't they?'

'Get your facts straight.'

'You weren't banished?'

'Exiled,' I corrected him.

'No longer welcome as a visitor to the country of Rumbago or her territories,' Bludwyn read the transcript with a smile. 'That must have hurt?'

'Yeah, I can't say I was best pleased.'

'So,' Bludwyn folded his arms behind his head and leaned back in his chair, 'what happened?'

- 72 -

CONFRONTATION

I cleaned my glasses on my dressing gown and peered out of the window. It was nearly 10pm. Orange sodium lights fell in spots on the darkened road. The streets looked quiet. There was no sign of the FBI. It looked like they'd given up and gone home.

Inside things were quite the opposite. The locals seemed to be warming up. The twenty-four hour Cockney-Oke had twenty more hours still to run, and we'd had five renditions of *My Old Man's A Dustman* already.

By the piano some old boy in a waistcoat came to the end of his song. There was a lot of clapping and playful heckling. He took a couple of mocking bows and shuffled off, giving the piano player a pat on the back. I had no idea what he'd been singing about. Either *rolling out Mother Brown* or *putting his knees up a barrel*. I dunno, all those tunes are the same. That's not to say they are the same, it's just the unique knack the piano player had of making it all sound like the same song with different words garbled over the top.

Next, the old woman with a face like a walnut grabbed the microphone. 'I want you to give a warm Cockney welcome to our Mockney, who's going to sing us a Chas and Dave in honour of his landlord...Jimmy Strongbow.'

There was applause and a few cheers. 'That's it!' cried someone, as I made my way forward. 'We'll make a proper Cockney out of you yet!'

'Go on, my son!' said another, patting me on the back as I passed them. 'Give it best! Make Jimmy proud!'

I reached the front and grabbed the microphone from the top of the piano. Feedback whined round the pub. My voice sounded strangely alien as it came out of the speakers. 'Listen...before I sing I'd like to say a few words...' I cleared my throat. I knew exactly what to do. I couldn't go in all guns blazing, I had to coax my audience round, let them connect the dots and within the next two minutes they'd call me a hero for revealing that their Pearly King was in fact a Pearly Killer.

'Now...Jimmy is missing, nobody's seen or heard from him, which we all know is most unlike *our* Jimmy.' *Our* Jimmy. Nice touch that, I thought. Makes them think I'm one of them, puts me on their side. The locals must have liked it as mutterings of *HearHear* drifted back.

'And what about Jaggers?' I continued. 'He was meant to run his legal surgery tonight, but he's not shown. Not even got on the dog to say he couldn't make it. Which is most unlike *our* Jaggers.'

HearHear said the crowd. Every pair of eyes was on me. I went for the kill. 'But, I ain't surprised Jimmy and Jaggers are missing, because there is someone I know, who we all know, that wants them both done in. In fact, he's said it to their faces, here, in this very pub.'

The room broke out into excited gossip.

'What's the Mockney on about?' said someone.

'This ain't singing,' moaned another.

'We want singing!' demanded someone else.

Taking that as a cue, the piano player started up. The crowd were turning on me. I had to think fast. I tightened my grip round the microphone and shouted the only thing I could above the boos. 'Listen! The Pearly King's a murderer! He's killed Jimmy and Jaggers!'

I can't really explain what happened next. It was like the world went on pause. The pub fell silent. The piano player stopped mid-jaunt. Jaws fell open. Pints were dropped in shock. I can't remember but I think one woman actually fainted. I took these as good signs that I'd reached through to them all and woken them up to the truth.

'What a load of cobblers!' cried Big Mick.

'You've got a nerve,' spat Berol. 'After all we've done for you.'

'The Pearly wouldn't hurt anyone!' called someone.

'Bloody Mockney doesn't know what he's talking about,' said someone else.

'It's true!' I protested. 'Ask him to deny it!' I looked over at the Pearly's sofa. A chill went down my spine. It was empty.

'Ere,' called someone. 'Don't you rent Jimmy's penthouse?'

'Yeah,' said someone else. 'He does.'

'I bet he's kidnapped him,' said another.

'Bloody Mockneys. Can't trust 'em.'

I tried my best to bring the mob round. 'The Pearly King has escaped!' I cried. 'Someone catch him!'

'What's happening?' asked a bloke who'd just come back from the gents.

'That Mockney's kidnapped Jimmy,' answered Big Mick.

'And Jaggers,' added someone else.

'Get him!' came a cry, and before I knew what was happening, some locals had stormed on stage and grabbed me. The pianist took this as his cue and struck up with Chas and Dave's *Rabbit*. As choices for exit music go, I guess it was kind of apt, what with the lines "You won't stop talking, why don't you give it a rest."

As I was manhandled out of the pub I shot a final glance over at the Pearly's sofa. I didn't know how long he'd been absent. But I felt you'd get good odds on finding him with his partners in crime, the pirates.

- 73 -

OUTSIDE

If tossing people out of pubs were an Olympic sport, The Eel would have a gold medal-winning team. They must have chucked me twelve feet or more before I came crashing down on the pavement, back first.

Sod this for a game of soldiers, I thought. It just doesn't pay to help people these days. No wonder the world is going down the swanny when you can't even do people a favour by pointing out that their favourite pearly-clad don may in fact be a psychopathic murderer. You'd think people might tip me thanks for pointing that out, rather than chucking me out on the street like a spent Christmas tree. Instead, I'd learnt my lesson not to put my beak in where it's not wanted, especially when it comes to Cockney affairs. Sod the lot of them, I thought. I had bigger things to worry about, like getting rid of an illegal chemical weapon that was still sat in my bedroom.

Laying still on the pavement I reached a hand down into my dressing gown pocket and pulled out a crumpled cigarette. Looking up at the black cloudless night, I sparked up and pondered my next move. A face suddenly appeared above me. 'I told you. We should have left it to Jaggers.'

I frowned. 'Don't you start.'

'Are you hurt?'

My spine was burning, but I didn't let on. I drew on my cigarette. 'I'll live.'

'Not for much longer.' Duncan looked back at the pub. 'They are really angry.'

'They'll get over it.'

He shook his head. 'You've not heard what they are saying. They are going to try and get a Chapwa on you.'

'A what?'

Duncan explained what a Chapwa was. I didn't believe a word of it. Apparently it was the Cockney equivalent of the Fatwa, a decree given by the highest in the Pearly hierarchy that effectively made you public enemy number one. As such, you were to be killed on sight. And then they'd be a celebration and free pie and mash all round.

'Trying to put a death penalty on me?' I looked up at him. 'You don't half talk it.'

'Serious,' said Duncan. 'Once you get a Chapwa you're in real trouble. I read a book on it.' He proceeded to explain what he'd read. That these death penalties were what gave the East End its criminal notoriety. The Krays, Jack the Hat, even Jack the Ripper…all apparently working on behalf of Pearlies, delivering Chapwas and dispensing foes of the Cockney faith in a range of gruesome manners.

'All they need to do,' drawled Duncan, 'is get the Pearly King to sanction it. And then you're a dead man walking.' He looked at me gravely. 'If I were you I'd get out to Zone 6 until this cools down.'

'No chance,' I said. 'Anyway, they've got to find the Pearly first. Did you see him leave?'

'No, I was watching you.'

'Well, it doesn't matter now,' I said. 'The fact he legged it whilst I was outing him is proof of his guilt. I mean, what innocent men run?'

'Lots,' answered Duncan. 'Harrison Ford in *The Fugitive* – he ran, and he was innocent. Guilty men like to stick around and see what happens.'

Amazingly, he had a point. I drew on my cigarette and had another look up at the sky. Cockney-Oke had resumed inside, the jaunty piano seeped through windows and crept under doors to reach us. The volume shot up a notch as the front door swung open. I heard somebody step out. Probably a local who wanted to finish me off.

I called out to the approaching footsteps. 'At least let me finish this smoke before you kill me.'

The moon disappeared, replaced by a toothy grin. 'Don't be a doughnut. I'm taking you home!'

I sat up and watched as Danny the ad-man crossed the road. I hadn't noticed it on my flying out of the pub but a huge blue cherry picker was parked opposite on double-yellows. Danny jogged up to it and climbed into the cockpit. He fed his keys into the ignition. The machine started up with a deep throaty roar. 'C'mon then boys!' he chirped. 'You coming or what?'

- 74 -

BREAKING BACK IN

The cherry picker crawled up the street with the engine misfiring every couple of yards or so. We passed along quiet roads and under awnings tied to street lamps, each one shouting about some pointless sport or other that would feature at the Games.

As we chugged up Water Lane I could see my flat looming ahead, the ad for Olympic condoms punched out across the skyline.

'I shouldn't go back in there in a hurry if I was you,' shouted Danny, over the engine.

'What?' I said. 'My flat?'

'No,' said Danny. 'The Eel! I think you're as welcome as a pair of sandy pants.'

'They want to put a Chapwa on him,' said Duncan.

'Oooh,' Danny offered me a hand. 'Nice knowing you, Oscar.'

'Don't be a tart,' I said. 'It's not that serious. It'll calm down. I'm just barred, that's all.'

'Exiled,' corrected Duncan.

He was right of course. Exiled was pretty much the last thing I remember being said to me and I seem to remember it was said quite aggressively in my ear, before I was sent flying through the air.

Not that it mattered now.

I didn't need The Eel anymore. In a few moments I was going to be home and I could start getting back on with my life. I'd start by getting changed. Twenty-four hours in a dressing gown spent sleeping rough and dodging down alleys and hiding in pubs was starting to take its toll. In fact, I'd noticed that Duncan was now only standing upwind of me so as not to damage his nose.

The cherry picker crawled to a stop. With a strained mechanical whiz and whir the platform rose, carrying the three of us up to my window.

I shot a glance across the street to the Pirate Shop. It seemed quiet. All the lights were off. A good sign. I didn't care where they were or what they were up to, just as long as I had five minutes to pop round the back, stuff the Junior Anthrax through their cat flap and scarper. I just needed five minutes.

The platform shuddered to a halt. Danny drew back a chain and helped me and Duncan out onto the window ledge. 'Watch how you go, Oscar,' he said, as the mechanical arm made its descent. 'I'd sleep with one eye open if I was you. Lovely-ol'-job.'

Duncan and I waved thanks and climbed in through the window. I couldn't see a thing. 'Watch your step,' I warned, groping about in the darkness. 'I've got buckets and stuff spread about.'

'Smells funny...' said Duncan, sniffing heavily. '...like onions.'

'Oi, did you hear me? I said watch—'

There was a slosh.

'Aww,' moaned Duncan. He gave a sniff. 'Is that Jimmy's piss?'

'Nah,' I said. 'It's just rain.'

'My foot's soaked. Why is it so dark in here?'

'Will you just wait a sec? I'm trying to get to the light.' I reached out for where I expected to find the edge of my bed.

'I can see in the dark at my place,' said Duncan.

'Good for you.'

'The standby light on my TV is so strong, it lights up the room.'

No sooner had the words left his mouth when I felt a chill. I froze and looked in the direction of my TV. There was no sign of power. Not even a light.

'Something ain't right,' I whispered.

'What?'

'My TV,' I replied. 'It's off. When I got locked out yesterday, it was on.'

'Serious?'

I looked back at him and nodded. I doubt he could see me. I could just see him, his black figure against the moonlight.

'Maybe a power cut?' he suggested.

'The rest of the street is still on,' I whispered.

'Do you think it was Jimmy?'

Creak.

Duncan and I fell dead quiet and listened. There was someone or something outside my room, on the stairs.

I called into the darkness. 'Jimmy?'

Something fell at my feet. My eyes started to sting. And then I was hit over the head and everything went black. Well, blacker than it already was.

- 75 -

BLINDFOLDED

I woke feeling groggy. My head was pounding and my eyes burned. Everything was black. It took a few moments to realise I was blind-folded. I reached up fast to remove it, but my hands snagged behind me. I was tied to something.

I called out. 'Hey? Is anyone there?' My voice echoed and disappeared, as if going down a tunnel. I listened for a reply, there was nothing apart from the sound of trickling water.

After a few more shouts I slumped back in defeat. Wherever I was, it certainly wasn't my flat. I was leaning against a sturdy wall, and my flat definitely didn't have a single one of those.

Something moved beside me.

'Duncan?' My voice echoed. 'Duncan, is that you?'

The reply was drawled and satisfyingly Kiwi. 'Oscar?'

'Yeah, it's me. What happened?'

'I don't know,' he replied, sounding more disorientated than usual. 'We were in your room. I smelt onions then I was hit with something. That's the last thing I remember...'

I shook my head. 'I can't believe this is happening. I was so close to getting rid of that bloody chemical weapon.'

But Duncan wasn't listening. 'I...I can smell something...familiar.' He began snorting, hovering up the damp air, trying to pick up a scent. '...Jaggers?'

'What?'

'I can smell Jaggers…' more snorts, '…and Jimmy. I can smell him too! And something else…'

'What?'

'I don't know…' more hurried sniffing, '…the smells are all over the place. They are all really strong. I smell onions.'

'Don't wind me up.'

'Serious,' he said. 'I can smell the others. My nose is never wrong.'

We called out for a bit, firstly their names and then just for help but nobody answered, our voices just echoed into the abyss.

I was seriously hacked off. Angry at being bundled. Angry at being in my dressing gown. Angry at not being able to have a cigarette. And, angry that I was so close to getting rid of the Junior Anthrax. But, most of all, I was angry that this was all Duncan's fault.

'Y'know…if you'd kept your hand out of that bloody cat flap everything would've been fine.'

'We might have been attacked by accident,' drawled Duncan. 'It might be a case of mistaken identity. Like in that film…*North By North-West*.'

'Dream on,' I said. 'We were jumped by someone who knew *exactly* who they were looking for and knew *exactly* what they were doing. You've said you can smell Jaggers and Jimmy, right? Two people who mysteriously disappeared, so, odds on, Poirot, we've been bundled by the same bunch.'

'You mean the Pearly King and his pirates?'

'Yeah,' I said. 'As unlikely as it sounds I put money on it that we've been kidnapped by a psychotic button-obsessed Cockney monarch and a bunch of landlocked no-good escapee mental patients who like to play dress up as seadogs. Pirate or Pearly, all of them are certifiable, which means you and I are as good as dead.'

'Wow.' Duncan sounded annoyingly unfazed by it all. 'You reckon they'll kill us?'

'I dunno. There's no telling what the Pearly will do. I mean, you heard what Jimmy's dad did about that bomb during D-Day, right? They are fanatical in their beliefs. Clearly ready to do anything to cancel the Olympics. Probably even die for the cause to defend his land. We got in his way, just like the others. And he's going to flush us the same way he flushed them.'

'No,' said Duncan. 'Maybe he needs our help?'

I laughed. 'A wallop over the head and a blindfold? He's got a funny way of asking for it. Face it, we're doomed. The only chance we've got is bargaining our way out.'

'Hey,' said Duncan, brightening. 'I know, we can offer them free video rentals!'

'No,' I said. 'How about something they want? How about intelligence?'

'But we haven't got any.'

'Exactly,' I said. 'And we tell them that. Make them understand that we've not seen any faces. We don't know any details. They can let us go and never hear from us again. We know nothing.' I turned my head about and flashed a smile in all directions.

'But what about all the details you heard in the Stratford Tanning Depot? About pirates wanting to sabotage the Games.'

'Shut up!' I hissed. 'They might be listening.'

'You said you heard them talking about treasure.'

'No I didn't!'

'You did! You said they were going to sack London.'

'I don't know what you're on about. I heard nothing. I know nothing. There is no plot. There is no bloody treasure. In fact, I don't even know who you are*OUCH!*.'

Something small and sharp hit me on the side of the head.

'What happened?' said Duncan

'I dunno. Something just hit me.'

'Like what?' he drawled. 'A bullet?'

'No, a stone or something. It—' I was hit again. This time on the temple. Another quickly followed, hitting me square on the forehead. 'Ouch! Bloody hell! Pack it in!'

'Never!' cried a new voice. 'Die, heathens!'

- 76 -

THE VOICE

I kicked out instinctively to defend my space, no doubt looking like a man on an invisible pedalo, but my bare feet hit nothing but air and wet stone. 'Who's there?' I called.

'Friend or foe?' added Duncan.

'You ain't my friends!' called the voice. 'You sound like Olympic spies! Die!'

Pebbles hailed around me. As I tried to squirm out of the way I could hear someone talking excitedly to themselves, well, it was more like gibbering really. I sensed this stone-thrower was a few DVDs short of a box-set.

I was busy kicking out in all directions when a worrying thought suddenly flashed into my head. What if this gibbering voice belonged to a pirate? And not just any pirate. What if it's the simple one who likes playing with his cutlass and dicing up captives?

'Wait!' I cried, replacing the kicking with a fake smile. 'We're friends!'

'No you ain't!' said the voice. 'You're heathens, come to steal my treasures!' And with that a large pebble hit me on the side of the head.

'Oi! Pack it in! Let's talk...' I was about to launch into some delicate questioning. Stuff that any sensible captive would ask, you know things along the lines of: What's going on? Where are we? Can you help us?

'What's your name?' asked Duncan.

Like that was a priority? We were hardly going to share out biscuits and look each other up online afterwards.

'Who cares what his name is? Just get him to stop lobbing stones!'

'I'm Duncan. I'm from New Zealand,' continued Duncan unfazed. 'And this is my friend Oscar, he's from Kent,' adding in a whisper. 'He's not a Cockney.'

'You're unbelievable,' I said. 'Why don't you tell him your star sign as well?'

'Sssh,' whispered Duncan. 'We need to win his trust. If you want to influence people you need their names. I saw it in a movie.'

'What a load of old cobblers,' I said. 'Why ask his name? Who do you reckon it is? Lord bloody Lucan?'

'Pah!' cried the voice. 'Don't insult me. I know all about you Olympic spies. Your tricks won't work, not on me. I'm a famous archaeologist, y'know! I'm Casper Macvittee!'

- 77 -

THE VOICE HAS A NAME

As revelations go, this was a bit of a biggie. I could feel Duncan beside me, spluttering like some unreliable Russian nuclear reactor.

'Serious?' he said, for something like the sixteenth time. 'You're Casper Macvittee?'

'You total git!' I cried, fighting with my restraints. 'You nearly shot my face off last night!'

'Ha!' scoffed the voice. 'You spies will have to do better than that.'

'Better than what?' I spat. 'I was at the Stratford Tanning Depot. I heard everything. I know all about the treasure and your plans to sack London. And I've told the Old Bill every word.'

'Serious?' drawled Duncan. 'When did you do that?'

'Shut up,' I hissed.

'I thought you said no police?'

'*Shut up.*'

'Lies!' snapped the voice. 'Damned lies! You can't trick me.'

'It's not a trick, you prat! I saw you!'

The stone throwing stopped. 'Don't play mind games with me, sonny. You ain't got the noodle. I ain't been seen by no one for over a year.' He laughed and began gibbering to himself. I tried to listen carefully to what he was saying, but couldn't make anything out, that's when something struck me about his voice. It was different.

I whispered to Duncan, 'How's this Casper meant to sound?'

'English.'

'Yeah, but is he high pitched, gravely or what?'

'I don't know. Why?'

'Because,' I whispered. 'The one I heard at the Stratford Tanning Depot sounded nothing like this one.'

I sensed Duncan bouncing up and down excitedly again, 'You think it's a different person?'

'Sssh!' I hissed. 'Keep it down. I don't care who this one is. Let's just see if he can help us.' I cleared my throat and called out. 'Oi, Casper!'

The voice stopped gibbering. 'Who's there?'

'Us.'

'Who?'

'You're new friends,'

'Who?'

'Duncan and Oscar.'

'Who?'

'The Olympic spies,' said Duncan. 'Remember?'

'Ahh!' cried Casper. 'Heathens!' And with that the stone throwing resumed.

'Duncan, you prat!' I cried, under a storm of pebbles. 'Shut up. Let me handle this!' I tried to think, fast. 'Casper, listen to me, we're not spies anymore. We've come to help you.'

'Help me? Ha! I'd like to see you try. I'm an archaeological genius!'

'We know,' I blagged. 'We know all about you.'

I can't explain where the following blag came from but being pelted with stones does make you think quicker than usual and before I knew what was happening I'd announced that Duncan and I were doing our PhDs on him. 'Yeah, we've been studying you and all your great work. Ain't that right, Duncan?'

The stone throwing stopped. 'Students are studying me?'

'Oh yeah,' I lied. 'There's hundreds of kids want to learn about the forefather of Cockney archaeology. They are naming schools after you and everything.'

'About bloody time,' said the voice. 'After all, I'm an archaeological genius.'

'That's right,' I said. 'And if you untie us, we can help you, with...erm...important archaeological stuff.'

Casper's mood changed. 'No, oh no, nobody can be untied. Not yet. Not until it's time. Definitely not.'

I didn't like the sound of that. 'Time for what?'

'You know,' said Casper. 'Being PhD students, you'll know all about it.'

'Erm...I think we missed a few lessons,' I said. 'Remind us.'

'Nobody can be untied until we uncover the Holy Grail,' said Casper. 'Duh, are you stupid or what?'

- 78 -

CASPER MACVITTEE'S STORY

This mention of a Holy Grail had Duncan salivating like a Saint Bernard dog. By contrast, I'd lost the plot somewhat, and wasn't sticking to my cover story of being a PhD student as well as perhaps I should.

'Oh c'mon,' I said. 'Is this a wind-up?'

'It's true,' said the voice. 'I proved it. The Holy Grail is buried on the Olympic site.'

'Yeah,' I said, sarcastically. 'And you're Casper Macvittee, the archaeologist who disappeared a year ago and nobody has seen since?'

'That's it!'

'Pull the other one,' I said. 'Where you been for the past year? On a cruise?'

'Keep it a secret,' he said, lowering his voice, 'but I've been in hiding.'

'You...don't...say.'

'It's true...I've been hiding with the pirates, working with them.'

'Sounds like it,' I scoffed. 'You're a prisoner as much as us, I bet.'

'Why are you hiding?' asked Duncan.

'The Olympic committee!' cried the voice. 'They want to assassinate me!'

'Serious?'

'Shut up, Duncan.'

'The pirates saved me,' said the voice. 'Without them I'd be dead.'

'Really?' I said. 'And how'd you work that out, Poirot?'

'I was causing mayhem,' said the voice. 'The Olympic committee couldn't handle me and my evidence giving them bad press. They wanted me out of the way. And they'd have succeeded if it weren't for the pirates. They put me in hiding and said they'd help me find the treasure. We became partners. And now we are going to find the Holy Grail together.' The voice started chuckling. 'We'll find it together, I tell you!'

I sighed. I felt like a remote control had died on me. I had no way of changing the channel and escaping this madness. I just had to suffer it until my brain turned to soup and bled out through my nose. Pirates? Treasure? The Holy Grail? All the rational questions I asked seemed to get weirder answers. Nothing made sense. But then, something clicked in my mind and I suddenly found a very good reason to care.

'Look, cut the crap,' I said. 'This Holy Grail...what's it worth?'

The voice started laughing.

'What we talking about?' I said, 'Millions?'

The voice laughed even more.

'Casper, you loon...answer me.'

'It's priceless,' crowed the voice. 'It can level continents, heal the sick – whoever has it can rule the world!!'

'Really?' I smiled, an idea was forming. 'And how big is this Grail? Is it heavy?'

'Oh no,' said the voice. 'The actual Grail is smaller than a box of cornflakes. It will fit in your pocket.'

'A dressing gown pocket?' I asked, casually.

'Easily,' said the voice. 'You could get two of them in there.'

'Are there two?' asked Duncan.

'No.'

I really can't explain it but I was suddenly very interested in this treasure. I mean, truth be told I didn't think it existed, but being as skint as I was I'd have got excited if it was a winning scratch-card buried out there on the Olympic site, let alone a multi-billion pound pocket friendly lump of loot. If I was being tied up, it was for a purpose, so from that point on I decided that I wanted in on the winnings. I deserved compensation.

'So, this Holy Grail,' I said. 'What exactly do you know about it?'

'Oh I know everything,' said the voice, seemingly forgetting that until two minutes ago we were spies he wasn't going to tell anything to. 'I'm an archaeologist. I've got an NVQ, y'know?'

I decided not to remind him that until his little stint at night school he was just a plasterer from East Ham, and that the stupid qualification he kept going on about meant nothing.

'What I mean is,' I said. 'How'd you find out about this Holy Grail?'

'Oh I found out about it through the pirates,' said Casper, matter of factly.

'The pirates?' I said.

'That's right.'

There was something of a confused pause. 'Erm…I thought *you* found this Grail thing? What do you mean you found out about it *through* the pirates?'

- 79 -

PLOT THICKENS

'I'd just graduated from the Academy,' began Casper, 'and was offering my services as an archaeologist, looking for my first big break.'

He claimed he'd been offered jobs in Cairo and Lima, but turned them down in favour of London. 'Y'know…I wanted to give something back…to the community.'

I found that a bit of a contradiction. I mean, don't archaeologists take stuff from communities? Anyway, I let it pass. It turns out he placed a card in a local newsagents saying:

Archaeologist for hire!
Foundation NVQ qualified in eras:
Jurassic, Roman, Grunge.
Competitive rates! No call-out charge!

Amazingly he gets a call. Some old seadog who said an uncle had died and left him an ancient parchment written in Latin. He needed the help of an expert to translate it.

'Can you speak Latin?' asked Duncan.

'No,' said Casper, 'That was Advanced Course stuff. But I am qualified in highly specialised translation techniques utilising a polylingual index.'

'What? Like a dictionary?' drawled Duncan.

'Ssssh!' cried Casper. 'Don't give it away! What's the matter with you?'

'Sorry,' said Duncan.

'Where was I?' said Casper. 'Oh yeah, I bought a dictionary and translated the parchment word by word. It was a time-consuming process, and the only reason I kept going was because the first line got me excited.'

'What did it say?' asked Duncan.

'It said, "Read here ye who shall learn the resting place of God's treasure, buried in the British Isles by his servant, King Arthur."'

Reading this, Casper sensed he was on to something. He painstakingly translated the rest but it didn't make too much sense. It was all too vague. When the Captain called, Casper asked if there was any more. 'I said, being that it was my first case, I'd work for free, for a share of the credit if I found anything.'

'And what did the Captain say?'

'He was fine with that. And he'd didn't mind me going public, y'know to the press…just so long as I never mentioned him. He wanted to keep a low profile. He was very insistent about that.'

'What was his name?' I said.

'Captain.'

'Captain what?' said Duncan.

'Captain bloody Birdseye for all we know,' I said, doubting the story more and more. I'd already given up mentally spending my winnings. 'What did he look like?'

'Oh, I dunno,' said Casper. 'I never met him.'

'You've never met him?'

'We did business by post mostly, and the occasional call. He just kept sending me pages, one at a time, to translate.'

'And this is when you were going to the press last year?' said Duncan.

'Yeah,' said Casper. 'That's right. The minute I translated a page I'd phone the paper and tell them I had more news. They liked that, the paper, and the more I was sent, the more interesting it got. I learned that the legend of King Arthur was real! And that Excalibur existed!

'The parchments told me that written on the blade of Excalibur was a grid reference pointing to the treasure. It took some time to piece it all together. Eventually though, I found it! It said that the treasure was buried on the meridian of his holiness Saint Ratford!'

'Saint Ratford?' I said. 'Who the hell is that?'

'Isn't he the patron saint of quality footwear?' asked Duncan.

'No, you prat,' I said. 'That's Saint Hubbins!'

Casper started laughing. 'Saint Ratford *is* Stratford. Don't you see?' He laughed some more. 'You wouldn't understand it. That's why they came to me to break the code. I'm an NVQ-qualified professional, y'know?'

Code? Hardly much of a code, I thought. Sounded like something straight out of a crappy film like *The Da Vinci Code*. 'So what happened next?' I said.

'Calm down, I'm getting to it,' said Casper. 'Next, things turned nasty. I got a death threat through the post from the Olympic committee. It said they were on to me and that if I breathed another word I'd be killed. They'd been intercepting my mail and all sorts. And they knew almost as much about the treasure as I did. The Captain said the Olympic committee would murder me and steal it from me if they got chance. He said it would be best if I went into hiding with the pirates and we work out the rest for ourselves.'

'Work out what?' drawled Duncan.

'It says that "only he who is clear of soul can find the Grail." So, being the archaeological expert that I am, I volunteered and I've spent the last year cleansing my soul.'

'How'd you do that?' I asked.

'By not seeing anything.'

'Eh?'

'The eyes are the window to the soul, so by not seeing anything for a year I've cleansed my soul ready for the Grail.'

'You've had a blindfold on for a year?'

'Serious?' said Duncan.

I didn't like the sound of any of this. Well, that's not true. I mean, I liked the sound of a piece of treasure worth a mint, if it existed, but the more this "Casper" spoke, the more he sounded like a complete fruitcake. In fact, the more he spoke the less he made sense. He was like some doddery old relative who can only talk in tangents. Although, there was enough in what he said to make you think nothing added up.

It sounded like he was being set up. I mean, think about it. A stranger comes to him. Gives him letters one by one to translate. The letters talk of a big treasure that gets him all excited. Then a death-threat turns up, supposedly from the Olympic committee. And then next thing you know he's agreeing to be blindfolded for a year by a bloke he's never met? Yeah, it stunk of a set up. The thing was, I couldn't work out why'd anyone would go to all that effort.

'Have you seen any of the people who kidnapped you?' I said.

'I ain't kidnapped,' said Casper. 'I'm a volunteer. A pioneer. The first man for two-thousand years to be pure enough. The only—'

'Nevermind all that crap,' I said. 'Have you seen anyone, ever?'

'Never,' said Casper. 'They take good care of me though. And I'll see them soon. The hour of history is nearly upon us, because tomorrow we all go public.'

'Go public?' I said. 'How are you planning on—' but I didn't get chance to finished. There were footsteps coming down the tunnel towards us.

- 80 -

SINBAD

'Who's there?' I cried out.

'Friend or foe?' added Duncan.

A smug chuckling came from down the tunnel, it grew louder as the footsteps approached.

'They're heathens!' cried Casper, suddenly remembering we were spies. 'Bloody heathens! Why'd you put them in here with me?'

I feared another stoning was imminent. 'Listen!' I said quickly. 'We know nothing.'

'That's right,' said Duncan. 'We know nothing about the Holy Grail on the Olympic site.'

I rolled my eyes. Even by Duncan's standards, he was surpassing himself. I suppose the trauma of being held captive was causing his mind to find new, previously unexplored, levels of idiot. I'd resigned myself at that point to being shot out of a cannon or spliced on a mainbrace or whatever it is pirates do when they kill people.

'Yeah, Holy Grail,' I said. 'We know nothing about it. You should just let us g—'

A sharp *SLAP* went across my face.

'Friend or foe?' repeated Duncan.

'Foe!' I cried.

'Serious?'

'Bastard, nearly broke my jaw.'

'Quiet!' barked a new voice. 'Or I'll keelhaul the pair of you.'

I didn't know what that meant. To be honest I still don't. But it didn't sound good.

'Are you a pirate?' asked Duncan, sniffing heavily. I don't think he knew what keelhauling was either, but it didn't seem to put him off asking his questions. 'You don't smell briny enough to be a pirate.'

There was a *SLAP*. I can only assume it was Duncan catching one in the chops for his stupidity.

'Y'arrgh!' growled the new voice. 'I'm as salty a seadog as they come!'

'You're a real man,' I said. 'Hitting a bloke when he's tied up.'

'Isn't there a pirate code?' drawled Duncan. 'I saw it in *Pirates of the Caribbean*. Parley! Parley!'

We were silenced with two quick slaps. It was clear this bloke had no interest in our questions. But then, I had no interest in these pirates. As far as I was concerned, they drew first blood. They broke into my flat. They bundled me. They brought me here. And for what? I was getting angry. My face stung from the slapping. I didn't care about being keelhauled or whatever. I decided to have a pop.

'You're no pirate! You're a pussy! Where I come from only girls slap. If you had any balls you'd punch, you—'

It's funny how you can sound tough when you don't know who you are talking to. That's why it's so easy to sound big on the phone or whatever, but when you actually see the person you're winding up, well, you kind of reassess things, which is exactly what I did when a punch to the face revealed one of my captors.

I don't know what happened. I reckon I must have had a Jedi moment or something because, sensing I was about to get a bunch of fives in the face, I jerked my head out of the way just as the punch flew through the air. He must have caught the blindfold somehow because next thing I know I'm staring at a big grinning face. Though not a friendly grinning face like the Mona Lisa, it was more an aggressive grinning face, with a few long decorative scars and a partially albino eye that looked like a peppercorn on a cue ball. This rather ugly head belonged to a hulking type dressed up like Sinbad, who looked like he ate nails for breakfast and shat steel at dinner. I sensed trouble.

'You're staying put, me hearty,' said Sinbad, mockingly slapping my cheek. 'Cap'n's got plans for you.'

'What plans?'

'You'll see,' he grinned. 'Now shut your cakehole.'

It's strange really, but as he tried to put my blindfold back on, I was suddenly aware I didn't have my glasses on. Everything was blurry. I tried focus. We were in a cell of some kind, made of crumbling brick. The only light came from the flaming torch held in Sinbad's hand, which cast a red glow over everything. I could see Duncan next to me. He still had his blindfold on. He was sniffing heavily.

'Is it time yet?' said a voice.

Across the room there was a dark figure slumped in the shadows. His body was half turned so I couldn't see his face properly. I tried to crane my neck.

Sinbad caught me trying to steal a look. I smiled at him. He smiled back. And, giving up on trying to make a blindfold, he went for the next best thing. He drew his muscular arm back and smashed it into my face, and everything went rather black, again.

- 81 -

AWAKE

I awoke with a tremendous sense of déja-vu. There was darkness and sniffing. Only this time the darkness wasn't as black. As for the sniffing, Duncan was hoovering up the room through his Kiwi hooter so hard, it was as if he thought he could work out what had just happened by scent alone. I reckon if you asked him, he'd tell you either he or his mum had been a bloodhound in a previous life. He believed in all that reincarnation stuff.

'Oscar?' *sniff,* 'You still there?'

I replied with a groan. My jaw burned. I tried to sit up. Something in my skull made a cracking sound.

'What was that?' said Duncan. 'Who's there?'

'It's me, you pilchard,' I said, my voice sounding weak. 'That git nearly broke my jaw.' I yawned a bit and tested things out. I'd live.

'What happened?'

I explained about being punched in the face and having the blindfold sort of ripped off.

'Serious?' said Duncan. 'Where are we?'

'I dunno,' I strained my eyes. I could just about make out the shape of Duncan next to me. 'It's too dark to tell.'

'Are we in a cave?'

'No, the walls looked like brick, but old…decayed.' My head was really hurting. 'How long was I out? I think I may have had concussion or something'

'What kind of brick?'

'Erm…house-brick.'

'Stretcher bond? Flemish bond or English bond?'

'What?'

'How were they arranged?'

'Does it bloody matter?' I asked. 'I was the one who was knocked out. How comes you're acting like a loon? Did Sinbad hit you too?'

'Sinbad?'

'Yeah, the bloke that was in here just now.'

'How'd you know his name?' asked Duncan. 'Did he have one of those nametag things like in the supermarket?'

'No, he just looked like a Sinbad. He had scars and a gammy eye.'

'A pirate?' said Duncan, somewhat unnecessarily.

'Yes, a bloody pirate!' I gave up on Duncan. Amazingly, I thought I'd get more sense out of Casper. 'Psst…Casper…you there?'

'I think they took him somewhere,' said Duncan.

'Good,' I said. 'He was doing my head in anyway. C'mon, let's make a break for it before they come back.' I began pulling against the ropes.

'Don't bother,' said Duncan. 'Pirates don't tie weak knots.'

'Oh, is that so?'

'All they do all day is tie knots, they'd get pretty good at it after a while I reckon.'

'Let's hope we were tied up a by a work experience then.' I wrestled with the rope, but after thirty seconds or so of pained straining, I gave up.

'Don't stress,' said Duncan. 'We just need to wait for the rats.'

'Rats? What have rats go to do with anything?'

'Rats eat rope,' answered Duncan, like it was obvious.

'That's your escape plan? You're going to wait for rats to rescue us? What are you the bloody Pied Piper?'

'Rats eat rope,' repeated Duncan. 'I saw it in a movie.'

'Why the hell would a rat eat rope? It's hardly a steak.'

'It's good for their teeth. They gnaw on it.'

'Oh, right, so I'll just wait for a plague of them to come along wanting a rope buffet or something.'

'Hey.'

'In fact I'll phone up the local rag and put an ad in the lonely hearts saying: PRISONER…WOULD LIKE TO MEET RODENT OR SIMILAR…FOR GNAWING…CHEWING…AND GENERAL ESCAPE ASSISTANCE…'

'Hey, there's no need to be rude.'

'Balls to being nice,' I said. 'Pussy-footing about is what's got us here in the first place. If I had more faith in the Old Bill I'd have gone down the cop shop and grassed this lot up.'

'I thought you already did?'

'Leave it out.'

'You told Casper you did.'

'I was bluffing, wasn't I? When have I had time? I've got enough on my plate with the sodding FBI hunting me down for being a chemical weapons dealer. You, on the other hand, had plenty of time to go to the police.'

'No, I've been busy.'

'Doing what?'

'Collecting evidence…and I've had the shop to run too.'

'That's the problem with the world today,' I said. 'Nobody's prepared to stick up for themselves. It's easy to duck your head and walk away. I lived on an estate like that. And you know what happened? The scum took it over 'cos nobody would stand up to them. I'm telling you, someone could have shut these pirates down before it got out of hand.'

'Maybe it's bigger than we think?' said Duncan. 'Maybe it goes right to the top!'

'Don't get excited. The government ain't in on this.'

'Maybe the Queen?' said Duncan. 'I saw a film once that said her great-granddad was Blackbeard.'

'Oh shut up,' I said. 'You're not helping.'

A silence fell between us. It dragged for a long minute or so. I felt bad for snapping at him. He can't help it, he's just one big dumb puppy.

'Duncan?'

'What?'

'Can you smell any new clues?'

- 82 -

THOUGHTS IN THE CELL

'Okay,' I cleared my throat, 'let's have a think.'

Five minutes or so had passed. Neither of us had spoken. Rather than sit listening to the water running nearby, I decided to try and have a stab at working out what was going on.

'Okay,' I began again. 'All we have to go on is what we've seen so far, and what that Casper told us. Though he sounded off his rocker.'

'He sounded genuine,' said Duncan. 'I liked him.'

'Well, if it is Casper, he's even more stupid than I thought. You buy any of what he said?' It was a stupid question. I knew the answer.

'Yeah,' said Duncan. 'Makes sense.'

'Makes sense? He reckons the Holy Grail is on the Olympic site!'

'It might be,' drawled Duncan. 'You don't know that is isn't.'

'I'd get bloody long odds that it is,' I said. 'Anyway, forget that. He says he's never seen his captors. Doesn't even believe he's captured. Thinks the blindfold is to block the window to his soul so it can be cleansed or something. He's being set up, why can't he see it?'

'He could be brainwashed,' said Duncan.

'Brainwashed? What, like they do in cults?'

'Yeah,' said Duncan. 'They could have hypnotised him and got inside his mind and are now controlling him like a drone. I saw a film once where some Russians tried doing that to the Americans in the Cold War.'

'Brainwashed, eh?' I thought about it. 'You know that's the first decent thing you've said since Chapter 12.' I cleared my throat, 'If he was brainwashed, that makes sense, because a lot of what he said didn't make sense. I mean, if the Pearly King wants to blow up the Games, why didn't he just strap a load of TNT to the stadium and press the plunger? Why'd he have to get the pirates involved? Why all this running about?'

'The pirates want the treasure. The Pearly doesn't. And he's got a reputation to uphold. Maybe you lose your Pearly King status if you go to prison. Maybe he wouldn't be able to pass it on to his son.'

'Has he got a son?'

'All Pearly Kings have sons,' said Duncan. 'It's the law.'

'Is it now?' I said. 'And which film did you learn that from?'

'Was there a *Carry On Cockney*?'

'No.'

'Well, maybe it was called *Carry On up the Lambeth Walk*. Sid James was definitely in it.'

'Like that narrows it down?' I couldn't be bothered to go through all the *Carry On* films to prove Duncan wrong.

We fell back into silence, which soon got boring. I decided that even though we were probably facing imminent death, I should spend my last moments trying to untangle the mystery that is Duncan's mind. 'So, you really reckon there is treasure on the site?'

'Yeah, the ley-lines make it possible. The site is on the Greenwich meridian, and there is a direct druid line that crosses it and goes to Leytonstone. That's how it gets it name, y'know? it's on a ley-line, and there used to be a holy stone there.'

'A holy stone?' I said. 'Like Stonehenge?'

'A stone altar,' he drawled. 'It was used during the Middle Ages to sacrifice witches.'

250

'Blimey!' I said, genuinely amazed. 'I didn't know that. Where's that stone now? In the Natural History Museum?'

'Tesco car park,' he replied, 'by the Green Man roundabout.'

'What? You mean that rock by the cash-point?'

'Yeah.'

'The one that's covered in graffiti? That's a ceremonial altar used for sacrificing witches?'

'Yeah.'

'Bollocks is it,' I said, my amazement going for a burton. 'It's a bloody stone, that's all. The only thing that's been sacrificed on that has been some bloke's virginity, I bet.'

'It's the truth,' protested Duncan.

'I'd love to see your copy of the encyclopaedia. I tell you what…if there is a Holy Grail on that site, you and I can split the money. I'll give you the lion's share, 70/30, just because you believed in it more than me.'

'I can't have 70%,' said Duncan.

'You want more?'

'What are you going to cut it with? A saw?'

'I'm not going to cut the actual Grail you prat, I meant the money.'

We fell back into silence, I imagined Duncan keeping his bizarre mind busy working out how to desecrate a holy artefact to get a perfectly even 50/50 split. My mind didn't hang on such pointless thoughts, instead it drifted to the Pearly King.

I was beginning to think it was maybe him who started the treasure rumour in the first place, hoping the Games would get shut down on grounds of archaeological significance or whatever. And when that failed, he had to rethink things.

I thought back to what Jaggers said. The Pearly King would stop at nothing to sink the Games, even hiring a bunch of mercenary pirates to help him. But how was he going to get away with it? He couldn't. Unless he was an evil criminal mastermind, which, based on his ideas for The Eel and his politics concerning pie and mash, was doubtful. He was a dunce. But even so, he was clever enough not to put himself in the firing line, I was sure of that.

Fuses popped in my brain as I started connecting things. Casper Macvittee, deluded and looking for a big archaeological scoop – he was the perfect scapegoat, all he had to do was to be lured in. I bet the Pearly couldn't believe his luck, especially when the local papers started covering things. Casper's treasure story really caught everyone's attention. And his disappearance sparked all kinds of rumours. People genuinely believed there was some treasure on the Olympic site. I mean people *genuinely* believed Casper Macvittee was leading an underground army.

I'd seen pirates writing "Viva Casper", hadn't I? Why were they doing it if only to build up the myth that Casper was running the whole show? This talk of going public was a sick joke. They were going to blow the site up. The Pearly King would pay the pirates off and Casper would take the blame. It was a perfect plan. Get a fall guy, create a cover story, do the damage and let him take the flack. Tell the fall guy whatever you want, so long as he believes it. And Bob's your uncle. And this Casper was perfect, he seemed to believe every word of it. He really had been brainwashed.

I paused for a moment, feeling chuffed with myself. I'd slotted it all into place.

Or, had I?

Had I in fact just done a "Duncan," racing ahead and connecting dots just because I could. I didn't know, but I felt confident I was on to something, and my interpretation seemed far more rational than believing King Arthur had buried the Holy Grail in E15. But then, if there really was something valuable on that site...

'Duncan,' I whispered, about to tell him everything, but I stopped. There were footsteps coming down the tunnel toward us.

- 83 -

COLLECTION

The room filled with light as Sinbad entered carrying a flaming torch. His hulking frame crouched down and tore off Duncan's blindfold.

'You're right,' said Duncan. 'He does have a gammy eye.'

Sinbad growled dissaparoval and looked down his misshapen nose at us. 'Y'arrgh! The Cap'n be ready for seeing you.'

At first I didn't think these pirates were the cleverest bunch. I mean, why bother blindfolding us if they were going to take the blindfolds off? You ever notice that in films? For example, take John Carpenter's flawed 1980s masterpiece *Big Trouble in Little China*. Two male leads are kidnapped, tied up, blindfolded and then when the main baddie wants to explain his cunning plan, the blindfolds come off and the truth comes out. I was only eight when I watched that, but even then I thought it was pretty cheap. Nobody was that stupid, right? Well, for half a second I thought these pirates might've been, but then I realised they needed us to see.

We were untied from the wall and yanked to our feet.

'How about cutting our hands free as well,' I said.

'Y'arrgh!' growled Sinbad.

'Was that a yes?' asked Duncan.

Sinbad pushed me in the back, 'Walk!'

'I can't,' I said. 'I need my glasses.'

I'd hoped this would stall things, so I was caught a bit off guard when he produced them from his pocket, all delicately wrapped in cotton wool. He unfolded them and put them on my face, gently.

'You scratched them,' I lied. 'You'll pay for that.'

'Walk!'

'Where?' drawled Duncan. 'We don't know where we are.'

Sinbad snorted and stepped in front of us. I figured he really wasn't the brains of the outfit, which was a shame because if he'd been in command, outwitting our captors would've been a doddle.

'Oi mate,' I said. 'You got a fag?'

Sinbad ignored me and led us down a short tunnel that had a trench in the middle that bubbled with black water. The stone floor felt cold and slimy underfoot and it was hard to keep my balance. A few times I nearly went arse over tit into the water.

At the end of the tunnel there were some short stone steps that led up to a trap door. Sinbad threw it open and we followed him up into a narrow room. It was dark and filled with chests. At one end there was whitewashed glass. Streetlight struggled to find it's way inside.

'This is the model shop,' I said, realising where we were.

'Pirate Shop,' growled Sinbad.

'What is a Pirate Shop?' asked Duncan.

Sinbad didn't answer. He pushed us both in the back towards a spiral staircase. 'Walk!'

I looked at the chests dotted about. One was open. It was filled with DVDs. I've got good at being able to identify a DVD at a glance, and in that quick half second gander I could see it was an impressive collection. Not a Spielberg in sight.

We followed the twisting steps and came up into a room of flickering shadows, lit by the glow of a small fireplace. As my eyes adjusted I could see the walls were lined with pirates, some sitting on the floor, some swigging from bottles. All of them looking at us with wide aggressive eyes. The old one who'd given me a soaking the other day was sat in an alcove, playing a slow haunting tune on his harmonica.

At the far end of the room there was a button back leather chair, turned away from us. Thin wisps of smoke rose from it making a sort of spaghetti pattern as they drifted towards the ceiling.

My eyes fell on a nearby chest, again to my surprise it wasn't brimming with doubloons. It was stuffed full of laserdiscs. Rare ones too. A double gatefold of a Belgian limited edition release of *Condorman*.

'You know maybe I should join your crew,' I said, nodding over at the laserdiscs. 'You've got the best collection of films outside of my own. Wait a minute!' I studied some of the other titles. 'Are these mine?'

'Ours now,' said a pirate.

'You thieving bastards!'

The pirates laughed. 'It's all booty.'

'Side booty we call it,' said one.

'Commission,' said another.

'Should bring us a fair penny on eBay,' added one more, with a wink.

My blood steamed. My fists clenched. They'd made things personal. That is, even more personal than kidnapping. My film collection was the only thing that mattered to me. It had taken me years to put together.

Sinbad stepped forward, throwing his flaming torch over to another pirate, and bent down to the chest. He picked out the very rare, very special, Swedish dubbed copy of *Weekend At Bernie's 2*.

He shot eyes at Duncan. 'What's it worth?'

'Lots.'

'Why'd you tell him that?' I cried.

'It's the truth,' drawled Duncan. 'It was a factory error. Only two hundred produced.'

'Will you shut up!'

Sinbad laughed and flexed his large fingers to show sharp looking nails. He pulled the disc out of the sleeve and went to scratch it.

'You bastard, you wouldn't?'

But it was too late. I gawped as he ran his nails down the disc with a piercing scrape, scarring it forever. The pirates laughed and cooed. Sinbad drew out his pistol.

'Enough!' said a voice from behind the armchair.

The pirates fell silent. Sinbad tossed the laserdisc into the fire. As the plastic crackled and shrank my body began to shake with rage. I wanted to Incredible Hulk and knock down the Pirate Shop, model shop, whatever you want to call it, I wanted to smash it into the dirt and make jam out of everyone in it.

'I know what you're up to!' I spat. 'And so do others. We've told them everything. They know about the underground army. They know about Casper not leading it. They know about the Pearly King paying for all this.'

The voice behind the armchair laughed a high haughty laugh. 'And how many people have you told? A hundred? A thousand? The more the merrier. You *know* nothing.'

'What do you want from us?' I barked.

Sinbad slapped me. 'You address the Cap'n by his name, you mangy cur!'

'What do I call him?' I asked. 'Captain—'

'—Jaggers,' said the voice. 'Call me Captain Jaggers.' The leather chair spun round and there sat the country's shrewdest lawyer, sucking on a cigarette holder, with a white cat on his lap. His creased face betrayed a satisfied smile. 'So glad you could join us, Oscar.'

- 84 -

THE CAPTAIN'S CHAMBER

'Whoa,' drawled Duncan. 'That's a twist that needs some explaining.'

'Jaggers!' I cried. 'What the hell are you playing at?'

Sinbad slapped me across the face. 'Cap'n Jaggers to you!'

'Y'arrgh!' went the pirates in unison.

'How come you're involved in all this?' I said. 'And why are you a bloody pirate captain?'

'Didn't you grow up in Sidcup?' added Duncan, somewhat cryptically.

Jaggers smiled. 'I was in the navy for over thirty years as a lawyer. It's fair to say I picked up a few bad habits during my service.'

The crew laughed heartily at that. 'Indeed,' continued Jaggers, 'for thirty years I've travelled every sea, ocean, and channel. All for one reason.' He paused, seemingly wanting us to ask what that reason could possibly be, but to be honest I couldn't be bothered.

'I'm not really interested,' I said. 'I'd sooner you just let us go.'

Sinbad gave me another slap across the face. 'You mangy cur!'

'Oh, Oscar, I can't let you go,' purred Jaggers. 'You've played your part too well.'

'What part?'

'Indulge me,' said Jaggers, stroking the cat. 'What's your favourite film?'

It may have been a hostage situation but questions like that are as easy as answering your name. You know your favourite film, just like you know what hand you write with and which side of your mouth you prefer to chew on.

'*The Wicker Man,*' I answered. 'The original.'

'Mine's *The Piano,*' offered Duncan, earning a slap from Sinbad, who clearly wasn't a Sam Neill fan.

Jaggers curled his thin lips into a smile. 'Ah, yes...*The Wicker Man.* How fortuitous, almost ironic in fact that *that* particular film should be your favourite. I think you'll find the plot very similar to your current predicament.'

Given the rather nasty end to that film, I didn't like where this was going. I hoped Jaggers had seen an alternative ending where, instead of burning the poor bloke to death in a huge wicker statue, it finished with jelly and ice-cream and everyone singing kum-by-ah. But somehow I doubted it.

Jaggers stroked the cat and continued. 'You see...in order to achieve what we're doing, we need to make a sacrifice. Only, we cannot just sacrifice anybody. We need someone special. Someone not of Cockney blood, born outside the sound of Bow bells, who has come to the area of their own volition, someone who would accuse the Pearly King in public,' he paused, a gleam in his eyes. 'Only the blood of a heathen will appease the gods.'

Duncan's mouth hung open. 'Serious?'

'No,' scoffed Jaggers, probably amused at his own genius. It was easy to see why he was a good lawyer. He could spin believability into the most far-fetched of stories. 'No, in truth, anybody's blood will do.'

'We just need a lot of it,' said Sinbad.

'Why?' asked Duncan. I sensed he was about to ask one of his stellar questions, really get to the bottom of the mystery and work out what was going on. 'Are you like vampire pirates or something?'

'Duncan, for fuck's sake!'

The pirates exploded into laughter.

'Is the fact we've just found out that a respected lawyer is moonlighting as a pirate not enough for you? What else do you want to throw into the mix?'

Duncan blinked. 'Erm...I'd like a bit more about the Holy Grail they found.'

'Don't be a prat,' I said over the continued laughter. 'Look at this lot. Do you really think this bunch were going to find the Holy Grail? They look like they'd have trouble finding their own bum crumbs.'

The laughter died down. Every pair of eyes stared at me, hard. Well, every available pair. Those with eye-patches and gammy-eyes did the best stares they could. For a moment I thought about asking whether those with just one eye would class themselves as cyclopses. But the moment went.

'We don't need to find the Holy Grail,' purred Jaggers. 'We've already found it. And tonight, we are going to take it!'

- 85 -

THE HOLY GRAIL

'You don't half talk a load of old cod,' I said. 'I don't know what you're up to but there's no Grail, I bet. And even if there is, there's no way it's buried in Stratford. Next you'll tell me Atlantis is under the Lea Valley River and Big Foot lives in Hyde Park.'

The room stiffened. I felt something sharp and pointy press against my back. I took that as a sign to be quiet.

Jaggers studied me. 'You don't understand, Oscar. Working in the navy I was privy to all kinds of secrets and I've read reports on projects you couldn't possibly imagine. But there is one project in particular that has shaped the course of my life.' He puffed on his cigarette holder, presumably waiting for me to ask him to continue, but given that I had a sharp pointy thing pressed against the base of my spine, I just sort of shut up.

Jaggers grinned. 'I don't suppose you're aware of The Chaffinch Project? It was set up in Oxford during the Second World War. Its purpose was to recover idols and artefacts, good luck charms to help defeat Hitler. Can you guess what they found?'

'The Holy Grail!' cried Duncan.

Sinbad slapped him.

'No,' purred Jaggers. 'They found nothing. They spent a year cataloguing every known treasure on the planet both mythical and actual. They covered everything from the four-leaf clover to the treasure in *Treasure Island*. But it counted for nothing. The only items they managed to obtain were some rabbits feet, horse shoes and lucky heather. Embarrassing to think that would stop the Reich.' Jaggers sucked on his cigarette holder and continued. 'But one member of The Chaffinch Project made some progress. A chap called James Jesus-Smythe. He was searching for Excalibur. And do you know what he found?'

Duncan gave Sinbad a furtive glance. 'Erm…the Holy Grail?'

Another slap.

'No,' said Jaggers. 'But he came close. Jesus-Smythe stumbled upon a ship's log from 1721 that spoke of a man being rescued off the west coast of Africa. He was adrift on a raft, been drifting for days, apparently. What was most striking was the manner of his dress. The log recalls the castaway as wearing "a full suit of armour as golden as the sun, resplendent with unusual crests and insignia." Across the breast plate were the words "Arthurus rex Albion". Do you know what that means?'

'The Holy Grail?'

Sinbad gave Duncan a belter, right across the chops. Knowing elementary Latin was clearly something he considered quite important.

'No…it means, King Arthur of Britain,' purred Jaggers.

'So what?' I said.

'Consider the implication,' enthused Jaggers. 'A suit of armour inscribed with the seal of the mythical King Arthur proves his existence. Furthermore, such a suit of armour would only have belonged to a knight of the round table.'

'I get it!' said Duncan, his cheek looking a little bruised. 'This castaway they found at sea was a really old knight. Just like that dude from *Indiana Jones and The Last Crusade*?'

'No!' cried Jaggers, followed by another slap from Sinbad. 'This was no knight. This was a Frenchman!'

'Grrrr,' went the pirates, a few spitting on the ground. Clearly not fans of the Entente-Cordial.

Jaggers continued. 'When asked where he found the suit of armour, the Frenchman explained he'd been shipwrecked in the Caribbean, on an island no bigger than a chamber bed that was permanently submerged beneath the waves by one clear foot of water. He said he'd been drifting when he'd been washed "ashore". Kicking about in the sand his foot stuck something hard. Curious, he dug it up, and do you know what he found?'

Duncan trembled, but he couldn't help himself. The words burst from his lips. 'The Holy Grail?'

Sinbad gave a sad shake of his head. *SLAP!*

'No,' said Jaggers. 'He found a golden suit of armour and a heavy gold chest. This evidence was extraordinary. It virtually pinpointed the next clue in the quest for the Holy Grail.'

'So what happened?' I said. 'If this department found all this out, why didn't they go looking for it?'

'It was too late,' said Jaggers. 'The war had finished. There was no need to continue funding the research.'

'Well what happened to that Jesus-Smythe bloke who found all this out? He was a scholar right? Surely he got excited and shot his mouth off to a few people, told them what he might have found.'

'Oh, he did,' said Jaggers with a grin. 'He told me. And he paid for it with his life.' He reached down beside his chair and picked up a skull. He examined it in his hand. 'Well, say hello, James Jesus-Smythe.'

- 86 -

SKULL

The pirates rolled about with laughter. Strange sense of humour these pirates, I thought. Really sick. The sort of sick sense of humour that finds Jennifer Aniston rom-coms funny. And in my opinion anyone that can laugh at that stuff is easily capable of murder, and much worse.

Jaggers sat the skull in his lap and began stroking it, much to the alarm of the cat who leapt off in panic.

I gestured at it uneasily. 'Is that thing real?'

Jaggers answered with a solemn nod. I shivered.

'You really killed that Jesus-Smythe?' gulped Duncan.

Jaggers gave a wide grin. 'I didn't have to. These seadogs did it for me.'

'Y'arrgh!' cried the pirates.

'You see,' began Jaggers, patting the skull affectionately, 'when the Second World War ended, Jesus-Smythe went hunting for the Grail on his own. For fifteen years he worked his way round the Caribbean but found nothing during his travels save a penchant for rum. As such he became known as something of a joke. A drunken Englishman who would roll from port to port, amusing locals and fisherman with his constant questions about an "invisible island", never answering questions about why he wanted to find it, for fear of giving up his golden goose, as it were. With that sort of notoriety preceding him, I didn't have too much trouble tracking him down.'

Jaggers puffed on his cigarette holder and continued. 'I recall our first meeting. It took place in a go-go bar on St. Lucia. He was drinking rum, well into a bottle I should say, as such his tongue was loose; it didn't take long for him to crack. I'd researched him well. Knew his weaknesses. He needed money. Manpower. Resources. And more importantly he needed someone in the navy. Someone with access to sonar and naval maps, to help speed up his search. But, most importantly, he needed someone he could trust. Given the sterling account I gave of myself he figured there was no safer bet than a top naval lawyer to provide all those things.'

'So what happened?' asked Duncan.

'Oh, I toyed with him,' grinned Jaggers. 'Said I wasn't interested. Said I thought he was mad. Said everything to dissuade him but that only fuelled his determination further. It was delicious. Before sunrise we had entered into a gentleman's agreement. I was to provide him with maps and documents as he needed, as well as naval support, if required. In exchange he would see to it that I be given a credit when the treasure was recovered, plus royalties from any book sales.'

'That doesn't sound like a fair deal,' said Duncan. 'Nobody buys books.'

'Yeah,' I agreed. 'Sounds like you shafted yourself.'

Jaggers frowned. 'In chess it's not about the small pieces you can steal instantly, it's about moving the small pieces to squeeze the larger ones into giving themselves up.'

I raised an eyebrow. 'What fortune cookie did you get that out of?'

Jaggers sneered and continued. 'The deal turned in my favour, as I knew it would, but by a most unexpected turn of events. We were out investigating a small island south of Tobago, that had strange magnetic properties, but upon landing it soon became clear it wasn't the correct island. We went to return to our boat when we were ambushed by pirates.'

The crew started to laugh. Jaggers himself could barely conceal a grin. 'Do you know what they wanted?'

'The Holy Grail?' asked Duncan.

SLAP!

'Shoes!' cried Jaggers. 'Can you believe that?'

'I can believe that.' I looked down at my own battered feet. 'Right now, I'd kill for shoes.'

'Well,' continued Jaggers, 'there must have been a crew of forty bloodthirsty pirates, not a pair of shoes amongst them. Lord knows how they were going to divide up the booty of our boots, as it were. "Your shoes or your life" they cried and soon Jesus-Smythe and I were surrounded. Scabbards pointed at throats. Pistols pointed at our private parts. A lesser man would have considered himself dead. However, I thought about their ultimatum and made them an offer.'

'What offer?' asked Duncan.

Jaggers grinned. 'An offer they couldn't refuse.'

- 87 -

THE OFFER

'You offered them wellies?' said Duncan.

'No!' scolded Jaggers. 'I offered them a simple exchange. Spare my life and kill their own captain, and I'd give them a share of the greatest treasure in the world.'

'The Holy Grail?' said Duncan, ducking instinctively.

'Yes!' cried Jaggers.

Sinbad gave a broad smile and patted Duncan's head.

'The Holy Grail!' continued Jaggers. 'The most powerful artefact on Earth, blessed by God himself, and imbued with such power it can level mountains, flatten armies and heal the sick.'

'Worth a pretty penny on eBay too,' said a wizened pirate with a white beard.

'Yes,' said Jaggers, considering his crewmember. 'Worth a pretty penny indeed.'

I frowned. 'And these blokes fell for it? They killed their own Captain and put you in charge? All because you said so?'

'Oscar, you are forgetting my profession. To this day have I ever lost a case?' Jaggers grinned and started tossing the skull about, spinning it on a bony finger as if it were a basketball. 'Admittedly, they were untrusting at first, but when I told them the power of the treasure that awaited them, they soon capitulated. Within five minutes of our meeting there had been a mutiny, their Captain killed and Jesus-Smythe was no more. Having convinced them that he was merely my servant, the crew took it upon themselves to use a blunderbuss and blow his head into a thousand pieces.'

'That still doesn't explain why you are here,' I said. 'This is the East End, not the Caribbean.'

Jaggers raised an eyebrow. 'Indeed, Oscar. How right you are. How happy I would've been to discover the Grail languishing in a chest buried on an invisible island, but it wasn't to be. When we finally discovered the chest there was nearly an insurrection when we found not booty, but documents. Scores and scores of papers that spoke of a secret chamber in Albion, in the vicinity of what is now London's East End.' Jaggers blew a thin trail of smoke above him. 'I promptly relocated to the area and for years I've been working my hardest to excavate five square miles in secret. You have no idea how impossible a task it is. We pirates set up building firms, landscape gardeners, everything we could think of that would allow us to dig in the area covertly. But it was just too slow. Finally, I hit upon a grand idea of mass urban renewal and, as fortune would favour it, the Olympic Games suddenly came into view and I pulled every string and every trick to bring them here, so we could excavate the site quicker.'

'A thousand pieces?' said Duncan.

'Pardon?'

'You say you blew Jesus-Smythe's head into a thousand pieces?'

'Indeed,' said Jaggers, now flipping the skull about on his arm, like that trick you do with an apple, rolling it down your arm and popping it up in the air.

'How did you glue his head back together so well?' asked Duncan.

My stomach suddenly went. 'That's not Jesus-Smythe's skull.'

Jaggers caught the skull and gave it a theatrical double-take. 'Good Lord! You know, Oscar, you're right! I don't think it is.' And with that he rolled the skull across the floor to the far end of the room, causing the pirates to cheer as it knocked over a previously unnoticed set of bowling pins.

'Well if it's not Jesus-Smythe's skull,' said Duncan, puzzled. 'Whose skull is it?'

They'd been planning this for years. They were ruthless. They'd kill to get what they wanted. And I'll admit, I'm no expert on skulls, but from the way it had bounced along the floor and taken those pins out I could tell it had a particularly dense forehead and I knew a man like that, even if there was no pork-pie hat attached.

'It's Jimmy's.' I looked across at Duncan. 'It's Jimmy Strongbow's skull.'

Duncan gasped and looked around the room in horror. His eyes sprinted from pirate to pirate, to their cutlasses, to their pistols, to the skull and the cat who was playing with it like a ball of yarn.

'This is serious!' he cried. 'Parley! Parley!'

And he would have carried on like that had Sinbad not silenced him with a right hook that sent him crumpling to the floor.

'This would never happen in New Zealand,' mumbled Duncan, before slipping somewhat overdramatically into unconsciousness.

- 88 -

A GUEST

'Why kill Jimmy?' I said. 'He was your friend, wasn't he?'

Jaggers studied me. There was a long silence. I took that as a good sign. He was considering my question. That meant he was listening to me. And from experience when people listen to you, you can turn them around.

'I wonder what your skull looks like, Oscar.'

'Now, wait a sec! We can sort this out.'

Jaggers shook his head. 'Over thirty years of planning has gone into tonight, you really think you can persuade me to stop?'

'I reckon it's worth a punt.'

In truth, the thought of trying to talk round the country's shrewdest lawyer was a dead rubber unless the subject veered towards *Welsh Blaxploitation* cinema.

Jaggers threw his arms wide. 'Oscar, this crew are the most loyal bunch of seadogs to ever sail the seas and yet I persuaded them to kill their own captain and appoint me as their leader in under three minutes. Can your CV boast as impressive a turn of minds?'

'The other day I persuaded a Polish bloke to buy *The Three Amigos,* saying it was based on a Jane Austen novel.'

Jaggers raised an eyebrow. 'Impressive, but it hardly compares to the masterstroke I played to save my life.'

'But why involve Casper Macvittee?' I asked. 'And why all the graffiti?'

But Jaggers didn't answer, he was distracted by a pirate with an eye-patch who'd come rushing up the spiral staircase.

'We've the last one, Cap'n!'

Jaggers smiled. 'Very good, Number Thirty-Six. Then everything is in place. Bring them up.'

Duncan stirred. First his outstretched boots twitched a little. Then his hooter drew a massive intake of air. Next thing I know he's sitting bolt upright, fresh as a morning lark.

'I know that smell!' He chimed.

And it was a hell of a smell. The room filled with a musky scent that burnt the nostrils, like a mix of urinal cakes and bad perfume.

'What the bloody hell is that?' I said.

As if in answer two pirates appeared, leading a prisoner up the stairs. Muffled groans and protests came from the bag over her head as she struggled with her captors, which probably would have earned a slap or two from Sinbad or one of his goons had they not been distracted by her outfit. It was a feeble slip of zebra print. Her gigantic fleshy orbs silenced the room as they swung back and forth like a Wimbledon rally. Even the fire stopped crackling and had a perv. It took Duncan a good few seconds before he could gain enough composure to call out her name.

'Tallulah!'

But before he could say any more he was silenced by a punch to the face from Sinbad, who then checked his breath and lurched towards the new prisoner, yanking the bag off her head. He grinned, flashing some horrible pointy teeth. 'Allo, my pretty.'

Stratford's number one prozzer screamed through her gag and tried to wrestle free. Everything that was womanly jiggled a bit. The pirates approved with a resounding 'Cor!'

Sinbad pressed his face close to hers and growled.

'Leave her alone,' said Duncan.

'Or what?' said Sinbad.

'Or...' Duncan stalled. He looked about the room for some inspiration. 'Or...or...I dunno...'

'Bloody hell, Duncan,' I said. 'Is that the best you can do? How many films have you seen?'

'Sam Neill doesn't do insults.'

'Stuff Sam Neill,' I said. 'What would Arnie say? What would Bond say?'

Sinbad grinned. 'Yeah land-lubber, what you go going to do to me?' He pressed his ugly face close to Tallulah and started licking her cheek.

Duncan's eyes fixed with a steely determination. 'I will have my vengeance...in this life or the next.'

The pirates fell about laughing.

'Ooooh,' said Sinbad, feigning fear. 'I'm shaking. I'm shaking.'

'I'd be bricking it if I were you,' I said. 'He believes in that reincarnation stuff.'

Sinbad snorted and hung out his tongue to give Tallulah's face another lick. She replied by jiggling a bit and swinging a mighty fine bronzed leg straight into his sea biscuits.

Sinbad moaned and bent double. '*Ooof*...Why you little—'

'Enough!' barked Jaggers.

Tallulah's eyes shout round the room looking for who had spoken and when she caught sight of the man in the chair she screamed through her gag for all she was worth. To be honest, I jumped too, as Jaggers was now wearing a mask. It was made of a dark wood and had a face engraved on it that looked a bit like Mr Punch, y'know from those crappy puppet shows you see as a kid. The mask was roughly finished. Around the crown were twigs and leaves. The hooked nose pointed out at us and the mouth was curved into a sneer. I could see two cold eyes peering out from behind two narrow slits in the bark.

Jaggers's voice became more screechy. 'Now, you will now learn the power of the Grail and do our bidding.'

- 89 -

THE POWER

Tallulah gave a pitying cry as Jaggers rose from his seat. He looked proper eerie, like some sort of devil. He muttered to himself as he approached, half crouching, his thin legs taking slow deliberate steps, the glow from the fire playing across his mask.

I'll admit, I was having trouble with reality at this point, but God knows what Tallulah made of it all. As far as I knew she hadn't had the convenient backstory me and Duncan had got. All she probably knew was that she'd been bundled by some blokes dressed as pirates and taken back to their lair to find me and Duncan tied up, me in an "Italian Stallion" dressing gown and a figure with a tree stump on his head prancing about menacingly. But, I guess as a brass she'd had weirder nights and clients.

Jaggers drew up to Tallulah, careful to keep enough distance to avoid having one of her legs strike him in the plums. He closed his fist and held it in front of her face. I could see a gold ring on his finger that held a red gem the size of a potato. I couldn't tell if it was the light from the fire or not, but the gem looked like it was glowing. Not inside, but radiating a sort of light around it. Thinking I was just seeing things due to nicotine withdrawal I did a double-take, but there was no denying it: a red mist was building up. Jaggers continued his muttering as he waved the ring in front of her eyes.

Suddenly, red light shot out of the ring. Not like a laser or anything, more like a headlamp, and Tallulah was bathed in it. Her body slumped as the light hit her and then she rose, slowly, as if on strings. She moved her hips seductively, craned her neck as if in ecstasy, pursed her lips, even groaned a bit. I swear I could hear music, very faint, coming out of the ring. High spooky notes, like a music box, underpinned by the 'cors' of the pirates who seemed to go a bundle on this floorshow.

As suddenly as it had started the red light ended and Tallulah's head rolled back.

Jaggers clicked his fingers. 'Her eyes.'

Sinbad pushed her head forward. Duncan and I jumped. Tallulah's tongue was hanging out, and her eyes were rolling up and down and left and right like some messed-up compass.

'What did you do to her?' yelled Duncan.

Jaggers stepped back, and stroked his ring. 'You doubt the Grail. You doubt its power. This…' he held the ring aloft, '…is but one lowly spec of dirt in comparison to what the Grail can do.'

'I'm not scared of your joke shop ring,' I lied. Things were getting increasingly weird. Weirder than I'd banked on at the start of this novel. I checked back in my head. The bright red light I'd seen pulsing behind the door in the sauna that night. It had to be this ring, hadn't it? Jaggers and his crew were putting people into trances.

Putting people into trances?

Yeah, that's what I thought. Bit far-fetched, innit? I was starting to sound like Duncan.

'Duncan,' I whispered. 'Can a crystal do that?'

A stupid question. After all, he believed animals can talk, what answer was I going to get other than: 'Oh, yeah.'

'Of course,' grinned Jaggers. 'The chest we found on that invisible island was full of more than just parchments and papers. We found the ring of King Arthur himself. The ring that had the power to unite the warring counties of Albion and form England.'

'One ring to rule them all,' I said, 'blah blah blah, heard that one before...'

Jaggers stormed close and looked down at me, pressing the bark of his mask against my face. 'Oh how I'll enjoy killing you, Oscar. You may have only moved to this area six months ago, but for me your presence has felt like a tortured life-time. How deluded you are in your self-perception, seeing yourself as a world-wise sceptic. How you mock others like your friend Duncan when you yourself know nothing of the planet you live on. How I've suffered hearing your ill-informed opinions often couched in the deluded realities of the movies you watch.' He pushed the mask hard against my face, butting me. 'Just before you die, you will see that you know nothing. Indeed, even now I can see in your eyes you've not pieced everything together, and that delights me. Your death will be the most delicious.'

'Ya mum,' I replied. A poor reply. But I couldn't think of anything to say. Sinbad slapped me for it. I should've known insulting a sailor's mum was a major no-no. After all, they're always depicted with tattoos on their arms declaring their undying love for their old dears.

Jaggers stepped across to Duncan. 'Hold his head!'

Sinbad did as instructed and put Duncan in some sort of half-nelson.

'It won't work,' drawled Duncan. 'I know about crystals. I know how to fend off their powers.'

'Yeah, Duncan knows all the tricks,' I blagged. 'He never goes anywhere without lucky heather in his pants. Tell them what you're going to do.'

'I'm going to close my eyes,' drawled Duncan. And he did. Smiling serenely.

'What!?' I cried. 'Is that it?'

'How clever you Kiwis are,' purred Jaggers. 'You've outwitted me.' He gave Sinbad a nod, who in turn gave Duncan a punch in the gut. His eyes shot open in shock, right into the path of the ring. The red light swallowed him.

'Duncan!' I cried, but it was too late.

Jaggers turned the evil grin of his mask towards me. 'And now for you, Oscar.'

'This is a bit stupid,' I said. 'You'll knock me out and then what? When I wake up I'll remember everything. In fact I don't know why you've told us any of this.'

'Fool,' said Jaggers. 'You expect to wake up?'

'Y—'

'Don't answer! It was a rhetorical question! Goodbye, Oscar!' Jaggers pointed his ring up to my face, my vision filled with a deep red light, I could see his lips moving behind his mask. I felt woozy but stayed conscious.

A pirate laughed. 'Cap'n, his glasses have gone dark.'

'Reactor lenses,' said a pirate who was probably good at quiz machines.

The red light continued burning into me, but nothing was happening. I felt a bit silly, so I decided to risk faking it. I rolled my eyes back and hung my mouth open. The red light in the room diminished, I tried to copy the way Duncan and Tallulah were breathing, taking long and heavy breaths. It seemed to do the job as Jaggers began barking orders. 'Take them downstairs for loading.'

'Shouldn't we wait for the Pearly King?' said someone.

'No,' said Jaggers. 'He's waiting for us at the site.'

- 90 -

CARRIED AWAY

A trio of giant pirates stepped out of the shadows. They looked like the sort of pirates that would have to go to a plus-size shop to buy their pantaloons. They scooped the three of us up and carried us over their shoulders. Holding flaming torches in their free hands, they made their way down the spiral staircase, through the trapdoor, and into the darkness of underground tunnels.

If we were being carried to our deaths, there was really bugger all I could do, slung over a bruiser's shoulder with my arms tied behind my back. The best I could do would be to take a bite out of his arse, which judging by the state of the crack that was swinging inches away from my face would probably lead to an even quicker and more unpleasant death.

Death.

Y'know, it's kinda funny the stuff that goes through your head when you think you're about to snuff it. I wonder what those blokes on death row think about? Things they never did? Things they shouldn't have done? Or do they spend all their time thinking about their last meal? I know what I'd order as my last meal. A salad made from flowers of the Amazonian jungle and a bottle of Coke from 1923 chilled with Antarctic ice brought from the magnetic South Pole that morning. Yeah, imagine the prison chef trying to round that lot up before they put you in the chair. Should put the stay of execution off at least a month, I reckon.

Anyway, I wasn't thinking of my last meal as I was carried down those tunnels. I was thinking about all the films I'd never got round to watching. And what, if I was given the chance, would I watch as my final film? Would I want to go out on a comedy? A thriller? A short? Or repent and go out on a Sam Neill? I can't explain it but for some reason, I felt right then I wanted to watch something with Chevy Chase. A *National Lampoon's* or something. Anything that would lighten my mood. Thinking about it now I can see the brain is a strange beast under pressure.

As we were carried deeper underground the sound of running water grew louder. The tunnel suddenly opened out into a large grey chamber lit with a dozen or so flaming torches. From my upside-down view I could see that we were on some sort of stone dockside, with a dirty green underground river running past.

The pirates dumped us by some large wooden crates. They exchanged words and then left. I didn't hear what was said, so I waited a good couple of minutes before jumping to my feet and kicking Duncan. 'C'mon, let's go!'

But he didn't respond.

I knelt down and looked at him. His hair was a tangled brown mess. Nothing new there. But his eyes were completely glazed, rolling around like a washing machine. His tongue was hanging out; an impressive and somewhat disgusting trail of drool hung off his chin. I'm no medic, but he looked out for the count. I wondered what the hell Jaggers had done to him. I looked across at Tallulah. She looked much the same, save for a far more impressive set of tits. But given the circumstances I didn't pay them too much attention.

I looked at the tunnel and toyed with the idea of making a break for it. But which way to go? It was a maze. I was sure whatever way I went, I'd soon run into the pirates.

I needed to think of a plan. I needed a fag.

Nothing motivates a smoker like the promise of a fag. If you're desperate enough, you'll do anything to get one. And when I discovered that with my hands tied behind me I couldn't reach into my pocket and spark up – well – I went kind of mental.

I stormed over to the crates and began looking for something sharp. Each crate was about 4ft deep and as long as a car. There had to be something I could use. Who knows, maybe I'd find a samurai sword. Or a mini-gun. Or at least a pair of shoes. But no, there was only fruit. Bananas. Apples. Oranges. All your five-a-day.

I swore and kicked the crate.

Something moved.

I looked up to see a rat on the crate edge, stood on it's hind legs, looking at me.

'What you bogging at, eh?' I said, still angry.

The rat rubbed it's face in reply and turned it's attention to an apple. It's teeth gnawed at the skin, making a horrible scratching noise.

An idea hit me.

'Hey,' I said. 'You're hungry? You want to eat some rope?'

The rat ignored me.

'Hey,' I said moving closer. 'I've got some rope here, yum yum.'

I tried to raise my arms into the crate for him to have a better look. Spooked, the rat bolted out of the crate and across the dock.

'Hey, come back!'

I chased him to a crate in a darkened corner. I went up to it, looked inside, and screamed. It was full of skulls, hundreds of them. The rat stood on top of one looking at me before turning his tail and disappearing down an eye-socket.

'You git!'

I'd never find him. It was too dark. If only I had more light.

More light!

I raced back to a flaming torch, and using my teeth, prised it from the wall. It fell to the floor with a thud. I was just working out how I was going to pick it up with my hands tied behind my back when I realised I was being a total prat.

Why was I chasing a rodent to gnaw my ropes? Why couldn't I just burn them off?

I set to work. It took a few attempts and a few burnt fingers, but eventually I got the ropes off. In triumph, I fished out a cigarette from my dressing gown and used the torch to light it. That first drag never felt so good.

With hands free, I carried the torch over to the crate of skulls for a closer look. I picked one up and examined it. It was light and made of plastic. I may have failed biology at school, but even I knew that wasn't right. In fact they looked like Halloween items you'd get from a pound shop.

I scratched my head and began pondering why the pirates needed so many plastic skulls, before giving up, deciding that finding a weapon was a better use of my time.

I moved to another crate. I wish I hadn't. It was filled with more of my films. My prized Japanese limited edition laserdisc of *The Running Man* peeked out beneath a sea of caseless Warner Brothers videos. It broke my heart. I'd been putting my film collection together since I was six.

I threw my fag to one side and reached in. I brushed aside the top layer of films to see what was underneath. My hand pressed against something soft and fleshy. I grimaced and felt deeper. I hoped to God I wasn't going to find a corpse. The last thing I'd want to find would be Jimmy's decapitated body corroding all my tapes. I pulled my hand out to find I was gripping a rat. A very dead rat. Its eyes were closed, its body arched in pain. I noticed it had something stuck to the very end of its tail – a piece of black and yellow tape.

- 91 -

CRATES

I put the flaming torch to one side and used both hands to dig deep. I found more dead things: rats, cockroaches – even a pigeon. But I also found the edge of a cardboard box. I prised it free and examined it.

I stared at the biohazard symbol. Next to it was a torn sticker that said "hazardous materials...this way up". Unless the pirates had chemical weapons of their own, this was definitely the box the Junior Anthrax had come in.

I scratched my chin and had a think. If the pirates had stolen all my tapes and DVDs, had they stolen the poison too? There was only one way to find out.

I rooted through the crate. I don't know why. I guess I thought a chemical weapon might make a good bargaining tool. I dug deep, leaning further and further in, standing on tiptoes to try and reach the middle when all of a sudden I felt my balance go and I fell into the crate face first. My glasses came off and bounced off somewhere. I swore and groped about for them, almost missing the movement in the corner of my eye.

I looked up. Lights were coming down the tunnel.

- 92 -

DISCOVERY

I froze. I didn't know what to do. There was no time to get out of the crate, so in panic I dived under the videos for cover. My body squirmed at the feel of dead rats and other dead things around me.

I couldn't hear much over the gurgle of the river, but I figured once the pirates realised I was missing they'd start hollering and shouting and firing their pistols and all that. My only hope was that they'd take off up the river or back up the tunnel in search of me. Do anything but look in the crates.

Careful not to make noise, I reached out with hands and carefully explored the crate. My fingers wrapped round what felt like a giant oozing rat. Throwing that in a pirate's face seemed as good a defence as any. I clutched it tight, held my breath and listened.

'This be the lot?' said a voice.

'Y'arrgh,' came a reply. 'One more crate to bring down and then Cap'n says we be good for taking all this to the site.'

There was a thump as something large was dumped on the dockside.

'Me and my family have been in pirating for nearly three hundred years,' said a voice. 'I never thought we'd see the day.'

'Think of the booty,' said one.

'Think of the women,' said another.

They laughed and walked off.

I gave it a minute or two before standing up. I spat and brushed myself down. My glasses fell off my dressing gown. Stupid things must have got stuck to me somehow. I picked them up and put them back on my face. I went to step forward and climb out of the crate when my foot struck something cold and metallic. I gave it a curious poke with my big toe before bending down to have a rummage. My hand clasped round a cool cylinder. I pulled it out. And there it was, in my hand, my Junior Anthrax, seals still intact.

I grinned.

I didn't know what I would do with it yet, but just having it felt good. Which was somewhat ironic since I'd been trying so hard to get rid of it. None of that mattered now though. Things had changed. The FBI be damned. This was now clearly a situation that warranted weapons-grade chemicals – the fate of the world was at stake. And more importantly, so was my life.

I pocketed the Junior Anthrax and climbed out of the crate. I extended my foot and reached for the floor, but instead of flat stone, it met something round and soft. My foot slipped and I lost balance and fell. I looked back to see that I'd fallen over a body. But not just any body. I'd fallen over the body of my landlord, Jimmy Strongbow, complete with head, and pork-pie hat.

'Jimmy!' I grabbed him. 'Jimmy, wake up!' but it was no use. His eyes were all glazed and rolling about the same as the others.

- 93 -

DOCKSIDE ORDERS

It looked like Jimmy needed urgent medical attention, so I gave it to him. I slapped him hard across the face. But it had no affect. It must have taken me ten or more slaps to realise that.

I stopped for a breather and glanced across at Duncan and Tallulah. They were both dead to the world, and it was starting to freak me out. I don't go a bundle on zombie films. But I'm sure I'd seen a few that had scenes like this. I decided not to turn my back on any of them in case they tried to pounce and eat my flesh, which, given all the weird stuff that had happened in the last twenty-four hours, didn't seem as unlikely as perhaps it should.

I tried to think of some alternative wake-up methods. I went to the edge of the dock, scooped up some water and threw it in Jimmy's face.

Nothing.

On impulse I decided to steal his pork-pie hat. He was so attached to the thing, I expected him to lunge at me instinctively, but there was no response. Disappointed, I squashed it back on his head.

I tried another approach. 'Jimmy, I'm moving out.' It was a stupid thing to say. What did he care if I lived there or not? There was only one thing he really cared about. 'Jimmy, I want to buy your penthouse. For five times the going rate. You've got ten seconds to accept.'

I waited for him to explode into life with a round of "lovely-ol'-job-cor-blimey-guvnor-love-a-duck" Cockney slang and shake my arm into submission over the deal. But he just sat there.

I stood up and scratched my head. Whatever mumbo-jumbo was in Jaggers's ring it was powerful stuff alright. I looked down at Jimmy. I wondered if he knew the uproar his disappearance had caused over the last twenty-four hours? And it had been uproar. Seemingly every cheeky chappy Cockney in a twenty-mile radius had heeded the call of The Blue Eel to help orchestrate a plan to find him, which was seemingly taken too literally as the best idea put forward was a twenty-four-hour pub sing-along. But, whatever way you wanted to slice it, people had turned out in force to find Jimmy Strongbow. This scheming, pork-pie hat-wearing, landlord was loved by many. And they made their feelings pretty clear when they threw me out of the pub and into the street.

I still couldn't believe they thought I was somehow responsible for him being missing. Some even wanted to kill me over it, if you believed Duncan. I didn't know if such a thing as a Chapwa existed, but I didn't really want to find out. And I didn't want to spend the rest of my life looking over my shoulder, waiting for a Pearly bullet to take me out. If I had any chance of clearing my name it would be to get Jimmy out of here and back to The Eel in one piece, preferably detranced.

I decided to give him another slap, this time favouring a back-hand, but there was no change. I didn't get chance to try any other combinations as the pirates were on their way back. I saw lights coming down the tunnel and quickly returned to my original place beside Duncan. Over the flow of the river I could hear footsteps growing louder. At the last minute I realised I had my hands out in front of me. I quickly fed them behind myself and started rolling my eyes about and drooling just like the others.

- 94 -

PIRATE CARGO

Sinbad strutted onto the dockside, barking orders at three other large pirates. I thought pirates might chat in a normal voice when nobody was listening, that their lingo was just for tourists, but straight up, when amongst themselves they still talk in that overly dramatic "Y'arrgh, Jim lad" voice. Which was a bit of a letdown, if I'm honest. I was hoping to discover they weren't pirates at all and we're perhaps all junior barristers from Battersea or something. It would've made them far less formidable and boosted my feeling of being able to beat them in a fight. But no, these seadogs seemed to be of the saltiest, meanest kind.

'You mangy bunch of tars!' barked Sinbad. 'You know the Cap'n's orders. Take the booty to the ship and get her ready to sail.'

'Splice the mainbrace?' enquired a pirate.

'Y'arrgh, three sheets to the wind, splice the mainbrace, cut the jib, buff the crow's nest and keelhaul Davy Jones, yo-ho-ho and a bottle of rum.' I can't remember exactly what Sinbad said, but it was something along those lines. It was all too nautical to follow. However, I did pick up that the pirate wearing the pink bandana wasn't happy.

'Why can't I help with the drilling?' he asked.

'Quit your moaning,' barked Sinbad. 'You have your orders. Now get loading.'

The pirates went over to the crates and threw back some tarpaulin to reveal a wooden row boat. They set it in the water with a splash. They then set to work emptying the crates. Items crashed and smashed as they were tossed into the boat. The pirates didn't seem to care. I wondered if they'd worked previously for the Post Office. Finally, we four "zombies" were picked up.

'Stop!' cried Sinbad. 'Cut their ropes. We need their hands free on the site.'

The pirates set to work.

'Y'arrgh!' cried a pirate, examining my hands. 'This ones ropes are already untied.'

I gulped.

'Y'arrgh!' cried Sinbad. 'That'll be Work Experience. He never ties a good knot. Get 'em on board!'

And with that we were tossed like dolls onto the mound of booty.

The boat cast off and Sinbad began rowing down the tunnel. The Pink Bandana held a torch out in front of the bow. The two remaining pirates on the dock faded away as we moved into the darkness. All I could hear was the slap of the oars on the water and the chat between Sinbad and his shipmate.

'Is it true, what the Cap'n said?' asked the Pink Bandana.

'What be true?' said Sinbad.

'The story about how we ambushed him on that island.'

'Course it's true!'

'But, did it really happen like that?'

'Aye!' cried Sinbad. 'Don't ye remember?'

The Pink Bandana shook his head. 'No, not really. I don't remember Jesus-Smythe or the ambush. In fact, I don't really remember the Caribbean. All I got in my head is London.'

'Y'arrgh! You've been on land too long. It's turned your mind to rot.'

'Maybe,' he paused. 'It's just…'

'What?'

'It's just…'

'Spit it out!'

'It's just…the more the Cap'n talks about the Caribbean, the less it seems real.'

Sinbad stopped rowing. 'Careful what you be saying. You're not calling the Cap'n a liar, are ye?'

'No.'

'Good…cos, that's mutiny if you is! And you know what happens then! The cat will kill you.'

'It's not mutiny!' said the Pink Bandana, looking about nervously. 'I just…can't remembering things.'

'You remember that tomorrow we're gonna be rich?' asked Sinbad.

'Y'arrgh.'

'Good, that's all you need to remember.' Sinbad resumed rowing.

'But how did it happen?'

'What?' asked Sinbad. 'The ambush?'

'Y'arrgh.'

'Well, it…' Sinbad went silent. 'Ah, I can't remember right now.'

'You can't remember any of it?'

'It was a long time ago. It happened like the Cap'n says it did.'

'But you can't remember?'

'Y'arrgh! What's all these questions? As Cap'n says – I ain't paid to think.'

'I think it's odd how nobody can remember.'

'Y'arrgh! Enough noise! Keep a look out there.'

We rowed on in the darkness. I looked down at Duncan. If this was to be the end of his life, then fate had been kind to him. Owing to Sinbad's slapdash cargo loading techniques, Duncan's body found itself tossed on top of Tallulah. Her body arched back over a chest, eyes rolling around and tongue hanging out, whilst Duncan's face was pressed deep into her ample bosom, his nose burrowed between her two enormous norks that heaved and jiggled with her long deep breaths. If we were to die I hoped he could take that memory into the next life.

By contrast, I had Jimmy Strongbow bent over in front of me with his builder's bum pointing up at the sky. I was amazed that, even being turned nearly upside down as he was, he still managed to keep that pork-pie hat on his head.

'I'm worried my memory loss will affect my appraisal next month,' said the Pink Bandana.

'Quit your yapping,' snarled Sinbad.

'It's okay for you. You're his favourite. Always have been. Why'd he send me down here with you? I want to be helping with the drilling.'

Sinbad snorted. 'What would ye rather be? A driller? Or a killer?'

'Killer!' said the Pink Bandana with pride.

'Y'arrgh! And what we be doing with these bodies?'

'Killin' 'em!'

'Y'arrgh!' cried Sinbad.

'Y'arrgh!' cried the Pink Bandana.

I looked back down at Duncan. Something wasn't right. Somehow his head seemed to be pressing deeper into Tallulah's rack. In fact, as I stared at him I could swear he was deliberately trying to burrow into her cleavage. I gave him a kick. In the flame light, two happy eyes flicked up over a round bosom and met mine. Somehow that Kiwi numpty had regained consciousness.

You okay? I mouthed.

Duncan nodded enthusiastically, which made Tallulah's boobs give a seismic jiggle. Oh, he was more than okay, I bet. Jaggers's ring clearly hadn't lobotomised him. In fact, given the result he'd had I wouldn't have been surprised if he asked Jaggers to juice him up again. Who knows, maybe he'd wake up next time and find himself on third base.

Duncan was still nodding his head unnecessarily, the wobbly waves of her breasts breaking against his face, and would have continued to do so had I not mouthed for him to stop. I shook my head a little to suggest he shouldn't attempt any Chuck Norris-style breakout just yet. Not that I think I could have persuaded him to do so for all the Sam Neill DVDs on Amazon. He seemed quite content where he was. I wondered how he'd woken up, but before I could give it too much thought, the Pink Bandana cried out. *'LAND AHOY!'*

Sinbad drew up his oars and we drifted a short way before a wall brought us to an abrupt stop. Duncan gave a small groan as the stop rippled through Tallulah's pillows.

Sinbad looked down at us. 'You hear that?'

'Hear what?' said the Pink Bandana.

Sinbad paused for a moment and listened.

'You're hearing things.' The Pink Bandana stepped out of the boat onto a ledge. Beyond him I could see a craggy tunnel, cut roughly into the rock.

- 95 -

THE CAVERN

The Pink Bandana tied the boat safe. 'Prisoners first?'

'Y'arrgh,' replied Sinbad.

'Y'arrgh!'

The Pink Bandana was so large he could scoop Duncan and I under each one of his briny arms, whilst Sinbad managed to take Jimmy and Tallulah in a sort of fireman's lift. Despite being captive I was so impressed with their physical strength I wondered whether their pirate ship had a gym of some kind or whether they trained *Rocky IV* style, bench-pressing anchors, pushing capstans and curling rigging. I mean, these blokes were in good shape. Although I suppose they'd spent so many years hanging about waiting for the treasure they had little to do but pump iron. I thought if they ever made this into a film, there'd have to be some pirate workout spin-off DVD. It seemed that with every new pirate I met my hopes of trying to fight them went that little bit further down the toilet.

As we were carried along the tunnel I noticed we were following a blue line spray painted on the floor. Despite the stone being uneven, the line remained dead straight. There were markings every few metres, numbers with small circles after them, like someone was measuring degrees or something. Ahead there was mechanical noise. The tunnel sloped upwards and we followed the line for a few hundred metres before we burst out into bright light.

We found ourselves in a cavern. It was huge and full of activity. There were a dozen or so telegraph poles set up and scores of crates spread about. Pirates hurried between them, carrying shovels and pushing wheelbarrows filled with rock. They seemed to be going back and forth from a large fireplace at the far end. The blue line on the floor seemed to run directly into it.

'Where's the Pearly King?' cried Sinbad.

A pirate by the fireplace turned round. He had a yellow hard-hat on over his tri-corn hat. 'Put them over the back!' he shouted.

'Where's the Pearly King?' repeated Sinbad, but the hard-hat had turned his attention back to the fireplace, looking up into the shaft at the falling rubble. 'Y'arrgh.' Sinbad threw Tallulah and Jimmy on top of a nearby crate. 'Let's be leaving them here for a while. Cap'n can decide later where he wants 'em.'

The Pink Bandana nodded and threw me and Duncan onto a different crate. I wasn't happy with the landing, not because it hurt, but because I ended up spooning Duncan.

'What's going on?' he said.

'Sssh!' I hissed. 'Play zombie.'

I took a closer look at the cavern. It didn't like what I saw. What I'd first thought were telegraph poles were in fact totem poles. Each one engraved with a grinning Mr Punch face, the hooked noses sticking out. There were skulls too, plastic ones, hanging up on the walls like Christmas decorations. The whole place was lit by flaming torches, which seemed a bad idea, considering the wooden crates were clearly marked with the letters: TNT. One crate was open. I could see red sticks of dynamite with fuses coming out. It looked like the stuff from cartoons.

'What's going on?' repeated Duncan. 'What are they doing?'

I looked over at the pirates. They were by the fireplace. I re-examined the cavern. The way we had entered seemed to be the only way out.

'Oscar.'

'Sssh...I'm thinking.'

'But what's happening?' he whispered. 'Is this a conspiracy?'

'Nevermind that. Just wait for my signal.'

'Signal?'

'Yeah,' I said, feeling the weight of the Junior Anthrax in my dressing gown pocket. 'We're going to break out of here.'

I was about to tell Duncan the plan when the drilling stopped. All that could be heard was the squeaky sound of wheelbarrow wheels and pirates murmuring shanties as they worked. Sinbad was patting the pirate with the hardhat on the back. He seemed pleased about something.

There then came a sharp nautical whistle. 'Cap'n's coming!'

Jaggers suddenly emerged from the tunnel, his black legal cape billowing behind him. Above the mouth of the tunnel I noticed some graffiti. In large red letters were the words: VIVA CASPER!

- 96 -

SPEECH

Standing amongst the crates, Jaggers sucked thoughtfully on his cigarette holder as his cold droopy eyes examined the cavern. 'Number 2.'

Sinbad hurried over. 'Yes, Cap'n?'

'Is everything on schedule?'

'Y'arrgh! Just a few feet be left.'

Jaggers grinned, he withdrew his cigarette holder and tapped ash on the floor, seemingly not bothered by the fact he was surrounded by several tons of TNT. 'Very good, have the men gather round.'

Sinbad put his fingers to his mouth and gave a whistle. Everyone stopped and looked up. 'Cap'n wants a few words!'

The pirates downed their tools and slowly assembled around Jaggers who had climbed on top of a crate to address his crew. I expected a rousing speech, but his tone remained chillingly even. He was on the cusp of pulling off the greatest caper the world had ever known and yet he was cooler than a snowman's cool bits.

'I'm informed that we are merely feet away from completing the shaft, which means that after nearly thirty years of toil, we'll finally set the treasure free.'

'Y'arrgh!' cried the pirates, a few of them tossed their hats in the air like they'd graduated from Pirate University or something.

'I'm proud of you,' said Jaggers, his thin lips twisting back into a smile. 'All of you.'

'Even me?' asked the Pink Bandana.

'Even you, you pitiful excuse for a seadog.'

The pirates cracked up at this good-natured mocking, although the Pink Bandana did mumble something into his chest about constantly being the butt of the joke, and taking it up with his union.

'Now, I've warned you about the treasure,' said Jaggers. 'We know what will happen when we move her.'

'All hell will break loose!' called a pirate.

'The walls will crack!' said another.

'Earthquakes! Eruptions! Tempests!' cried a pirate with what I hoped was an overactive imagination.

'Aye,' said Jaggers solemnly. 'She sits on a nexus of powerful ley-lines,' he crossed his thin arms over his head to illustrate the point. 'One of which being the Greenwich meridian, the most powerful ley-line of them all.'

The pirates crossed themselves at this. Jaggers continued. 'We know that moving her to port or starboard will cause catastrophe, gang and aft the same. Which leaves us two directions to take her in. Up or down. When the drilling is finished we'll be winching her directly up out of the hole, two hundred feet to the surface, without changing her longitude or latitude a single degree,' Jaggers's face adopted a grave look, 'For if she lists Davy Jones will be the least of our worries, for fire, brimstone and hell itself will open up and take us.'

The pirates crossed themselves repeatedly.

'Now...' Jaggers fixed a smile. '...am I a good Captain?'

The pirates looked at each other, sensing a trick question. 'Y'arrgh,' they mumbled.

'Have I always done right by you?'

'Y'arrgh.'

'Been the best Captain you ever had?'

'Y'arrgh!' they cried, confidence growing.

'Well, they say a Captain should go down with his ship. And whilst this cavern is further from the sea than we'd like, it could be here that we all go down. I don't want to lose any men, so I want you, all of you, to go up the shaft first. Get topside and then winch me up with the treasure, and under the cover of night we'll escape together.'

'But Cap'n,' said Sinbad concerned. 'You could be killed.'

'Aye,' Jaggers patted Sinbad's shoulder, 'but it's the right thing to do. I want my crew out of harm's way before we try and bring the booty to the surface.'

'Oh, Cap'n,' said Sinbad. The other pirates looked tearful. They were a stupid bunch. I knew Jaggers's game. As soon as they were topside he was going to bugger off back through the tunnels. All this talk of hell breaking open and tempests and earthquakes was just to scare them off. It was a blatant stitch-up. Even Duncan could see it.

'Seems legit,' he whispered.

'But me hearties,' continued Jaggers. 'We all know what happens next. Before we complete the drilling...'

'...we must prepare for the killing!' chimed the pirates in unison.

I didn't like the sound of that. Not at all.

Jaggers clicked his fingers. A large pirate bent down behind a crate and came up holding two bodies, both gagged and blindfolded. One was a man with a beard so huge it looked like he was hiding behind a privet hedge. He was dirty and dishevelled, his skin a horrible white colour. I figured this was Casper Macvittee. I didn't know what he was supposed to look like, but I guessed he'd seen better days.

However, the other prisoner was much easier to identify, for whilst many people are portly with round faces like the moon, few of them go about wearing a black suit covered in a sea of shiny buttons.

- 97 -

CALL ME A MONKEY'S UNCLE

Well, call me a monkey's uncle...the Pearly King wasn't behind everything after all! I never was good at whodunnits.

- 98 -

THE PEARLY KING

Blindfolded, Casper and the Pearly King were marched across the cavern. Casper walked without protest but the Pearly wrestled with his captors for all he was worth.

Jaggers's thin lips twisted into a grin as they approached. He slipped on his weird tree stump-style helmet as the prisoners were set on their knees before him.

A pirate ripped off Casper's gag. 'We beat them, didn't we Captain!' he cried. 'The treasure is ours! The Olympic spies never caught us.'

'Yes!' replied Jaggers, his voice screechy and hysterical. The mask made him a different person. 'Dear Casper, how we admire you. You've made the ultimate sacrifice, shielding your eyes for an entire year, blocking out the world to prepare your soul, to make it pure enough to receive the Grail. Your name will go down in history. Are you ready?'

'I'm ready, Cap'n!' cried Casper. 'I've got an NVQ. None of your crew are qualified for this…it has to be me, the expert. I'll tell you when it's safe, I will.'

'Good,' purred Jaggers, stroking his ring. 'In a moment we'll take off the blindfold. You know what you have to do?'

'Yup!' chimed Casper. 'I read the parchment. Look forward and ye who is pure of soul shall receive the light, the truth, the way.'

Jaggers gave a nod. Casper's blindfold was whipped off and in a flash there was red light. Casper screamed and went limp. A burly pirate picked him up and threw him onto a nearby crate.

Jaggers clapped his hands excitedly. 'Now, for the final piece of the puzzle.' The command given, the Pearly King's blindfold was taken off. Kneeling amongst a circle of pirates he blinked around him in panic, shooting worried eyes at the burly sword-waving mob surrounding him. His eyes fell on the tall slender character standing on a crate, wearing a tree stump for a helmet. Instinctively, sensing something bad, the Pearly King tried to break free, but it was no good.

'What's your game?' he cried, as his gag was ripped off. 'I always knew you were a wrong'un.'

I smiled. It was good to hear the Pearly King have a pop at someone else for a change.

'You want to let me go, you Mockney git!'

Mockney?

'I'm telling you,' continued the Pearly King. 'I've already got a Chapwa on you, boy. When the others find you, you'll be pie and mash before sun up. You really don't know what you're messing with, Oscar.'

Oscar?

I looked at the Pearly King, but he wasn't looking in my direction, he was staring at Jaggers. That Pearly prat thought it was me wearing the mask! How the hell he'd pieced everything together to find me the ringleader I'll never know. The man was a total duffer. But then again, I thought he was bang to rights throughout. It's fair to say that the pair of us wouldn't be up to much at Cluedo.

The Pearly continued slagging me off. Trying to scare me. Or rather, trying to scare the bloke in the tree stump mask he thought was me. I wished I'd shouted out that it was Jaggers. It would've saved so much trouble in the long run. This is why you'll find so many people think I was behind it all. Just goes to show how much faith people round here put in the Pearly King. His word really is gospel, even if he has been a total noddy and got the wrong end of the stick.

But I didn't know what was to come. And so from the ungraceful position of spooning Duncan, I just had to watch helplessly as the red light shined from Jaggers's ring, fading away moments later to leave a zombiefied Pearly King. Eyes and tongue out to lunch.

'And now,' said Jaggers. 'We put them in their places, ready to vanquish them when the drilling is complete.'

'When will that be?' asked a pirate, who I felt was a bit too keen.

Jaggers checked his watch. 'Not long now. Avast ye! Continue drilling!'

'Y'arrgh!' went the pirates and once again the sound of pneumatic drills rang round the cavern. All of a sudden my mouth felt very dry and I got the feeling that, unless I acted fast, I'd soon be witnessing my own closing credits.

- 99 -

ESCAPE PLAN

Duncan turned his head. I could see his lips moving but could hear nothing over the drills. I dipped my head closer.

'What are we going to do?' he shouted.

'I thought about waiting to see if they change their minds.'

'Serious?'

'No!' I hissed. 'Let's get the hell out of here!'

'How?' replied Duncan. 'There's too many of them.'

He was right. I don't know how many men it took to crew a ship, but there was plenty of salty-looking bruisers in the cavern, although I noticed they had all gathered around the fireplace in a sort of scrum, those closest to the shaft used their hands to clear the debris, whilst those at the back stood on tiptoes trying to get a look.

Duncan said something.

'What?'

'We need some ninjas,' he said. 'They fight pirates. They are sworn enemies. They'd get us out of here.'

'No need.'

Duncan brightened. 'Are you a secret ninja?'

'Leave it out.' I pulled the Junior Anthrax out of my dressing gown pocket. 'I've got a plan. You see the pirates are all stood around that fireplace thing? I reckon if we open this and lob it at them we can make a break for it.'

'Will it be safe?'

'How should I know? The instructions never said anything about letting it off in a cavern full of pirates two hundred feet beneath the Olympic site. But if we don't do something soon we're going to be brown bread.'

He nodded. 'And after we escape, we come back?'

'What?'

'With ninjas.'

I ignored him. Once he gets an idea into his head it's hard to let it back out again. A bit like a rain cloud, you've got to suffer a bit and hope that the breeze moves it on eventually.

'What about the others?' asked Duncan.

'We leave them.'

'I'm not leaving Tallulah.'

'Duncan, don't be a prat. We've no chance getting them out of here on our own. Not whilst they are in that weird trance thing.'

'Sam Neill wouldn't leave them.'

'But you're not leaving them,' I said. 'You're going to come back and save them with an army of ninjas.'

'You mean...*we're* going to come back.'

'That's what I said.'

'No, you didn't.' Duncan studied me. 'You're not going to come back are you? You're going to leave them down here to die.'

'No, I'll come back as soon as I find some ninjas,' I lied. 'It just might take a while to round them up.'

'What happened to the British sense of fair play?'

'Duncan, this ain't a game of Kerplunk. Those crazy loons are going to kill us! Now, how good is your aim?'

He was silent. I thought he was ignoring me but then I noticed his chest was rising and falling rapidly. I braced myself for the worst.

'You better not be about to go into a Haka.'

He shook his head. 'Can you smell that?'

'Smell what?' I sniffed. 'Is it good or bad?'

Duncan sniffed again. 'It's faint. It smells of—'

'Don't say ninjas.'

'No, it smells...cold.'

'Cold?' For what it was worth I had a proper snort, but I could smell nothing apart from the stale cavern air and the odd waft of pirate like BO that seemed to have gotten stronger in the last few moments. I looked around us. The flaming torches were flickering.

'There's a breeze!' I hissed. 'They must be nearly done with the drilling. We have to get out now!' I went to pass him the Junior Anthrax. 'Go on, throw it.'

'Why can't you do it?'

It was a good question for which my answers were poor. Firstly, I've never been good at sports. At school I was rubbish at PE. I got a detention once for writing quotes from *The Exorcist* on the desk of the Religious Studies teacher. My punishment was to serve an evening as a ball-boy for the school football team. My throwing the ball back to the players was as accurate as their shooting, and I threw the ball back to them a lot that night. After my performance the head of PE told me even the lowly athletic requirements of a ball-boy were way beyond me. I think I told him that his Mrs was as round as the ball, or words to that effect. Whatever it was I said, I got another detention for it.

And so I learnt that night that I couldn't throw. And it's been something I've steered clear from since. The prospect of trying to throw now with the pressure on was idiocy. I should point out my decision to let Duncan throw it had *nothing* to do with wanting to avoid being collared for throwing an illegal chemical weapon at a group of people in a city suburb. Nothing whatsoever.

'Okay,' said Duncan finally. 'I'll do it.'

'Good man.' I handed him the silver flask. 'Can you throw?'

'Yeah,' he replied. 'I've got good aim. I play darts a lot. On my laptop.' He looked over at the fireplace. The pirates were still preoccupied, the drills busting through rock as the crew brushed rubble away.

'On three,' said Duncan. 'One...'

I glanced at the black tunnel by which we had entered. It was unmanned.

'Two...'

I swallowed. Took a deep breath and prepared to run.

'Three...'

The drilling stopped. But it was too late. The flask of Anthrax was already airborne.

Duncan and I froze as we watched the silver cylinder fly through the quietness of the cavern in a perfect parabolic arc. I'm sure everything went in super slo-mo. The cylinder crashed down on top of a crate full of TNT before bouncing off with a loud metallic *TING*!

Jaggers's head snapped up. 'What was that?'

The rest of the pirates turned and looked about them. Several dampened tings followed as the flask bounced to a stop. I closed my eyes and waited for the pirates to begin cursing, coughing, spluttering and generally panicking as the Junior Anthrax poisoned them.

There was silence.

Silence was good. Perhaps the poison was instant?

There was a noise.

I opened an eye. All the pirates were still standing, looking about them.

'Must've been rubble, Cap'n,' said the pirate with the hard hat.

Jaggers looked suspicious. 'Get it clear! We can't have rubble falling on the treasure, for just one slight movement will cause her to rip London in two. Get on with the drilling!'

And with that the drill started back up.

'Duncan,' I whispered. 'What happened?'

'It must've been a dud.'

'A dud? That stuff pretty much wiped out my cockroaches, unopened!'

'Maybe it only works on insects.'

'Did you open it?'

He looked blank. 'I thought you opened it?'

'Why would I open it? It's a chemical weapon!' I ran my hands down my face. 'I can't believe you threw away our only chance of escape.'

'You wanted me to throw it away.'

'Please,' I buried my head in my hands, 'no more.'

'We can still escape,' said Duncan.

I looked up. 'And how we going to do that, Einstein?'

Duncan shrugged. 'Let's just walk out.'

I glanced about. The pirates were still huddled around the fireplace in a scrum. The flaming torches were now flapping fiercely. I could feel cool air rushing around me. The shaft had to be nearly finished. Walking out wasn't exactly the escape plan I had in mind, but as it might be the only one we got to try, it was worth a punt.

'Okay,' I said. 'Let's go.'

- 100 -

ESCAPE

I got up slowly, keeping a watchful eye on the fireplace. The drilling continued. Pirates were now kneeling, throwing rocks haphazardly over their shoulders.

I turned for the tunnel. The cavern floor was gravely in places. With no shoes on I had to hobble carefully. It wasn't a graceful getaway, but I didn't care. I wasn't looking to win points on style. My life was at stake.

I zigzagged between the totem poles, checking I was safe before breaking for the next one. The blackness of the tunnel drew closer. I was just starting to feel that I might make it when the drilling stopped and Jaggers yelled something that didn't exactly turn me on.

'Seize them!'

'C'mon, Duncan!' I looked back. There was no sign of him. 'Duncan?'

I spotted him on the far side of the cavern, trying to carry Tallulah over his shoulder, but he wasn't strong enough. Pirates quickly surrounded him with their evil grins and swords drawn. They were going to cut him to pieces. 'Go get help!' he cried. 'Get the ninjas!'

I turned and hobbled for the tunnel, boots pounding behind me. I pushed on. I could taste freedom. The black mouth of the tunnel yawned before me. I was going to make it.

But then I saw something. In the darkness ahead there was something shiny. It danced before me in mid-air. I then saw it was connected to an arm. Which was connected to a pirate. He emerged from the shadows with a grin and began swinging his cutlass at me.

I back-peddled. I hit something hard behind me. I turned to find it was a totem pole. I quickly stepped round it and continued back-peddling, keeping my eyes on the approaching pirates. I hit something hard again. I turned in panic and felt the cold rock behind me.

'You're trapped,' said a pirate.

'Surrender,' said another.

I looked around. The pirates advanced. The glow of the flaming torches played across their ugly features. Desperate for a weapon, I turned and lunged for a nearby torch. I pulled it from a totem pole and began to wave it about wildly. 'Stay back!'

The pirates laughed. They reached into their breaches and drew pistols. 'Surrender!'

'No chance.' I held the torch toward a crate of TNT. 'You surrender.'

I expected the pirates to suddenly come over all nervous, maybe a little frightened, but instead they just started laughing. And I mean proper belly-laughing, holding their sides, whooping.

'I mean it,' I said. 'I'll blow us all up.'

'You landlubber ain't got the guts.'

They stepped closer.

In reflex I tossed the flaming torch. I wished my PE teacher could've seen it. It landed square in the box. A fuse caught light with a furious fizzing spark.

I expected to run. But I didn't. I didn't do anything. I just froze in fear. I didn't even say anything meaningful, I just stared at the fuse as it sparked down into nothingness, and waited for the explosion to tear through me.

- 101 -

BANG

There was a bang. Not the cataclysmic bang I was expecting. More a sort of firework bang. It reverberated loudly round the cavern but didn't do any damage.

'Have you quite finished?' asked Jaggers, like I should have better manners when trying to escape.

'What?' I said, totally confused. 'It didn't explode?'

The mob grabbed me roughly by the dressing gown and pulled me towards Jaggers. Two or three pirates attended to the crate. The fuses gave a damp hiss as they extinguished them with the contents of their hip flasks.

Duncan and I were dumped unceremoniously in front of Jaggers.

'I don't get it,' I said. 'Why didn't it explode?'

Jaggers didn't look like he was in a giving answers kind of mood. He fought hard to keep his tone even. 'How did you shake off the trance?'

'We're ninjas,' answered Duncan. 'We've ninja skills.'

The pirates laughed at this.

'Serious,' protested Duncan. 'Our ninja clan will be here any minute to rescue us.'

'My dear boy, forget your ninjas. Not even God, be he a seventh-dan black-belt, could save you now.' Jaggers drew a sword from his robes. The circle of surrounding pirates began to cheer.

'Cap'n,' said Sinbad, aghast. 'What about the plan?'

'This pair seem determined not to fit in with our plans, Number 2.' Jaggers waved his sword at us. 'We should kill them now.'

'But, Cap'n. I thought timing was crucial?'

Jaggers shot his crewmember an angry look. 'I've told you before, Number 2, you're paid from the neck down. Leave the thinking to me.'

'Sorry, Cap'n.'

Jaggers tapped his thin grey lips in thought. 'The problem is...how do you kill a man on land?'

'Tar and feathers!' chimed a pirate.

'Y'arrgh!' cried the others.

'A favourite,' agreed Jaggers. 'But there is not enough time.'

Nor, did I hope, enough feathers. Or tar. But given how resourceful these pirates were I wouldn't put anything past them.

'We can't even make 'em walk the plank,' moaned someone.

'Or keelhaul 'em,' moaned another.

'Why didn't that dynamite go off?' I said.

'Yeah...and why are you wanting to kill us?' added Duncan.

'None of this makes sense,' I said. 'What's really going on?'

Jaggers started laughing. 'Oh, Oscar, can you really not see? Is my plan so perfect that you *still* haven't got a clue?'

'Your plan's not perfect,' I spat. 'In fact from what I can work out it's total cobblers. You're after the treasure, right? So, why not just take that and go? Why bother kidnapping people?'

'My dear Oscar, once we move this treasure, the world will want to find us.'

'But they can't find us if we are dead!' cried a pirate, who I reckon always blurts out punch-lines when someone else is telling a joke.

'Dead?' I said. 'You're going to kill yourselves?'

'What?' said Duncan, suddenly brightening. 'Are you like kamikaze vampire pirates of the undead?'

'You fools,' said Jaggers, coolly. 'Your pitiful little minds couldn't even begin to imagine how to commit the perfect crime. I've been a lawyer for almost forty years and let me tell you that, try as hard as they might, there is only one way for a criminal to commit a crime and maintain his freedom.'

'I get it!' said Duncan, excitedly. 'You're going to hide on the Costa del Sol?'

'No!' bellowed Jaggers. 'Running from the law is a fool's errand. If you are running it is because you are wanted. And if you are wanted it is because the police think you did it. The trick is to make the police think you didn't do it. The trick is to frame someone else. The best person to frame is someone who won't fight back. Who offers a weaker defence of themselves than the dead?' Jaggers straightened with a satisfied grin. 'When the police piece all the clues together they'll arrive at the conclusion that Casper Macvittee's army was behind everything.'

I smiled and looked at the pirates. 'You do know he's talking about you? He's going to frame you all.'

The pirates started laughing.

'How very droll Oscar, you believe I'd kill my own crew? How wrong you are. Let me show you Casper Macvittee's army. I think you'll be greatly amused.' He walked towards me and pulled something out of his pocket. He held it in front of my face. It was a mirror.

'There,' said Jaggers, waving my reflection of me. 'Can you see Casper's army now?'

'Us?' I said.

'Ah,' Jaggers grinned, seeing the penny drop. 'Welcome to the perfect crime. So glad you could play your part.'

'Nobody will believe it,' I said.

'I think they will,' said Jaggers. 'When the police discover your bodies down here it shouldn't be too hard to piece everything together.'

'Piece what together?' I said. 'We've no connection to each other.'

'But of course you do,' grinned Jaggers. 'You've all got a motive for destroying the Olympics: Casper Macvittee, embittered by the treatment he received at the hands of the Olympic committee, who rubbished his claims in public and made him a laughing stock, goes underground for a year to prepare his revenge. He recruits the Pearly King, a man who believes the Olympic development to be a cancer that will kill his Cockney heritage. Jimmy Strongbow, a Pearly Prince who would follow the Pearly King out of duty. Tallulah Funbags, local Madame, concerned that political efforts to clean up the area will lead to a police crackdown that will drive away her livelihood.'

'What about me?' said Duncan. 'I'm not a Cockney.'

'No,' smiled Jaggers. 'You are an immigrant. Which in the eyes of the law already makes you a suspect. When your body is recovered you will just happen to have a copy of the Koran about your person. I don't think the police will look any further, do you?' Jaggers smiled. 'Prejudice is a cruel thing.'

'You evil ba—'

'And as for you, Oscar,' interupted Jaggers. 'Your criminal record speaks for itself. A repeat youth offender from a broken home. No qualifications. No prospects. Looking for trouble.' Jaggers tented his fingers. 'Yes, it's a masterplan. They'll find your bodies down here, surrounded by explosives.'

'But the explosives don't work!' I cried. 'You've shot yourself in the foot!'

Jaggers grinned. 'No, Oscar...*you* have shot yourself in the foot. You have no idea how hard it has been for me to think like you imbeciles and plan things as you would plan them, stumbling over every hurdle. Your final undoing will be your lack of knowledge of explosives. One crate will go off, killing you all and opening up the cavern for the world to discover. Which is why it is so important that you die at the right time.

Forensics could be the undoing of me. If your bodies don't die at the same time by the same cause it will sink the whole caper.'

I turned to Duncan. 'Well, go on then.'

'What?'

'You heard what he said. If we don't die at the same time it will ruin everything. You have to kill yourself.'

Duncan looked around himself helplessly. 'With what?'

'Enough!' cried Jaggers. 'I tire of the pair of you. If you excuse me, I have a Holy Grail to steal.' He turned, but stopped. He clicked his fingers, 'Spray paint their hands.'

'Spray paint?' I said. 'Why?'

'Forensics,' said Jaggers. 'When they find the bodies of Casper Macvittee's army, don't you think their hands should be covered in the paint used to put up the graffiti all over Maryland?' Jaggers grinned. 'I have to ensure you are caught, red handed.' He let out an evil laugh.

Two giant pirates stepped forward with toothy grins and set to work. The red paint felt sticky on my fingers. When they'd finished it looked like we'd been given a manicure by a rabid ape.

Duncan and I knelt there, helpless. I watched Jaggers. He walked over to the fireplace. I could now see there was a sheet of metal at the bottom of it, covered in rubble. Four pirates brushed the rubble off and moved the sheet clear. The fireplace suddenly filled with light, but I couldn't see any torch. It seemed to be coming from under the ground. A golden glow hung like a fine mist an inch or two above the floor.

Jaggers produced a brush from somewhere and began dusting. The glow grew stronger, his face was bathed in it. His grin was wide. 'Number 2. The winch.'

- 102 -

WINCH

Sinbad poked his ugly head in the fireplace and called up to the surface. *'WINCH!'*

Jaggers sucked contentedly on his cigarette holder and turned to his crew. 'Remember, once we've secured the treasure, you get yourselves topside. It's not worth the risk. We'll all meet back on the ship.' Jaggers glanced at the fireplace. 'I don't see a winch, Number 2.'

Sinbad put his head back in the fireplace. *'WINCH!!!!'*

As if by magic the winch arrived on cue, right in Sinbad's face. Fortunately for him it wasn't a face you could make uglier.

'I'll keelhaul you for that!' He waved a fist up the shaft at someone before handing the hook to Jaggers, who had placed some strange towel around his shoulders and waved a finger in the air, almost as if he was crossing himself, but it was something else, like a figure four or something. Jaggers then began saying incantations. I can't remember it word for word. I don't even know what language it was, but it sounded something like "budda-raaam...sidda-raaam..." and he did it in a low voice, genuflecting, if that's the word for it, as he did so. When he finished he pulled the hook low to the ground.

Everything shook. Rock yawned.

'It's fixed!' Jaggers took the towel off his shoulders and turned to face his crew with a grin. 'Number 2, the rope ladder.'

'ROPE LADDER!'

'What about the prisoners?' asked a pirate who looked a bit like Lemmy from Motörhead.

'Let's kill 'em,' said someone.

'I don't like that one's dressing gown,' said one.

'Or his glasses.'

'Or his face.'

'Let's pickle 'em and feed 'em to sharks!' said a pirate, who seemed to think sharks like pickled stuff.

'Skin 'em alive,' said a pirate who probably found things were easier said than done.

'Wait a sec!' I said. 'Don't we get any last requests?'

'No,' said Jaggers.

'Oh,' I said, deflated. 'I thought that's how it works.'

'As always Oscar, you've watched too many movies.'

'Whatever happened to the British sense of fair play?' asked Duncan. 'Parley! Parl—'

The cavern shook again. Only this shake was stronger than the first. It made everything move. The totem poles wobbled and the crates of TNT seemed to leap off the ground, even my sphincter jumped a bit.

'Wait, God damn you!' Jaggers raced to the fireplace and yelled up to the surface. 'Do that again and I'll send you to hell in pieces!'

'ROPELADDER!' added Sinbad.

I slumped my head forwards. There was no way out. I, Oscar Hume, was going to die in London's East End at the hands of a crazy bunch of pirates.

Jaggers said something. I glanced up. His lips were moving, but I couldn't hear him, I was distracted by something. Something silver.

Between the legs of the encircled pirates I could see the flask of Junior Anthrax. It was too far away to grab, maybe a dozen feet or so, but if I could just get my hands on it somehow.

'So, it's decided,' said Jaggers. 'We tie them to the crate of explosives and burn them alive. All those in favour say "Y'arrgh!"'

'*Y'ARRGH!*'

'Wait!' I said, an idea forming. 'Look, gimme a last request. All I want is a cup of tea.'

Jaggers grinned. 'How very English of you.'

'A cup of tea and a cigarette. Then you can kill us both.'

'But I don't smoke,' said Duncan.

'Listen,' I said, under my breath. 'This might be one of the few times when smoking *adds* minutes to your life.'

'I'm afraid I can't grant you such a pitiful last request,' said Jaggers. 'We pirates don't care much for tea.'

'We drink grog!' chimed a pirate.

'Rum!' cried another.

'Archers and lemonade!' said a pirate who had his hair done lovely.

'I brought tea with me,' I said. 'Look, it's over there.' The pirates turned to follow my pointing. Having noticed the flask, one of them stepped over to examine it.

'Give that to me!' Jaggers snatched the flask. 'Who brought this here?'

'I told you,' I said. 'I brought it.'

'Did you, indeed?' Jaggers turned it over in his hands. 'Pray tell, why is it covered in biohazard symbols?'

'Erm…'

'Because he makes really bad tea,' lied Duncan. Or at least I assume it was a lie. I never make a bad cup. Ever.

Jaggers went to open it.

'No!' I cried, my stomach going. 'Let me pour it.'

'I think not.'

'C'mon, it's my final cup. Let me pour it. You don't know how I like it.'

'A cup of tea is a cup of tea,' dismissed Jaggers.

'You haven't tried Oscar's,' said Duncan. 'His are really bad.'

'Will you leave off!' I reached into my pocket and pulled out my cigarettes. 'Look, you've got us beat. How about it? A final smoke and a cup of tea?'

Jaggers studied me. I knew what I was doing. I was trying to work on smokers' solidarity. You band together when you smoke. Always happy to lend a light. Always happy to lend a fag. It's like the freemasons bond. If that couldn't momentarily blind his evil genius, nothing would.

He considered me before extending his arm and offering the flask. 'Enjoy your tea,' he said coolly. 'It will be your last.'

- 103 -

JUNIOR ANTHRAX

'Tricked you, Jaggers!' I jumped up with my cigarette dangling from the corner of my mouth and waved the cylinder above me in triumph. 'Stand back! Or we all die!'

The pirates laughed at this. Even Jaggers grinned. 'Oh, Oscar, I'm sure your tea is not so bad as to be able to kill me and my entire crew.'

'I mean it,' I said, backing away from them. 'You don't want to mess with me. I'll kill us all.'

'We'll kill you first,' said a pirate who I reckon always liked to win at things.

'I mean it!' I said. 'This is Junior Anthrax. It's a grade-three chemical weapon. If I open this in here, we all die.'

'It's a bluff,' cried Jaggers. 'Seize him.'

The pirates advanced.

'I'm serious,' I cried. 'This stuff is the real deal.' Despite my warning the pirates continued to fan out towards me. They looked like they meant business. Now was the moment of truth. Was I really going to open it? I didn't know. In panic I started to talk, fast. 'Cockroaches! How many dead ones in my flat, eh? Tell me that.'

'Distractions,' said Jaggers. 'Ignore him.'

'Answer me,' I shouted. 'When you broke in, how many dead cockroaches were there?'

'Thousands of 'em,' said a pirate.

'They was everywhere,' said another.

'Well, this is what killed them,' I waved the cylinder. 'And I haven't even opened it yet!' I put my hand on top of the flask and got ready to break the seal. The pirates stopped dead. A sunken look filled their faces. Some even began to step back. I had them!

'You're not so clever now, eh?' I waved the flask about. 'Not when I've got a deadly American military made illegal chemical weapon in my hands.'

There was something very odd about the way the pirates shrank away from me. They backed towards the fireplace, exchanging nervous looks with each other and then back at me, only I realised they weren't looking at me, they were looking past me, over my shoulder, to the tunnel by which we'd entered.

A voice came from behind. 'An illegal chemical weapon? Well ain't that something.'

I glanced nervously over my shoulder. From the accent I already knew what I'd find. There to my horror stood five men in black suits, each with sunglasses, side-partings and earpieces. The one nearest held up his ID. 'Freeze! FBI!'

I dropped the Junior Anthrax and held up my hands. I was nicked.

- 104 -

THINGS HEAT UP

To this very moment I have no idea who the FBI were actually after. Whether it was me, with my illegal chemical weapon, or Jaggers, with his plot to steal the Holy Grail, I'll never know, as moments after they announced their arrival the cavern descended into a full-scale riot.

Well, that's not strictly true. There was a momentary stand off. Fingers danced above holsters as the sides eyed each other up. I reckon there must be a gaping hole in the FBI handbook though when it comes to dealing with pirates, as the men in black were caught a bit off guard when a cannon was wheeled out of nowhere and fired at them.

The lead FBI agent's face filled with surprise, as anyone's would, given that the cannonball struck him square in the gut and carried him across the cavern. He flailed with it in mid-air before crashing into the "Viva Casper!" graffiti above the tunnel. That sort of set the tone of what was to come.

Pirates charged forward with their pistols drawn, firing in all directions. Smoke quickly filled the air. Cries of "Y'arrgh!" and "FBI!" sounded all around us.

I ducked for cover behind a nearby crate. 'Duncan?!?'

'Oscar!'

'No, Mr Bunger!' I shouted, suddenly remembering my alias. 'Where are you?'

'Over here.'

I scurried across the battlefield and found him crouching beside a crate of TNT, with a grin on his face. 'I said they'd have a cannon? Didn't I say that?'

'Well done, Marple,' I mocked. 'Now...*let's get out of here.*'

'Why?'

'*Why?*' I spat. 'What do you mean "*why?*" Look!' I pointed into the gun smoke that surrounded us. 'We're in the middle of a massacre!'

'No,' drawled Duncan. 'We're safe. The FBI are here to rescue us.'

I grabbed him hard and shook him. 'They are not here for the pirates you numb-nut! They are here for me! We have to escape!'

At that moment the ground shook with a deafening roar. Around us rock split and yawned, coughed and rumbled. From somewhere American voices rang out in pain. As the dust settled I could see the tunnel had collapsed, burying several Feds beneath it. Despite their predicament they still waved their badges about hoping to collar someone. 'FBI! FBI!'

'Great!' I said. 'We're trapped.'

'I thought we were already trapped? You mean we're more trapped?'

'C'mon. We have to find another way out of here.'

Duncan started twitching his nose. 'Wait...I can smell something.'

'Never mind that. Think. How are we going to get out of here?'

Duncan raised his head and pointed his nose in different directions. 'I know that smell. Smells like...detergent.'

'Like what?' I pulled him down as another volley of gunfire went over our heads. I looked over at the fireplace. A rope ladder had dropped down. 'Go!' I pushed him forward. 'Get to that ladder!'

'No, you go,' he cried. 'Go get help.'

I looked at him. He had a boyish grin on his face. I felt somehow this was the last time I would ever see him. I shook his hand. 'I'll be back.'

'With ninjas?'

I nodded. 'With ninjas.' I patted him on the shoulder. 'Good luck.'

He sank into the gun smoke. I didn't like leaving him in the middle of a shootout, but we were probably safer apart. I've watched enough war films to know what happens when comrades try to rescue each other. I decided I'd get to the surface and make an anonymous call to the police or army or whatever, tell them what was happening, and then go into hiding and hope they never found me. That seemed like a good plan, but one thing was stopping me: my feet.

With gritted teeth I limped, and then my limp slowed to a hobble which then slowed to a stop. In agony I ducked down behind another crate. There was the boom of the cannon and the explosion of rock being blown apart. Pops of gunfire continued overhead. A sharp yell of pain rang out nearby. I turned round to find the pirate who looked like Lemmy from Motörhead. He lay on his back. A still expression on his face. A smoking bullet-hole in his chest.

From somewhere Jaggers gave a rallying cry. 'Fight, me hearties! They are outnumbered and cut off!'

'We'll never surrender!' called a lone American voice.

'Damn your American spirit!' cried Jaggers. 'Slaughter the Yankee lubbers!'

And with that the gunfire increased. I know nothing about firearms, save for what movies have taught me, but I swear I heard an Uzi 9mm being fired as well as a phase plasma rifle with a 40watt range. All of which weren't helping the floor situation. It was still as sharp as a piranha's dentures and now covered with a carpet of razor sharp rock chips and splinters.

I glanced at the fallen pirate beside me. His shoes looked like something from a panto. Black leather with a silver buckle and a curly toe.

Stealing off a dead man was a new low.

Under the crossfire I leaned forward and pulled off his boots. They were a little on the roomy side. A bit like flippers to be honest. But I didn't care. It's not as if I wanted to escape in style. I drew up to a crouch and got ready to run, but an idea stopped me.

I ducked back and stole his hat. It was a tri-corn job with a skull and crossbones on the front. I stole his sword too. The more I looked like a pirate the better chance I stood of getting up that ladder. In the heat of battle would anyone notice me? I would soon find out.

I stood up and made a break for it. I could see the rope ladder dancing in the fireplace. Someone was smart enough to be escaping. I swallowed hard and moved forward.

A leg appeared, coming *down* the ladder. Gun-smoke drifted in front of me and I lost sight momentarily, but when it cleared I was amazed to see Berol stood in the fireplace, her face a no-nonsense gurn, her white spiky hair looking more aggressive than ever, her fingers covered in cheap sovereign rings that gleamed. She gave the cavern the once over before shouting up to the surface. 'Blimey! It's a proper bundle down here!'

- 105 -

FIGHT OR FLIGHT

I was saved!

'Berol!' I cried. 'Over here!'

'Who's that?' She scanned the cavern, peering through the smoke. 'Oscar, that you?'

My heart was pounding. I couldn't quite believe it. I don't know how they'd found us, but the Cockneys had pieced it together and come to our rescue. As I've always said, they are a clever bunch of people, Cockneys. They may be misunderstood but they really are some of the smartest people on the planet. And I'd never say a bad word about them again. Ever. They could call me a Mockney muppet and have me serve them pie and mash morning, noon and night, I wouldn't flinch. I'd be forever in their debt. Mine eternally to repay.

Berol poked her head back into the fireplace. 'You were right!' she called to the surface. 'The Mockney is in on it! He's dressed up like a pirate and everything!'

'Wait!' I cried, quickly pulling off the tri-corn hat and throwing the sword to one side. 'It's not what you think!'

'And his hands are covered in blood too!'

'It's paint!' I yelled.

But it was too late. Cockneys dropped down the rope ladder like commandos and charged into the cavern. From here on it was a blur.

Everywhere I looked there was slugging and punching, with bullets singing through the smoke.

Berol was swinging her right foot into the balls of any FBI agent or pirate stupid enough to get near her. Danny the ad-man was fighting three pirates at once with his mop and bucket, using it like a lance to fend them off. And Big Mick, barman and bare-knuckle fighter extraordinaire, had his charcoal grey suit on and his fists up, looking for someone to hit, but he wasn't having much luck. Every time he'd try and engage someone, they'd run away like they didn't understand what he was on about. To be honest, that's no surprise, as Big Mick kept repeating the baffling line: 'Who fancies the job?'

I backed off and tried to keep out of trouble. I made my way to the collapsed tunnel, nearly tripping over Jaggers's cat, which was cantering about the battlefield with it's snotty head held high, seemingly oblivious to the carnage happening around it.

'C'mon!' came a cry over the gunfire. 'Someone must fancy the job? Anyone?'

From somewhere the cannon boomed, and there was a fierce clang of metal.

I weighed up my options and decided to take evasive action.

I moved over to a crate and began emptying it of explosives. At first I did it carefully but then I started chucking them out by the armful.

Jaggers was right, these weren't proper explosives at all. They were fireworks, and cheap French ones at that. Stencilled on the side of each stick were the words "le dynamite" with small print beneath it that read "les petit explosives pour la famille. EU Tested."

Once I'd emptied the crate I climbed in and pulled the lid over me. Hiding, I peered out through the wooden slats at the subterranean battlefield. It was still a smoky no-man's land peppered with shouting and shadows running back and forth, with gunshots and ricochets coming in all directions. Occasional cries of "FBI!" would be met by the

"Y'arrghs" of the pirates and "Lovely-ol'-jobs," of the Cockneys. It was hard to say who was winning.

'Does anyone fancy the job, or what?' cried Big Mick, still struggling to find someone willing to take him on.

The smoke cleared a little and I suddenly caught a glimpse of Duncan. He was running about in a manner that can be best described as headless, pushing pirates over who weren't looking and then running away again. He wasn't exactly James Bond.

'Duncan!' I called.

He looked about him. 'Oscar?'

'Mr Bunger!' I shouted. I stuck my hand out of the crate and waved to him. 'Over here!'

'Oscar! You're back!' he skipped across to me. 'Where are the ninjas?'

'Sold out,' I said. 'You'll have to settle for Cockneys.'

'Great! C'mon, help me grab Tallulah.'

'Forget it.'

'I can't move her on my own,' said Duncan. 'She's in that trance.'

'I ain't moving. Now, quick, get in here and hide.'

'I can't hide,' he drawled, a ricochet zinging off the wall behind us. 'I've got to rescue Tallulah. C'mon, help me.'

'I can't! I've got everyone in this cavern either wanting to make me walk the plank, turn me into pie and mash or put me in the electric chair – I'm staying put!'

'You can't stay in this crate.'

'I'm going to give it a bloody good try.'

'C'mon,' he pleaded. 'I need your help.'

'Look, I got you some Cockneys. What more do you want?'

'If you don't help, I'll tell them where you are hiding.'

'You wouldn't d—'

'OVER HERE!!!' shouted Duncan. 'Oscar's hiding over here!'

- 106 -

RESCUE

I reached out of the crate and grabbed Duncan by his dusty leather jacket. 'What the hell are you playing at?!?'

'I'm not leaving the others down here to die.'

'You're going to get me killed!' I said, 'Now, quit pratting about and get in here and hide with me.'

Duncan looked over his shoulder at the battlefield.

'I'll take the blame.'

I raised an eyebrow. 'You'll do what?'

'I'll take the blame…for the Junior Anthrax. I'll tell the FBI it was me.'

'Serious?' I said.

He nodded.

'Sold!' I leapt out of the crate like a jack-in-a-box. 'You grab her feet, I'll grab what wobbles.'

Our journey across the cavern to Tallulah was perilous. It was all gunfire, ricochets and smoke. We scurried, using the crates and totem poles for cover. We had to keep our wits about us at all times and remain completely focussed.

'Hey, where did you get those shoes?' asked Duncan.

'I'll tell you later.'

'Did a pirate sell them to you?'

'I'll tell you later!'

We scrambled over some rubble and reached Tallulah's crate. She was still out for the count. Amazingly, the chaos and cannon fire had failed to wake her. I suppose there was something a bit Sleeping Beauty about her, or at least their would've been had Jimmy Strongbow not been laying beside her with his arse hanging out of his trousers, waiting for someone to park their bike.

'We need to get Jaggers's ring,' said Duncan. 'It's the only way to wake them up.'

'You don't know how to use it.'

'I read a book on crystals once.'

'You'll never get that ring,' I said. 'You'll have to chop his arm off.'

Duncan scratched his head. 'There must be a way to wake them up. How did you wake up?'

'I didn't need waking up. I never went into a trance. I think my glasses saved me.'

'What about me?'

'You went out like a light,' I said. 'One shine of that ring and it was good night Vienna. Although, dunking your head in Tallulah's norks seemed to wake you up a treat.'

Duncan sniffed. He stepped close and dunked his face in her chest.

'You dirty git, like that's saving her? You should be ashamed of yourself.'

A muffled cry came from between her melons. 'It's her perfume!' He withdrew his face with a triumphant look. 'It must have myrrh in it!'

'What's that got to do with anything?'

'Myrrh is holy, like the Holy Grail.'

'What?'

'Opposites attract. Like and like repel.'

'What are you on about?'

Duncan grabbed Jimmy's arm. 'Pick him up. We need to put his head in her...' he waved at his chest. '...her lady apples. So he can sniff the perfume.'

I stared at him. 'Serious?'

'Serious,' he repeated. 'C'mon!'

We grabbed Jimmy and, holding him like a battering ram, ran at Tallulah. His face disappeared amongst her huge flesh pillows.

'Lovely-ol'-job!' he cried.

We pulled him up and sat him on the edge of the crate. His cheeks seemed rather red. He straightened his pork-pie hat and looked about the cavern.

'Cor blimey!' he cried, over the gunfire. 'It's the rapture!' He knelt down, grabbed rock and legged it to join the battle.

'See!' said Duncan. 'I knew her perfume would work! Quick! Let's grab Casper.'

We moved on to the next crate. Casper's dirt-covered body lay in the foetal position with hands up by his eyes.

'I'm not touching him,' I said. 'He's probably not had a bath in a *y*—

,

'Y'arrgh!' A hand clamped on my shoulder. I was spun round and came face to face with the pirate with the harmonica. He pointed a pistol in my face and prepared to fire.

I closed my eyes, expecting the next sound to be the gun.

'*AWOOGA!*'

I opened my eyes. The pistol dropped to the floor. As did the pirate. Duncan wiped his hands and surveyed his work.

I should've been grateful. Thankful, perhaps. But I was running on shock. 'Duncan, what the hell did you just do?' I cried.

'James Bond karate chop.'

'I never thought that actually worked!'

'Oh yeah,' drawled Duncan. 'If you do it to the back of the neck. Knocks them out cold.'

'Well, bugger me,' I said. 'Every day is a learning day. Thanks.' I stooped to pick up the gun. I'd never held one before. It felt heavy.

'Careful,' said Duncan. 'Give it to me.'

'Why?'

'I know about guns.'

Given everything I knew about Duncan, it didn't seem improbable that he was trained in fire-arms. I handed it over.

'Thanks.' He threw it off into the smoke.

It took everything I had not to punch him in the face. 'What the hell did you just do that for?'

'Guns are dangerous,' he drawled.

'But, we could've used it!'

Duncan shook his head. 'They kill people.'

'But...but...but...' I couldn't even find the ability to argue.

'C'mon,' said Duncan. 'Help me with Casper.'

We gave Casper the battering ram treatment and shoved his head between Tallulah's norks. He didn't say anything, but his legs seemed to twitch. We pulled him out and stood him upright. Somewhat confused he squinted at me and Duncan. 'You ain't the treasure!'

'No, we're—'

'Heathens!' he cried. And with that he turned and legged it into the gun-smoke.

I fished a cigarette out of my dressing gown. 'Y'know, I kind of thought people would be a bit more...grateful.'

Duncan swatted the fag out of my hand.

'Oi!' I protested. 'What did you do that for? It was my last one!'

'We're not finished yet. We still have to rescue the Pearly King and Tallulah.'

I stooped to pick up the cigarette. 'I can smoke and rescue,' I protested. 'Besides, I'm stressed. I nearly had my face shot off just now. That's twice in two days!'

'You smoke when the job's done. Fat ladies and cigars, remember?'

Duncan was clearly showing early signs of battle fatigue or combat stress or whatever it is that causes Vietnam vets to return home and shoot up police stations or become taxi drivers. 'It's the rules,' he added.

'What rules?' I said. 'What the hell are you on about?'

'*Independence Day*,' said Duncan. 'They smoke cigars at the end of the film, *after* they've killed the aliens. Not before.'

'Listen,' I waved my now humpback cigarette in his face, 'this is not a cigar. And these...' I waved at the cavern. '...these are not aliens. They are pirates. And they are fighting Cockneys. Is that not weird enough for you?' I put the fag to my lips and sparked up.

'You shouldn't do that,' warned Duncan. 'It's bad luck.'

'The luck I've had in the last twenty-four hours, I'll chance—'

The ground shook violently. Duncan and I lost our balance and fell to our knees. Several rocks crashed down from the ceiling. One fell and hit a totem pole, knocking it over with a crunch that kicked up a cloud of dust. A strong Cockney voice ripped out from somewhere. 'Retreat to The Eel!'

- 107 -

RETREAT?

In the chaos it was hard to pick out what was happening. There were clouds of smoke and dust and a mix of voices shouting in all directions as rubble came crashing down. I'm sure I heard someone shout "Apone! Where's Apone?" but I can't remember. I was more worried about the shout of "Retreat!" It sounded like the Cockney's were beaten.

The smoke cleared a little. I looked across the cavern to see Big Mick bounding toward the fireplace with the Pearly King slung over his shoulder. Berol was running alongside with a look of panic, seemingly disturbed to find her illustrious leader under some demonic trance. I couldn't be sure but I swear someone else was running alongside with a plate, trying to feed him pie and mash.

The cannon was fired again, which was a bad idea to start with, but worse now the cavern was falling apart. I thought I heard Jaggers shout something, but couldn't make it out. Whatever the command, the pirates were now giving up on the fighting and were chasing the Cockneys up the shaft. The smoke quickly cleared. The cavern stood empty. Pops of gunfire could be heard coming from the surface.

'What do you know?' I said. 'Those silly sods have gone topside, perhaps we should just wait down here until it's finished?'

But a shout from behind hinted at the reason everyone was so quick to get out.

'FBI!'

- 108 -

FBI

'FBI! FBI!'

I looked about for the source, but couldn't see anyone. The cavern was empty.

'FBI! FBI!'

We traced the cries to the collapsed tunnel. The entrance was completely sealed with fallen rubble. A mix of large fallen boulders and loose chippings. A few dead FBI agents lay still, crushed under the rocks.

'I don't hear them anymore,' said Duncan.

'Maybe they've gone back?' I whispered. I leaned forwards for a closer listen.

An arm burst through a gap in the rubble, waving a badge. 'FBI!'

I jumped back in shock.

The badge waved helplessly at my face. It was clear the agent was trapped, but I didn't like the idea of hanging about. There could be more of them, all wanting to break through.

I grabbed Duncan. 'Let's get out of here.'

'One sec.' He stepped forward and put his hands on his hips. 'Hi....FBI!'

'Duncan!' I hissed. 'What are you doing?'

He ignored me and continued. 'FBI…I know you want to lock Oscar up, but he's innocent. The illegal chemical weapon he got off eBay, the Junior Anthrax, it was me. It was all me.'

Whatever his intentions, Duncan's guilty plea only seemed to stir up the nest of Feds. A dozen or so fresh arms punched through the rubble, waving badges in a futile attempt to collar someone.

'C'mon,' I said, grabbing Duncan. 'Didn't you hear me? I've said it like three times now…*Let's get out of here!*'

'Tallulah!' he cried.

We ran back to her crate and picked her up. Together we carried her across the empty cavern, toward the ropeladder. Her womanly figure was lovely to hold but a bitch to carry over rough terrain. 'When we get topside,' I huffed. 'We get as far away as we can.'

Duncan nodded. 'Zone 6.'

'No, you prat!' but as the words left my mouth something went very wrong. Duncan's body suddenly crumpled. He let go of Tallulah and fell to the floor with a quiet groan, clutching his back.

- 109 -

DUNCAN

'What's wrong?' I cried.

'My back.' He was short of breath. His eyes confused.

'Are you hit?'

'Maybe,' he drawled. 'Maybe, a little bit.'

I looked around but couldn't see anyone. The cavern floor gave a short shake. I peered round a crate toward the fireplace. The winch was tightening. The pirates were ready to lift the treasure out, which probably meant it was time to escape, as if any of their mumbo-jumbo was to be believed, moving the treasure was going to cause earthquakes and all sorts. And I didn't really fancy having an Olympic stadium fall on top of me.

From somewhere a gun fired. I dived back behind the crate. Duncan lay nearby, with effort I inched along the cavern floor towards him.

TING! Another ricochet.

Duncan lay on his back with his eyes fixed on the cavern roof, his brow contorting between puzzlement and surprise 'My b-b-back...' he stammered.

I knelt by his side. I went to turn him over and have a look at his wound, but there was no need. A red puddle was already forming beneath him.

'Oscar, my back...'

At that point it was just like a film. The realisation of what was happening hit home. Noise all around me tuned down to nothing. I looked up, I don't know if I cried out a defiant "Nooooo!" or what. I remember watching, almost in third person, as my trembling hand extended toward him. I grabbed him, 'You have to get up! We have to get out of here.'

'But my b-b-back,' he protested.

'You're fine,' I lied, pulling at him. 'Get up! I'll get you to a hospital.'

Duncan grabbed my arm. His eyes fixed on mine with a seriousness I'd never seen before. 'You have to help me stop the bleeding.'

'No,' I said. 'You're walking out of here.'

Duncan tightened his grip on my arm. 'Pressure,' he spat. 'Put pressure on it.'

'You're the designated first aider! I'm not trained for this!'

'Pressure...' he wheezed. His grip on me loosened and he lay back. His chest was rising and falling heavily. The pool of blood grew beneath him. 'Pressure...' his eyes flickered, the light was going from them fast. His head tilted back.

I knelt beside him, completely frozen. I'd have probably stayed that way if it weren't for the gunshot. It tore into the crate near us, sending wooden splinters everywhere. Normally I'd have run. I say normally, like I made a habit of watching friends get shot in the back. I half expected instinct to take hold. Get as far away from the danger as possible. But something within made me stay.

Duncan's body started to shake.

It wasn't first aid but I did the only thing I could. I dragged his body a few feet, towards Tallulah, and dunked his head into her cleavage. As his nose caught the smell of her perfume he sighed, then he tensed. It didn't look good. I've never seen anyone die in real life, but in films this is what they do just before they croak it. Final words are always something profound. I really hoped Duncan's weren't something stupid about foxes.

'I'm going, Oscar,' he wheezed, rolling back from her cleavage. 'I'm going away...'

I shook my head. 'Don't die...we have to make it to the closing credits together.'

His face filled with a half-smile. 'Avenge me...' And with that his head dropped back, his eyes closed.

'Don't go! Don't go!' I begged, my eyes filling with tears.

He didn't reply.

He didn't do anything.

He was still.

I pushed him. I shook him.

Nothing.

I reached into my pocket for a cigarette. My hands were shaking, but I managed to find my mouth. I was about to light up...but stopped. I took the cigarette out and examined it. I put it back in the packet and placed it on his chest.

'Thank you,' I whispered. 'You were the only friend I've ever had.'

I wiped my eyes and looked about the cavern. Someone was going to pay. 'You bastards!' I cried. 'You killed him!'

A low chuckle drifted toward me. 'Then that's one down, two to go.'

It was Jaggers.

- 110 -

SHOWDOWN

'Come on out, Oscar. I won't hurt you.' Another bullet tore into the crate, showering me in splinters. 'I promise, I'll shoot you stone dead.'

'It's over!' I cried, trying to place his voice. 'The FBI are here. You're as good as nicked.'

Jaggers laughed. 'I put it to you, that you are all as good as dead.'

He sounded off to my right, close to the fireplace. I thought about taking a peek but the sight of Duncan's still body made me think again. 'Why'd you shoot him?' I shouted. 'He'd done nothing to you!'

'I can't afford to let any more of you escape.'

'Too late!' I said. 'There's dozens of witnesses. The Cockneys will spill the beans. The Pearly King is probably chatting to the Old Bill right now.'

'My dear Oscar,' Jaggers voice stayed calm and chillingly even. 'It doesn't matter how many witnesses there are if they don't know what they are witnessing.'

'I know what I've seen,' I said. 'And I'll tell the rozzers every word of it.'

'Which is why you must die!' He fired another shot. It hit the cavern wall with a loud *TING!* showering me in dust.

I spat and rolled closer to the crate. I reached a hand over the top and groped about for some fake dynamite. I took out my lighter and lit one, throwing it like a grenade across the cavern. I didn't expect it to kill anyone or anything. Knowing my aim I wouldn't even get close, but that didn't matter, I just wanted to confuse Jaggers for long enough to find out where he was hiding.

The fake dynamite went off with a *BANG!* Like a jack-in-a-box I popped up and had a gander. Jaggers was standing by the fireplace, a silver pistol in his right hand. I ducked back down, confident he hadn't seen me.

I chewed a finger. If I was going to get out of here it was going to take more than giving him free video rentals for life. I was going to have to tackle him. I looked about for a weapon. There was nothing but bodies and rock chips.

'Attempting to fight back is useless,' cried Jaggers. 'Accept the verdict. You will die here.'

'Why'd you start shooting now?' I asked. 'You've watched too many Bond films, they never kill anyone when they have the chance.'

'I put it to you that it is you who has watched too many films,' purred Jaggers. 'Not everything is a nice linear plot that ties up neatly at the end. Sometimes situations change. Unexpected events occur. It's called life, Oscar. And I'm extremely good at getting what I want from it.'

'You ain't half as clever as you think,' I said. 'The FBI were on to you all along.'

Hearing their name caused a ripple of excitement from the collapsed tunnel. The arms sticking out of the rubble began waving their badges again. 'FBI! FBI! FBI!'

'No, Oscar they were on to *you*. Or to be more precise, they were on to Casper Macvittee's army. Which, when they excavate this site and find your body beneath the rubble, they'll naturally conclude that's who they've found.'

'And they'll find me with your bullet in my back.'

'I'm glad you are finally getting it,' said Jaggers.

'That doesn't make sense. I put it to you that your bullet being in my back implicates you.'

Jaggers laughed a high haughty laugh. 'Oh, Oscar, you're priceless. I put it to you that you were shot by the FBI with your own gun, because there will be no witnesses to say differently. And whilst I can't wait to bury you beneath several million tons of earth and steel, I'd enjoy it so much more knowing I'd killed you first.'

- 111 -

AN AMAZING PLAN

Frankly, I don't know why I was bothering to try and work out what Jaggers was thinking. All I knew was he had a gun and he was shooting at me. His reasons didn't matter. It could've been that he didn't like Mondays or that he hated short-arse video store workers in glasses. I don't know. All I knew was that if I wanted to get out in one piece I had to get past him. I had to outwit the greatest legal mind the country had ever known.

I grabbed some more bangers from the crate and threw them to the fireplace.

B-B-B-BANG!!!

I gave up my hiding place and legged it to the other side of the cavern. I crouched down behind a totem pole and listened.

'You can't win, Oscar,' purred Jaggers. 'You should just give yourself up. It will be the kinder sentence.'

I tried to think of a plan. I looked back at the far end of the cavern with the collapsed tunnel. Given that they'd just heard that several million tons of soil was about to bury them alive, the FBI had stopped waving their badges as enthusiastically. They knew they were going to die. And there was nothing they could do about it.

I looked around. A few pirates lay dead, with eyes closed and blood in their beards. One held a cutlass. I wasn't a swordsman. But it was better than nothing. If I could distract Jaggers, maybe I could get close enough to stab him and then climb up the shaft to freedom. I leaned over and prised it out of his hand.

His eyes opened.

I stumbled backwards and pointed the sword at him. I realised it was the pirate with the Pink Bandana.

'One word,' I whispered. 'And I'll kill you.'

He nodded, and stayed quiet.

I kept my sword on him and peered over the crate. Jaggers was standing by the fireplace, looking away from me. He didn't know where I was. Perfect.

The Pink Bandana moved by my feet. I turned sharp and thrust the sword at him, the point pressing him to the floor by his neck.

'Don't kill me,' he gasped. 'I'm on your side.'

'My side!' I hissed. 'I've just seen my best mate killed! I should slice you up into kebab meat.'

The Pink Bandana closed his eyes. 'Not my face, please!' he begged. 'I want to leave a beautiful corpse. I can help you. Please, not my face!'

'Help how?'

'Escape…I know of a way to get out. There's another tunnel that—'

Meow!

From nowhere Jagger's cat leapt onto the Pink Bandana's face and began fiercely clawing at it, ripping his looks to shreds. The Pink Bandana screamed in pain, but I doubt anyone heard as at that point the cavern began shaking. And I mean proper shaking. Not only did rubble fall from the ceiling but the crates themselves seemed to jump off the floor. It was one of the oddest things I've ever seen. That and the sequel to *The Mask*, which was called *Son of Mask*, that was pretty odd too.

'No!' yelled Jaggers. 'Wait for my signal, damn you!'

I peered over the crate and saw him pointing his pistol up the shaft. His face was flushed red.

I ducked back down and tried to think. Jaggers was smart, he wasn't going to come and find me, unless…

I looked at his cat. It was sitting on the Pink Bandana's bloodied face, licking his paws as if nothing had happened.

An idea suddenly presented itself. Oh boy, this was perfect. I grabbed the cutlass and peered over the crate. But it was too late, Jaggers had gone.

- 112 -

ESCAPE

No more hanging about. I was escaping. I leapt over the crate and legged it toward the shaft. As I drew close it became clear that Jaggers had gone. I sprinted into the fireplace and went to reach for the rope ladder.

That was gone too.

All that remained was the winch, hooked to the treasure. I went to grab it when, out of the corner of my eye, something moved.

Instinctively I held out the cutlass. There was a fierce clang of metal and before I knew what was happening I was boxed into the shaft, Jaggers pressing down on me, his blade pushing against mine, a dead disinterred look in his eyes. I tried to push him off but for a thin man in his sixties, Jaggers was surprisingly strong. Whether he was on some special Holy Grail gym regime or had drunk some Holy Druid tonic or what I don't know. But he was getting the best of me. So I did the only thing I could. I kneed him one in the plums.

'*Ooof.*' He stumbled back. I went to grab the winch but he raised his sword. I stepped back out of the fireplace.

'That's for Duncan,' I said, as he rubbed his groin.

Jaggers advanced towards me. 'Don't be upset about your friend. You'll be joining him very soon.'

I wish I could say that our fight was epic, but it wasn't. I'd had no training with a sword and was pretty much picking things up on the job, as it were. I swung. Parried. Jousted. Even pirouetted at one point.

Basically my fighting style was cobbled together from lightsaber battles and any film where a knight single-handedly sacks a castle. Had there been a big rope tied to a chandelier, I'd have probably had a go swinging on that. But there wasn't. There were lots of crates. And for a while we took turns to jump on them, and then jump off them again, the whole time our swords were clanging and banging. At one point, to spice it up, I grabbed a flaming torch from the wall and threw it into a box of bangers. That went down a storm. The explosion was so massive it knocked both Jaggers and I off our feet. He fell against the wall. Whilst I back peddled until I hit a crate, which caused me to fall over backwards in a feeble sort of roll.

My face hit the floor with a crunch, whilst my stomach hit a smooth and strangely cold object. I got up and saw I'd landed on the Junior Anthrax. Fat lot of good that was going to do. I picked it up anyway and stuffed it in my dressing gown.

Jaggers was still trying to get to his feet. I decided I'd had enough swashbuckling and made another break for it. I sprinted into the fireplace and grabbed the winch. I gave it a firm tug.

It went taught.

I held tight and felt myself being lifted off the ground. The cavern began to shake. I mean proper shake. Stone fell and everything cracked and roared. I looked down. At the end of the winch, rising from the ground, was a black box, not too dissimilar to a coffin. A bright light was streaking out from it.

The cavern continued to roar and shake. Loose stones fell on me from above. I squinted and looked up the narrow shaft to the surface. I couldn't believe it. I was escaping. I'd outwitted Jaggers. Not only that, I was escaping with the Holy Grail. I was going to be rich for life. Everything was going to be okay.

The winch snagged. I looked down to find two dull eyes climbing towards me.

- 113 -

FIGHT

The winch swayed back and forth and the chimney filled with the rumble and roar of rock falling in the cavern. The glow from the coffin seemed to be getting stronger. Despite having reactor lenses, it was still hurting my eyes.

Jaggers was now barely ten feet below me, holding on to the rope with one hand whilst he held a shiny object in the other. I knew instantly what it was. In slow-mo I saw him cock the hammer and point the pistol up at me. He shouted over the roar. 'Time to settle this case! Goodbye Oscar!'

I closed my eyes and tensed. The gun fired with a loud *BANG!* followed by a very loud metallic *TING!*

I opened my eyes. Jaggers looked up at me curiously. He hurriedly examined his pistol. Had he missed? I didn't feel pain. I didn't feel anything. Maybe a bit light-headed. That's when I noticed the hissing.

It sounded like gas. Like an aerosol. I looked about me. A thick yellow cloud seemed to be piping out of my dressing gown pocket. He'd shot the Junior Anthrax! As impossible as it sounds, a chemical weapon had just saved my life.

I fished the cylinder out of my pocket. The thick yellow gas billowed out of the top. Coughing and spluttering in the smoke I threw it down the shaft at Jaggers. He pulled hard on the winch. The cylinder sailed past him and hit the chimney floor with a muted boom, causing a small mushroom cloud, as if someone had just dropped a few bags of yellow flour.

He began laughing hysterically. 'Oscar! Time to die!'

Holding onto the rope, he began to reload his pistol. I looked up. The surface was still fifty feet away, I'd never climb it in time. I looked down. The coffin was now glowing brightly. The yellow mushroom cloud of Junior Anthrax bubbled away beneath it at the base of the shaft.

No escape.

This was it.

The game was finally up.

I reached into my pocket for my final cigarette. There was nothing there. Only my lighter.

MY LIGHTER!

I pulled it from my dressing gown and held it to the winch. The rope instantly started to smoke.

I heard the hammer snap down on the pistol. I looked down to see Jaggers pointing it up at me. A grin on his face.

I don't know what happened next. There was a *SNAP!* and a *BANG!* I don't know which one came first. But one was the sound of a pistol being fired and the other was the sound of the rope breaking.

Jaggers face filled with surprise as he began falling down the chimney. The glowing coffin hit the floor with a colossal *BOOM!* Everything went white, I mean supernova white. The chimney shook violently. It was as if the walls had turned to molten clay. I felt a sudden rush of air around me. It screamed past my ears carrying with it the sound of crashing, banging, smashing and all sorts.

I closed my eyes and held tight. When the wind died down I looked beneath me, but I could see nothing. It was pitch black. There was no light. No sign of Jaggers. No sign of the treasure. Just darkness.

- 114 -

SURFACE

Slowly, I scaled the winch to the surface. As I climbed upward I could see the black velvet of the East London night stretching out before me. I've never seen stars in London, but that night, I swear I could see them twinkling above me.

I inched my way up with all the strength I could muster, grunting like a female tennis player as I went. As I drew close to the lip of the shaft a hand thrust out to help me up. I couldn't see who it belonged to, but the sleeve was blue. I decided not to trust it and made my own way up and out. I belly-flopped into the cool night air and closed my eyes.

'I'm free,' I groaned. 'I'm free!'

'No, sunshine. You're nicked.'

- 115 -
HOW THE STORY ENDS?

Now, you pretty much know the rest.

I looked up to find myself surrounded by a team of police officers, each one in riot gear with those scary masks and batons. In front of them stood a middle-aged copper with a moustache, accompanied by a younger officer who looked a bit lanky.

'Evening, sir,' said the older officer. 'Would you mind explaining what your business is here at the Olympic stadium.'

'Olympic stadium?' I looked around. There was nothing but rubble. Mountains of rubble. Girders like fallen Jenga pieces. Mud and rock spat around like half chewed walnut whips.

'Wait a sec—' I began. But the officer with the tash was having none of it. He grabbed my arm and threw some cuffs on me. 'You're coming with us.'

I was led away across a torn-up field. Under the moonlight I could see bits of what used to be running track. I looked about for the pirates, but I couldn't see any of them. I didn't see any Cockneys either.

'Watch your step,' barked the lanky one.

I looked down into a gigantic hole. I can't measure, either in imperial or metric, but I'd say this hole was about the size of an Olympic stadium. I could tell that with some accuracy, as I could see most of the Olympic stadium in it.

I remember at that point I started yelling. 'I'm innocent! It's the pirates! Ask them!'

But the police officers didn't listen. They marched me to a waiting car.

'Get in,' growled the tash.

I stopped and took one final look at the site. Beyond the fallen cranes and rubble I noticed a large mound of dirt with a fox standing on top of it. I can't be sure, but I think it winked at me.

- 116 -

FILM THEORY

'So,' I said. 'That's it. That's my story. And every word is the truth.'

Bludwyn and Peasworth sat in silence. There was something about their expressions that suggested they weren't overly satisfied.

'So,' I said. 'You can let me go now, right?'

Bludwyn looked across at his rookie. 'He's a clever one, isn't he, Slick?'

'Very clever, sir. A classic Keyser Soze.'

'Oscar, you must think we are stupid,' said Bludwyn. 'You've been leading us on a merry dance from the very start.'

'Merry dance,' repeated Slick.

'What?' I said. 'I've told you the truth.'

'British film.'

'Excuse me?'

'British film,' repeated Bludwyn. 'You said yourself there is more to it than gangsters...'

'...*Carry On* movies...' added Slick.

'...and Bond films,' concluded Bludwyn. 'And yet, your story of what really happened is nothing more than a combination of those ingredients poorly tied together.'

'What?!?' I said, pretending to be hurt. 'You think I'd make all this up?'

'No,' said Bludwyn. 'We believe you. We really believe that pirates went hunting for the Holy Grail in East London. We believe that you could get people out of a trance by having them sniff the cleavage of a local prostitute.'

'Very *Carry On*,' nodded Slick.

'...And we believe you when you say Jaggers was a Bond-like villain who, despite ample opportunity to kill you, disclosed every facet of his plan before trying to murder you in an elaborate fashion in an underground lair.'

'Trademark James Bond,' added Slick.

'We are smarter than you think,' said Bludwyn, 'You can't pull the wool over our eyes that easily.'

'You can't be serious?' I said. 'Listen to me, I'm not making this up. It's all true.'

'But nobody can corroborate your far-fetched story,' said Bludwyn. 'The Cockneys say you were in on it. They say they saw you in pirate clothing, which you were.'

'Nono,' I said. 'Berol thought she saw me in pirate clothing. I was in my dressing gown. I stole the shoes and hat to escape. I told you that.'

'Your prints have been found all over the site on cutlasses and explosives,' said Bludwyn.

'And,' said Slick, 'the Pearly King believes it is you who put him in a trance. He's still got a Chapwa out on you.'

'Wait!' I said. 'There's evidence I'm innocent. What about all the dead pirates you found at the site? Surely that proves I'm telling the truth?'

Bludwyn looked at Peasworth. 'How many dead pirates did we find beneath the Olympic stadium, Slick?'

Slick consulted his notes, carefully. 'Seventeen at last count, sir. All unidentified.'

'See,' I said, 'that proves it.'

'That proves nothing,' said Bludwyn. 'If anything, it's seventeen reasons you were behind it all.'

'And we've recovered over two hundred unidentified skulls,' said Slick.

'You can't pin that on me! They're plastic!'

'Forensics still have to examine them,' said Bludwyn. 'Just like they have to examine the Junior Anthrax. How comes a grade-three chemical weapon didn't kill you?'

I shrugged. 'I don't know.'

Bludwyn looked at an evidence sheet. 'Preliminary tests show your dressing gown pocket to be rich in a particular pesticide that was banned in the 1970s.'

'I've told you. It was called Junior Anthrax. I got it through eBay. I don't know what it was, I just know what it did.'

So far so good on my part, they were going round in circles. They hadn't mentioned Duncan.

'And,' added Slick. 'We have yet to recover the bodies of either Jaggers, Duncan or Tallulah. Though each has now been registered as officially missing.'

'Though, we strongly allege you killed them and hid their bodies to preserve your own freedom,' said Bludwyn.

'Still no sign of Duncan, eh?' I smiled. 'Now, that *is* interesting, isn't it? You think he could've escaped?'

'You said he was dead.'

'Did I?'

Bludwyn's face flushed red. He smashed his hand on the table. 'No more games, Oscar! Tell us the truth! What did you do with the Holy Grail?'

I smiled. 'Search me, Inspector. I have no idea.'

I picked up my empty mug and waved it at them. 'Time for some tea,' I said. 'Mine's a Julie. I've a feeling you're going to want me to tell you this all over again.'

THE END...?

HOLY GRAIL

Item Condition: **Used**
Time Left: **6d 08h**

Current Bid: **No Bids** (Reserve not met)

[ ] Place bid

Postage: **None**
Delivery: **Buyer to collect**
Payments: **Cash**
Returns: **No returns accepted**

Enlarge

Sell one like this

Description	Postage and payments

Seller assumes all responsibility for this listing

Item Specifics

Condition: Sorry for the pic...the camera on my phone isn't very good. Item in good condition. Only used once. Check out some of my other items. My girlfriend is selling some large bras and a zebra print dress.

A NOTE FROM THE AUTHOR

Hello. Nice to meet you at last. Congrats on making it to the end of my book. I hope you enjoyed it. This may be cheeky, but I'd like to ask a favour. If you liked the book, please leave a review, tell your friends, tell strangers, tell cold-callers who pester you with offers of *new, improved* double-glazing, tell everyone. It really is word of mouth that keeps a self-published book alive.

And if you think this book stank – well, you never heard of Dot Gumbi, okay?

Thank you,

Dot Gumbi